IN A
DARK
AND
LOVELY
WOOD

NC JAMES

In A Dark And Lovely Wood

NC James

 Formatted with Vellum

This is to all the fans of the 1985 masterpiece Clue and to my sister who woke me up far too early when I was far too young so we could watch it.

Author's Note

Dear Reader,

Thank you so much for being here. This book is by far the most challenging one I've ever written and I'm very pleased with how it's turned out. I hope you love it.

A few things...

One: There is an actual Lost Lake Campground. I have spent many warm summer days floating in a raft on the lake. I love it there. This is not that place. It shares many of the same elements but the lay out and location are different.

Two: Content warnings. This books contains language, sexual situations, cheating, and murder. None of the descriptions are gratuitous but there is violence in this book. Please take care of yourself and if that's not for you I completely understand.

Three: None of the people, social media accounts, or cases in this book are real.

Again thank you for being here and have fun reading. ☺
—NC James

Lost Lake Camp
N
W
E
S

"*The woods are lovely, dark and deep.*
*But I have ~~promises~~ **secrets** to keep,*
And miles to go before I sleep,
And miles to go before I sleep."

Robert Frost

Channel Four News Report July 28, 2004

"Several were found dead this morning in one of the most horrific scenes the Hood River has ever witnessed. Stay tuned. We'll keep you up-to-date as we find out more."

Gabe

One week earlier

A snake. That's all I see as lights pulse through a thick haze of smoke in time to the music. The woman on stage runs her hands down her body, undulating her stomach. Tiny muscular movements. Like a snake.

My mind flashes to another stomach, slightly softer. I can practically feel the velvet skin under my fingers.

Ben claps me on the back as he sits, setting another drink in front of me.

"It's your wedding, I should've got this for you." I shift in my seat, the cracked vinyl of the stool snagging on my jeans.

He shakes his head, sipping his whiskey. "Nah. It's on me."

From the outside, this would seem a friendly gesture. Brothers getting along. But I know he's rubbing it in my face that he can afford the top-shelf shit.

"Where'd the other boys go?" I grab my cigarettes from the bar and flick my lighter. The flame popping to life.

Ben shakes his head. "You know Nick, he's getting a lap dance. And I think Joe may have taken off. I haven't seen him in a while."

I nod. Honestly, I don't really care where they went. I just want a buffer.

"Do you want a lap dance?" I reach for my wallet. I should buy him one. That's what people do for the groom to be, right? It isn't really his bachelor party. That was a few weeks ago. But still, if he's getting a lap dance, we don't have to suffer through small talk.

"Nah. I don't want to cheat on Jennifer."

Something between a grunt and a scoff escapes me along with a plume of smoke. Ben looks at me quizzically. I shake my head. "A lap dance is not cheating."

Ben frowns and sips his drink. "We clearly have different views on it."

He's giving us an out of this conversation, but for some reason, I can't let it go. "Did Jennifer say she thought it was cheating? Did you talk to her about it?"

"No. But I know how she feels. I didn't get this far in life without the ability to read people, and trust me, I can read my wife. She wouldn't like it."

My wife. I clench my teeth. "Not your wife yet."

"What about Sheila? I mean, I know you two aren't as serious as me and Jen, but... Don't you think she'd care if some hot girl was grinding on your crotch?"

I raise my eyebrows. Not as serious. It's true, but it feels like he's saying it to rub it in my face. "I'm pretty sure Sheila wouldn't give a shit."

Ben lifts his glass, so his words are slightly muffled when he says, "People care about what you do more than you think." He downs the rest of his drink. "We should probably go, this place is about to close, and we have an early morning."

I throw the drink back and follow my brother through the crowd, the music loud enough to drown out my thoughts.

* * *

My mouth is practically wearing a sweater when I wake up on Ben's couch, bright white light pulsing through the open window. I put the pillow over my face to block it out.

I'm never drinking again.

Maybe I should just keep the pillow here. Can you suffocate yourself or will you instinctively stop?

"Wake me up before you go-go!" Ben's insufferable voice sings out as he lifts the pillow from my face. "Come on. It's time to get up. We're late. Coffee is on and your shower awaits!"

"Okay, I'm up, I'm up." Sitting on the couch, I turn my neck, every vertebra popping on the way.

Ben is the only person who can be this chipper after closing down a strip club only a few hours earlier. He's already showered and dressed in his favorite shirt with a picture of a skeleton drinking a beer on it and a clean pair of jeans. I don't know why he wears that shirt so often; it doesn't really go with his finance guy style during the week, but maybe that's the reason. It makes him just one of the guys. Not so buttoned up and straight laced, even though underneath the shirt he's still both of those things. It certainly fit in more at that house he and Nick shared with a bunch of people off Alberta than at this swanky prefab condo.

But he had the money for it after his big promotion. It's crazy to spend that kind of money on a condo, why not get a house, with a yard? But this is what he wants. Strike that. It's what Jennifer wants.

Ah, Jennifer.

Fuck.

I place the pillow back over my face. Now I'm ready for another drink.

"Come on. We have to get moving."

I throw the pillow at Ben. He flips me off then takes his mug out onto the small balcony. I drag my bones into the kitchen, make myself a coffee and take it into the shower with me.

Ben knocks on the door twenty minutes later. "Dude. We gotta go pick up Nick and Joe."

Turning the water off, I step through the steam then throw on the same smoke-drenched jeans I wore the night before. I grab a clean shirt from my bag then down the rest of my coffee, the caffeine clearing the cobwebs in my brain but doing nothing to ease the tension in my chest.

Ben knocks again. "Are you ready?"

Despite his grown-up job, his fancy condo, and his upcoming nuptials, he's still my pestering little brother.

"Yep. All set to go."

Forty minutes later, we're all in the car headed for Hood River. Nick and Joe had both been sleeping when we picked them up, as anyone who stayed at the strip club until after three would be, so it took longer than expected. They stumbled into the car and immediately both fell back asleep. To Ben's credit, he didn't seem that annoyed by it, or he at least wasn't letting it show.

The silence between us echoes through the car. What should we talk about? We've never been the chat it up about our lives kind of brothers. Whenever we start talking about jobs, or relationships or our lives, it turns into a game of who has more. I don't need it rubbed in my face that Ben is winning on all fronts at the moment.

Ben turns up the radio, flipping to a top forty station.

The truly terrible music on the radio stops and a news report comes on with a loud beep, beep, beep.

"State officials are looking for any information on the escape of Wyatt James, recently convicted of multiple murders. James always claimed innocence..."

Wyatt James. I haven't thought about him in years.

Nick yells from the back, making the muscles in my neck tighten. I didn't even realize he was awake. "Change it! Too sad. I brought my CDs." Nick flips through the plastic pages of his CD book then hands me one. "Put this on."

I push the disk into the slot, and after a few whirs, Jay-Z's *The Black Album* fills the car. Leaning back, I close my eyes, the thump of the base reverberating in my chest. I place my hand on my phone in my pocket, waiting for it to vibrate.

Allie

I hate the woods. I hate the dirt. I hate the trees. And I fucking hate weddings.

But there's no way out of it. I have to go. Which is why I'm currently trying to ferret out my black bikini from my massive laundry pile, morning sunshine pushing obnoxiously in through the sheet covering the window. When Jennifer told me they're having a camping wedding, I tried to find some plausible reason for why I couldn't go. Work isn't a good enough excuse. She knows I don't give a shit about my job. And she'd never buy a family emergency.

I should be developing the roll of film in my Holga. How am I supposed to get a solo show if I never have any time to actually work on my photos? And what the hell am I supposed to pack for a wedding in the woods? I should've packed before, I realize this, but in my usual style, I have been putting it off. And last night after my closing shift at the bar, the other bartender, the new bus boy, and I got a teensy bit hammered.

My head pounds now. Is that why they call it hammered?

What I need is just a little nip of something to take the edge off the headache. I pad lightly to the kitchen downstairs and notice my roommates are all gone, off to work already. They all have real jobs that they go to in the daytime and have weekends off to go to farmer's markets and run 5Ks. A pulse thunders behind my eyes at even the thought of running right now. I grab a bottle of Prosecco and the Simply Orange from the fridge then a jelly jar from the dish drying rack.

The cold champagne bubbles into the glass, sparkling in the light. I add a splash of OJ, just a splash. If my grandmother taught me anything, it's how to make a proper mimosa. When I take a little sip, sweetness fills my mouth first then the bite of the alcohol. Grandma'd cringe at the bottled OJ, but she'd approve of the ratio. The cool liquid is refreshing, but the drink won't stay cool long. It's only a little after ten and already eighty degrees. It seems like since I moved to Portland, each summer is hotter than the last.

There's a knock at the door, making me dribble the last sip onto my shirt. *Shit.* It must be Dana. She's early, and in other news, we need air to breathe. She's literally *always* early.

I plop an ice cube in while the knocking continues, this time louder.

As I open the door, fully expecting an earful from Dana on how I'm not ready, I yell out, "Christ woman. It's a forest. It's not going anywhere."

But it's not Dana. The bus boy is on my doorstep, his beautiful light-blue eyes, made all the more startling by his dark lashes and light-brown skin, are directed right at me. What is his name and what was he doing here? He has a backpack slung over one shoulder.

"Hey, I'm not late, am I?"

"Late?"

He glances down at my bare legs. I haven't yet put on pants, so I'm hanging out in my black underwear and a black and gray tie-dye tank top.

"Or too early? I thought you said 9:30 last night."

I shake my head and immediately regret the motion.

"For the wedding."

Did I invite the bus boy—was it Ernie?—to come with me to the wedding? I don't remember a lot about the end of the night. It's entirely possible.

Shit.

I don't even know this guy. I can't take him on a multi-day camping trip with a bunch of people I used to be close to in college, but now all look their noses down at me with their fancy jobs and five-year plans.

He's still staring at me with his startling blue eyes. I hold up my glass, at a loss for what to say. I must have invited him, otherwise why would he be here? Fuck it. We'll sort it out over a drink. "Want a mimosa?"

"Yeah!"

Ernie follows me into the kitchen, throwing his bag down. He wipes his face with the edge of his shirt, and I snag a glimpse of his cut stomach underneath. Maybe this isn't such a bad idea after all. I for the champagne and he claps his hands together. He's *fun*.

It'll probably make the whole trip a lot more exciting. Drunk Allie is very smart, inviting him along. People don't give her enough credit.

I hand Ernie his mimosa.

"Are you sure you can go the whole time? We're not coming back until Sunday. You don't have any shifts at the bar?"

Ernie swallows his sip of mimosa. "I got my shifts covered when you asked me to come. I'm free as a bird."

Asked me to come. Something's still nagging me about that, but before I can poke at the feeling any further, there's another knock.

Opening the rickety front door, Dana stands before me in

low cut jeans and a purple satin spaghetti strap tank top, just the bottom of her flat stomach showing.

She emits a high-pitched squeal that nearly splits my head in two. "Allie! Are you so excited?"

Her face pinches a little as she clocks Ernie behind me.

"I am," I say flatly. "I'm almost ready. Can I get you a mimosa?"

"Umm, no. Jennifer and Lauren are waiting in the car. We have to get going. You're not even dressed." That last part, she says in a whine that makes me regret even agreeing to ride with them in the first place. But I don't own a car so, not a lot of other options.

"I'll throw on pants, then we can grab our stuff."

"Our stuff?"

"Oh yeah, this is Ernie. He's my date for the wedding." I smile and sip my champagne.

"I wish you would've let us know. He should've gone in the boys' car."

"The boys' car?"

"The girls are going in my SUV. The boys went in Ben's. We're all meeting in Hood River for lunch at a brewery, then we'll ride the school bus the rest of the way." She claps her hands, her sparkly nails accentuating the movement. "Isn't that fun?"

I march over to the coffee table and pick up my flip phone where I left it last night, ready to text the boys. "Has Ben already left?"

"They did, yeah. They wanted more time at the brewery." Dana clicks her tongue and brushes her layered dark-brown hair over her shoulder.

Downing the rest of my glass, I snap my phone shut. "He'll just have to go with us. Don't worry, he won't ruin our estrogen vibe."

Boys' car and girls' car. *Ridiculous.*

Before she can protest, I run upstairs, throw on some jeans, and slip into my Van's I'd left by my bed. Then I head to the kitchen and fill a travel mug with the rest of the champagne, a bit of juice, and screw the lid on.

Ernie's sipping on his drink, looking completely relaxed on the couch, while Dana's making eyes at the car waiting on the street.

"All ready."

We pile into Dana's brand new Mercedes SUV, a graduation present from Mommy and Daddy. Jennifer sits shotgun, her long blonde hair tied in a messy bun, aviator glasses perched on her button nose. Lauren doesn't look very pleased as I scoot into the middle seat to make room for Ernie.

"Allie!" Jennifer says. "You look great! Oh my god, look at your arms, girl! Where do you work out?"

Half laughing, I beam a little. They do look good. "Just moving kegs at the bar. This is my friend Ern—"

Ernie whispers in my ear next to me. "It's Eric."

I look at him sharply, my cheeks warming, and whisper back, "Eric? Really?"

He nods, smiling. I cringe and mouth, *Do you hate me?*

His eyes flash as he shakes his head no. I look away, the intensity in his gaze a bit much this early in the morning.

"This is my good friend, Eric. Eric, this is Lauren, Dana, and Jennifer. Hope you don't mind him riding with us. I wasn't aware of the segregated vehicles."

The car is suddenly so silent you can hear a baby crying somewhere off in the distance.

Murder? What murder? Episode 189 July 20, 2024

"Okay, it's time for everyone's favorite game? Murder? What murder? Are you ready, Jules?"

"Yes, Barbara, I'm dying to play."

"And it's our very first livestream!!!!!"

"Woot! Woot!"

"Okay, this murder just had its twentieth anniversary and took place in the woods in Oregon."

"Hmmm, is it murder? Or murders?"

"Ders. definitely ders."

"Ummm, The Lost Lake murders?"

"Ding, ding, ding. Got it in one. This one is really crazy, do you know much about this case, Jules?"

"Only what my eleven-year-old brain clung on to from the news at the time. Honestly, I'm not sure how much of that I even made up. Wasn't it at a wedding or something?"

"It was, sort of. Nine people set off on an adventure to Lost Lake for a glamping summer camp type wedding. The rest of the guests were supposed to join them in a few days, but the wedding never happened. Look, here's a picture. They were all young and hot and just having a good time, you know."

"Oh, it's so much worse when they're hot. Don't you think? Like more is lost somehow?"

"Uh yeah...Or it's the cases we hear about over and over again for years because of society's implicit bias to favor attractive people."

"Oh, shit, or that."

"Obviously I'm no better. I'm the one pulling out photos for a podcast. If you're listening and not watching on YouTube, the photo will be up on our Substack. I'll link it in the show notes. Anyway, this case is fascinating. I can't even begin to tell it without first talking about the one, the only, the infamous Wyatt James."

"Wyatt James? I've heard of him, I know I have, but I can't remember..."

"Oh boy. Well, sit back and let me tell you a story."

"A story before the story, my favorite."

Eric

This trip is starting to look like a mistake. But Allie is *so* hot. With her patch of shaved hair on the side near her ear and her forearm tattoo, she reminds me a little of Natalie Portman, only an edgier version. Basically, my dream girl.

It's more than that, though. What I'm feeling goes deeper than physical attraction. When I saw her, I heard violins. Actual goddamn music played somewhere in my brain, like one of those cheesy romance novels my mom used to read. Every time I hear them, it makes me think of that Burroughs quote, "Love is a haunting melody..."

I don't remember how the rest of it goes, but I do remember his other one that says it's our duty, "to love and feel without defense or reserve."

So, here I am.

I'm not one to turn down an adventure very often to begin with, but one with Allie? No way in hell would I pass that up. Not that it would've been me turning it down really.

How I got here is not the important part.

Her and me, alone in the woods, might be the start of something beautiful. That's what matters.

But now I'm in a car full of women that clearly don't want me here.

I clear my throat. "It's cool. I don't have to go." I actually do have to go. I need to be there. "We just thought—"

Jennifer laughs, almost an evil laugh. I wouldn't be surprised if she said something like "foolish mortal boy." A beat passes, then Dana and Lauren join in the laughter, and it starts to sound a little less maniacal.

"It's fine. You're already here, right?" Jennifer says with a tight smile and a glare in Allie's direction.

"It should only take us around an hour and a half or so to get to Hood River from here. I'm pretty sure we missed all the traffic," Dana says as she pulls the car onto Burnside headed toward the 30.

"How is the bar?" Jennifer asks. "I've been meaning to stop in, but it's been so busy with the wedding and the new job."

"Oh yeah, I saw something on MySpace. Where is your new job again?" Allie takes a big swig of the travel mimosa like she's self-medicating.

"It's at Wieden and Kennedy. I just started last month as a junior marketing strategist. I'm really learning a lot." She dips her head in what I think is supposed to be a humble gesture. Who is this woman? Anyone can see from a mile away that she is anything but humble.

"That's great." Allie takes another large sip. It's like the more she has to talk to the girls in the car the more she has to drink to compensate. Why have friends like this? Allie can do so much better than these plastic people.

"So, Eric, is it?" Lauren asks, leaning over Allie.

"Yessir." I salute.

Lauren appears unamused. Her light-brown hair with

blonde highlights is pulled back in a tight ponytail, and she throws it over her shoulder to face me. "What is it that you do?"

"I work at The Bonfire with Allie," I say. "What about you, was it Laura?"

I know it's Lauren, I just don't like the way she asked me what I did, as if she expected the answer to be nothing, or I work at Taco Bell or something. Which I have done, and aside from going home smelling like chalupas, it's not a terrible gig.

"Lauren," she corrects me. "I teach second grade."

I flinch. "Ugh, scary."

A loud laugh erupts from Allie, and a swell of pride warms my chest. She has a great laugh, her whole body laughs, and I made her do it. My mind slips into thinking about all the other noises I might be able to make her do, when to my surprise Lauren laughs too.

"Yeah, it really can be."

"What about you, Dana?" I say, feeling warmed up. Maybe these girls aren't so bad. At the very least, they can be characters in my next novel.

"I'm in law school, and I'm interning at Smith, Voorhees, and Lincoln."

"Voorhees? As in Jason Voorhees?" *Friday the 13th* is one of my all-time favorite movies. "So, he turned to law after all this time."

Allie laughs then covers her mouth. "It's her last name. Dana Voorhees. She's interning at her father's firm." Then lowering her voice, "She hates those jokes."

"Don't worry," Dana says with a tight smile I can see in the rear view mirror. "I've heard them all."

"We're willingly going to camp in the woods with a Voorhees?" I whisper to Allie and make an exaggerated, frightened face.

She laughs again, and the golden glow that blooms in my chest makes it clear this was a good idea.

Dana turns the station on the radio, and a news report fills the car. She reaches for the scan button again, but Lauren says, "Wait, I want to hear this."

"...looking for any information on the escape of Wyatt James from custody on his way to a sentencing hearing. James was—"

Dana flips the station.

"Hey, I wanted to hear that," Laura whines, and it sparks a red-hot anger in my stomach. Does she have to say it in such a childish way? We're all adults.

"No," Dana says flatly.

Dana's clearly the mom to Lauren's pouty child routine.

"Too dark. We all know why Wyatt James was convicted. I'm sure they'll find—oh yeah." Dana stops on a station playing Maroon Five and cranks it up.

Allie turns to me and mouths, *Kill me now.*

I make a gun with my finger and mime shooting her then myself.

She giggles, nearly spitting out her mimosa. Handing me the travel beverage, she lays her head on my shoulder. The soft scent of lavender and oranges floats off her hair in intoxicating waves.

Dana

Allie's snoring softly in the backseat. Of course she's asleep. I'm driving, and she's sleeping. As per usual, I'm doing everything and she's doing nothing. It's probably better. It's not like we have anything to say to her, anyway.

Conversation has always been stilted with her, but it's been nearly impossible since we all graduated. Actually, even before that, when she transferred to art school.

I check my rearview mirror as I pass a slow moving vehicle and am startled by Eric's light-blue eyes staring back at me.

I glance away. I cannot believe Allie brought him along. Who invites someone to their best friend's wedding at the very last minute? They can't have known each other long either; none of Allie's gentlemen friends last. Although, sadly, I have no room to talk on that front. But it's not that I don't try. My life just makes it challenging to get close to people. Allie, on the other hand, pushes people away.

I glance over at Jennifer typing something into her phone, her engagement ring sparkling, a soft smile on her face, and a pang of jealousy hits me so hard it's like a punch in the face.

I turn my eyes back to the road.

It should be me getting married. It's in the five-year plan that I made when I graduated high school. I was supposed to get married last year at twenty-four, but I still haven't found the right guy. And I refuse to settle.

Joe could be the one. He's definitely cute and manly in a way I don't normally go for. I usually date the thin, tall, polished type. Like Ben. Joe, on the other hand, is thick. His neck, his muscles, his... Let's just say he's definitely the most masculine man I've dated. He's also extremely quiet. It's like pulling teeth to get him to talk about anything, especially himself.

"You okay?" Jennifer asks as she closes her phone.

I slap on a fake smile, one I use so often these days it's hard to tell anymore if it's really false or if this is just my smile now—an unfeeling, forced grin.

"I'm fine." And I am. We've spent months planning this weekend. I just need to shake off this funk. It's going to be amazing. I lower my voice to a whisper. "Are you okay? With the unexpected guest?"

Jennifer shrugs and leans in. "There's not a lot we can do about it now. It's..." She rolls her eyes. "Whatever. Typical Allie, right?"

I nod. It *is* just like Allie. I don't know why I'm surprised anymore. Especially with what happened at the bachelorette party. After that mess, I half thought that Allie would make up some excuse not to come to the wedding at all. Honestly, I wish she did.

I've put so much effort into planning this. Not just me—me, Jennifer, Lauren, and the wedding planner Melanie. Allie better not fuck it up.

Allie

Rubbing my eyes, I stretch my arms out wide, before I remember I'm sitting bitch in the backseat of Dana's car.

Lauren bats away my arm. "Watch it!"

"Oops. Where are we?" Out the window dark-green clumps of trees pass by. My stomach turns. I swallow back the saliva filling my mouth, let out a slow exhale, and look out the front windshield, staring at the semi-truck ahead of us.

"Shh. We're nearly there," Dana whispers and points at Jennifer sleeping in the passenger seat, her golden hair flowing over her shoulders, rosebud lips parted ever so slightly. She looks like a Disney princess for Christ's sake.

I grab the travel mug from Eric. It's considerably lighter than when I handed it to him, but not empty. As I lift it to take a sip, the car drives over a bump and the cup hits my teeth instead. "Motherfucker!"

"Are you okay?" Eric puts a hand on my knee, sending little electric pulses through me.

"Didn't see the pothole."

Jennifer stirs in the passenger seat.

"Oh no," she says, her voice still thick with sleep. "I didn't mean to nap. That's totally against shotgun rules."

"No problem," Dana says with a facsimile of a smile.

Is she getting work done? Is that why her face looks pained every time she expresses an emotion other than judgment?

"You can nap a little more if you want."

"No, I'm awake." Jennifer sits up and ties her hair in a messy bun with a hair elastic she'd been wearing as a bracelet.

"How's the art stuff, Allie?"

I cough as uncomfortable beads of sweat prickles the back of my neck. I haven't shown anything since my BFA show over two years ago. Once I graduated, I upped my shifts at the bar to pay back loans and for things like food and rent. It's not like I wasn't creating anything. I've been working on a project in my off hours. But I'm not quite sure how to put it into words yet, and even if I could, I'm positive Jennifer wouldn't get it. That sounds pretentious, and it's untrue; Jennifer's very smart. I guess what I mean is she won't approve of it.

"It's going great."

"What are you working on?" Jennifer turns slightly, her eyes locking on mine. Then her gaze drifts to the back window, her face changing, brows knitting together.

Following her line of sight, I turn. A light-green truck missing its muffler is speeding down the road behind us, swerving this way and that to get around.

Dana lets out a sigh.

She slows down, but the pickup keeps making erratic motions with no real effort to pass. Dana blows out another breath. "Go around, already."

I fucking hate asshole drivers. Up ahead, there's a sign for a scenic viewpoint in two miles. I point at the sign. "Pull over. Then this jackass can pass."

"Okay." Dana speeds up. The beat up truck does as well.

"Where's the turnoff?" Jennifer asks as the truck gets closer to our bumper.

"It said two miles on the sign back there."

A small tunnel built into the side of a hill looms up ahead. I hate tunnels on a good day, with no cars around. So far, today has involved so many things I hate, when I could be home binge watching my roommate's box set of *Twin Peaks* with a mimosa.

"Hold your breath!" Lauren says.

"What?" I ask.

"You have to hold your breath through the tunnel. Otherwise, it's bad luck. Quick. 1, 2, 3."

There's a collective gasp for breath then complete silence in the car through the dark tunnel. Each overhead amber light illuminates the interior ever so slightly, making it feel like we're in a stop motion animation film.

My lungs burn. The rumble of the truck echoes through the tunnel surrounding us. I squeeze the travel mug in my hand, close my eyes, and try to calm my rising panic. Underneath the truck's engine in my left ear, there's the faint, but undeniable sound of breathing.

I open my eyes to find Eric looking at me, the corners of his lips turned up ever so slightly.

The turnoff comes into view. Dana takes a quick left, sending stray gravel spraying. For a brief moment, it looks like the truck is also going to turn in, but it swerves at the last second and keeps barreling down the 30. Dana pulls into a parking spot.

We all sit motionless.

Eric slaps his knees. "Well, that was nuts." He waggles his eyebrows at me and gets out of the car, walking toward the railing.

"Whew. Nice driving, Tex." Jennifer places a hand on Dana's shoulder. "I'm going to use that bathroom."

She points to a small stone building in the corner of the scenic viewpoint.

I join Eric. Past the guardrail is a huge drop off, leading into a valley with light-brown grass and dark-green trees, an odd mixture of moist and dry, desert and forest. But the real view is the river, little currents of white caps offsetting its deep blue color. It's a terrifying size.

Eric's staring at me, again. I haven't decided if his constant gaze is flattering or annoying. I turn away from the view to meet his eyes. "You didn't hold your breath, in the tunnel."

He gives me a sheepish grin and shrugs. "I make my own luck." He motions over the railing at the view. "Don't you want your camera? It's gorgeous."

"It is and I don't." Landscape photography is definitely not my thing. I don't have the knack for it, and to be honest, I don't care to learn.

Eric looks at me puzzled and laughs.

"How can you not like this?" He holds both hands out toward the river like he's offering it to me.

"I like it." I squint my eyes, turning the landscape into abstract shapes. "Sort of. I just don't want to photograph it. My work is more Merry Alpern than Ansel Adams."

"Merry who?"

"She's a photographer from New York. She made this amazing series called *Dirty Windows*, where she took pictures through her friend's apartment window into the neighboring building. It looked right into the bathroom of a sex club that a bunch of Wall Street guys hung out at."

Eric's eyebrows shoot up. "Whoa."

"Yeah. The images are really grainy, black and white. They show girls stripping, counting money, lots of cocaine, but despite the flashy subject matter—"

"Pun intended?" Eric interrupts with a smirk.

I shake my head and plow on, intent on my point. "The images themselves are quiet. They're human and sad. Vulnerable, you know."

"I'll have to look it up."

"You should. There's one where a woman is looking out the window. I think she's probably looking at her reflection in the glass. It's such an intimate moment. One we've all had. Where we look out and end up looking in instead. What am I doing with my life? What is anyone doing? Why do we exist? Just this pure moment of introspection and existential crisis. And we're the assholes watching it."

Eric laughs again, and I'm not sure why. What I said wasn't particularly funny. "Did the people in the club know they were being photographed?"

I shake my head, my eyes searching his face for a reaction, judgment, but there is none.

"What are your photos like then?"

Lauren yells at us, saving me from answering that last question.

"We should take a group photo! Did you bring your camera?" She and Dana are standing on the other side of the car.

I nod. "Is the car unlocked?"

Dana throws me the keys in a large high arc. They keep going past my outstretched fingers through the blue sky. Dana's face falls in slow motion, and Lauren screams, "No," as the keys sail past the railing, over the cliff, and into the gorge.

Gabe

Sun sparkles on the water out the window, like a beautiful girl winking from across the room. Light snores fill the car from the back.

"We're almost there," Ben says, never taking his eyes off the road. "We just have to stop for gas real quick."

He signals and exits the freeway. A few minutes later, we were pulling into a 76 station.

I hop out and unhook the pump.

"Whoa, dude!" Ben laughs. "Have you really been out of Oregon for that long?"

Shit. I hang the hose back on the hook and put both of my hands up as an attendant comes running over to us.

"Sorry, sorry." I completely forgot in Oregon you can't pump your own gas. "Is there a bathroom?"

The attendant makes a motion somewhere between a salute and a wave. "Key is at the counter."

I walk inside while flipping off my brother, who's still laughing. The 76 is bright and airy, but for some reason, it still reminds me of that movie *The Vanishing*, where the creepy guy kidnaps Sandra Bullock. I shake it off, grab the key to the bathroom, and make my way down the hall.

The bathroom's as clean as a roadside bathroom gets. Black graffiti covers the white plastic walls, but it smells more of soap than urine, so that's a good sign. The mirror is clouded over, like someone used Comet to clean it. Even through the film, I look like shit. Dark bags under my eyes and a heavy stubble. I run my hand over my chin, letting the scruff poke my palm. I probably should've shaved. Hopefully, I can somewhere before the wedding Saturday, or I'll never hear the end of it from mom. She'll go on and on about how I need to take better care of myself. Then she'll pop some of her little white pills and get really quiet. I tilt my head to the side, on second thought, maybe I won't shave.

She's probably already going ballistic about a camping wedding.

Only Ben. He freaking loved summer camp as a kid. Him and Nick even became counselors. It surprises me Jen went for the whole theme, though.

Nope.

None of my business. I wash my hands, disappointed but not surprised to find no paper towels. Wiping them off on my jeans, I return the key, and then get a drip coffee.

Back in the car, I blow some of the steam off my paper cup, full to the brim.

"Better drink up." Ben puts down his printed MapQuest pages and starts the car. "We're only about a five minute drive to the brewery."

"Oh, I didn't realize it was that close." I check the time—a little before noon. "Are they open this early?"

"They open at 11:30," Nick chimes in from the back.

"I was hoping we could rent some mountain bikes and

throw them in the bus, we should still have time, I think," Ben says as he flips the radio station.

"Cool, cool!" Nick says through a mouthful of chips.

"I've heard there's great trails around Oregon," Joe says, his voice so deep and gravelly it sounds like he's putting it on. Maybe part of it is just waking up. "I've never been in this area before."

"Really?" I'd never been to Lost Lake, it's definitely off the beaten path, but Hood River isn't a far drive from Portland. Most people make the trek there for camping or a concert or to float the river. Joe looks like a real outdoor kind of guy. The flannel he has on looks lived in.

"Yeah, I just moved to Portland a few months ago." Joe takes a gulp from his Nalgene.

"Huh." The information sounds familiar, like a conversation I only half paid attention to last night.

"That's so nuts. You really aren't from around here?" Nick asks. "I know I already told you, but you really do look exactly like this kid we went to high school with."

Joe shifts in his seat, his knees knocking into mine. "Just one of those faces, I guess."

"He sounded like you, too, like Tom Waits," Nick says.

Joe laughs. "I get that all the time. I must have a doppelgänger."

I check my phone. No texts. Sipping my drink, I nearly spit it out. It has coffee undertones to it, but the dominant flavor is rot. Why do I always get gas station coffee? I can count on one hand the amount of times it's been good enough to actually drink, and this time is not one of them. When will I ever learn?

The town passes by in a whirl of antique shops and restaurants. When we park, I dump the rest of my "coffee" in the parking lot then follow the boys inside. Nick and Ben are bounding in and slapping each other on the backs like excited puppies. Joe follows behind with his hands shoved in his jeans pockets, shoulders hiked to his ears.

A girl in a black Full Sail tank top and cut off shorts stands next to a podium at the front door. "Four for lunch?"

Nick moves a little too close to her and says in a low voice, "Hey."

Still a lech, I see.

The girl backs up immediately, and Ben jumps in. "There's going to be eight of us. We have a reservation under Ramirez."

"Ahh yes. Come on in, we have a gorgeous table for you on the patio."

Ben beams and claps me on the shoulder a little too hard. He's awfully handsy lately. We were never affectionate as children, but since my plane from Austin landed, it's been all high fives and back slaps. He's probably excited about his wedding, but I prefer our more hands-off approach to brotherhood.

We follow the hostess to our table. On a different day, in different company, the view would be calming. Rolling golden hills dotted with trees and the Columbia River rushing by.

The hostess hands us some menus.

"We'll start with four flights," Ben says.

The hostess smiles tightly. "I'll let your server know."

Ben takes a deep breath, a grin on his face from ear to ear. I don't think he noticed the hostess's annoyance with him, not that I would expect him to. My brother is a lot of things, but perceptive isn't one of them.

Joe motions out at the river. "This is rad, man."

"If you think this is beautiful," Nick says, "just wait until you see Lost Lake."

The waitress comes over, followed by another server with our beer tasting flights.

Nick holds up his glass. "To Ben's last days."

Ben rolls his eyes. "You make it sound like I'm dying."

"Better you than me, my friend."

We clink and drink. The beer is light and crisp on my tongue, so much better than the gas station coffee.

After the first two tastes are gone, my shoulders relax.

"So, where is the bride-to-be and crew?" Nick asks.

Ben swallows the beer he'd been considering. "On the way. They should be here around one or so, I think."

Nick nods.

"And then we're riding a bus?" Joe asks, sipping his sample size beer.

Ben says, "Yep, a big yellow school bus, well, except it's painted white."

"Wild," Joe says. "I don't think I've been on a school bus since fifth grade."

"Where did you go to school again, Joe?" Nick asks.

"Here and there. We moved around a lot. What about you?"

Nick motions his beer toward Ben. "Me and this fucker both went to Sabin Elementary. Met on the first day of second grade and been buds ever since."

He holds out his beer to Ben, who clinks it with his.

The waitress comes over and asks if we want food. We say we're waiting for our party but order full beers as everyone's flights are almost gone.

The day heats up as the drinks pass with superficial talk of sports I know nothing about and some show I've never seen. We're just finishing our second round when Ben stands up with his phone, holding it this way and that, fixated on the screen. It reminds me of gramps with his metal detector.

"What are you doing?" I say.

"Trying to find service. The girls should be here by now." Ben walks over near the railing, his phone pressed to one ear and his finger pressed to the other.

Pulling out my own phone, I flip it open. I have service. There are two notifications: one missed call, one voicemail, both from Sheila.

I shut the flip phone with a satisfying snap and take a large gulp of beer. I knew this call was coming. The last thing I need to hear is Sheila's excuses about why she can't make it.

Ben comes back to the table, shaking his head. "Nothing. No messages or texts. It goes straight to voicemail when I call."

"They could be out of service," Nick says.

Ben sighs. "Maybe. But what if they had car trouble? Should we go find them?"

"Um, no." Nick holds up his beer for emphasis.

Ben slumps in his chair, his shoulders sagging.

"They probably just got a late start or stopped to do some shopping. I'm sure they're fine." Nick plucks the menu from the table. "Let's order some food, I'm starving, and I wouldn't mind talking to our server again. She is smoking hot."

Ben shakes his head but picks up his menu. "You're right. They're probably shopping."

Dana

My flip-flops smack hard on the concrete as I run over to where Allie and Eric are standing looking out over the railing. Each slap sounds out a chant in my head, *stupid, stupid, stupid.* Lauren follows closely behind me, her Uggs soundless in comparison. What was I thinking throwing the keys? To Allie of all people. She's the least athletic person here.

"Still don't believe in bad luck?" Allie says dryly to Eric. I can't believe she's joking right now. Except I can. Typical Allie.

"What are we going to do?" Lauren says, panic making her already high voice an octave only dogs could really appreciate.

And that's when it hits me; I'm going to have to fix this. Just like I fix everything. I'm the planner. I'm the problem solver. In every situation, I'm always the one who has to take care of the hard tasks.

Allie's completely frozen, not moving or doing anything, and the overpowering smell of alcohol hovers around her like flies on shit. Her travel mug is probably filled with some kind of cocktail she learned to make at her bar.

I snap.

"Why didn't you catch the keys?" I yell.

"Um, hello, it's me. Why did you throw them?" She flings her hands in the air.

I run a hand through my hair and sigh. She's right, of course, everyone knows she can't catch. "Fair point."

Lauren says, "What about that guy you're dating, what's his name?"

"Joe," Eric answers without a moment's hesitation, his eyes still focused on the cliff.

A cold shiver ripples down my spine. How does he know who I'm seeing? We all direct our attention to him. He takes his eyes off scanning the hillside. "You mentioned it in the car earlier."

Did I?

Lauren looks at Eric like he's sprouted another head, then turns back to me, her brows knitted together. "Yeah—Joe, does he have a spare key?"

I shake my head. "No, we've only been dating a couple weeks."

Jennifer walks over and joins the group. "What's going on?"

"Dana threw the car keys over the cliff," Allie says.

I gasp.

That bitch.

Of course she's going to make this my fault. I'm about to protest—I never back down from a fight—but when I open my mouth to argue, a sob comes out instead. Fat tears roll down my cheeks.

"What?" Jennifer says. "Why?"

"I didn't mean to," I say.

Lauren rubs my shoulder. "It'll be okay. We'll figure it out."

I sniff and wipe my eyes. It must be the stress of the occasion. All the planning, my job, all my plans fraying at the seams.

This is so unlike me. I never cry in front of people.

"I think I see them." Eric points off in the distance.

Eric's gaze into the abyss had, apparently, been him looking for the keys.

We all look in the direction of where his finger is pointing. Beyond the railing, the hill, covered in brown grass and brambles, thrusts out for a few feet then plummets sharply down. On a little ledge just beyond a sagebrush something silver glints in the sunlight. The keys.

I clap my hands. "Perfect. I'll call—"

Quick as a shot Allie jumps over the railing.

Allie

Without another thought, I hop over the rusted metal guard rail to the cries and protests of the group.

"Whoa!" Eric grabs for my arm, but I pull away before he can catch it.

"Maybe, I should go." He lowers his voice. "I've had a lot less of our travel beverage."

Is he implying I'm drunk from a little mimosa? "I'll be fine."

Possibly plummeting to my death is better than standing there while Dana blames me for the whole thing, then lords it over me all weekend that she's the one that got us out of the trouble I put us in, again. Plus, her solution is to hire people to fix it. We'll be stuck here for hours waiting.

"If I fall, someone has to go after me and pull me up. That's your job." I give Eric a smile and a wink.

Gingerly, I make my way down, my stomach lurching each time the smooth sole of my Van's slips on the patchy grass.

Don't look down, don't look down. Just look at the keys.

A surprised scream escapes me as my worn out sole slides again, and this time, I end up on my ass in the dirt, skidding down the hill. Cries echo from above, but I ignore them, focusing only on not descending into the gorge. I put down both feet and dig them into the dirt, slowing my slide. Once my descent is more in my control, I scoot the rest of the way on my butt. Not glamorous, but effective. Finally, I reach the keys.

When I turn back toward the railing, Lauren and Dana are hugging and Jennifer is jumping with her hands in the air. Only Eric isn't celebrating, he's leaning over the railing, watching me intensely.

Glancing at the trail that I traveled down, my stomach flips. I slid more of the way than I thought. How am I supposed to get back up? Should I crawl? My shoulders sag as I try to work out the problem I got myself into. It's an apt metaphor for my life, really. How many times have I found myself at the bottom of a cliff I just flung myself over?

I stand on trembling legs, feeling like a baby deer trying to walk. Shaking my head, I take a deep breath and throw my shoulders back. I can do this. I've gotten myself out of all the other sticky situations I've been in. Like when I was cornered in the club by that smelly guy twice my size. A swift kick to the balls and I was back by the bar taking another shot, no worse for wear. This hill just needs a swift kick to the balls.

Scanning the landscape, I try to find a rock or something that might give me more purchase than the slick dead grass and dirt combo. Instead of going straight up, the way I came down, I pick my way back going left and then right, sticking near the plants so if I fall at least, I'll have something to hold on to.

When I make it up to the railing again, I'm on the other side of the car than where I started. The group joins me.

Eric gives me a hand over the rail. "When I pointed out the keys, I didn't mean for you to go."

Shrugging, I hand the keys to Dana. "Who needs a drink?"

I brush the dirt off my legs.

Dana unlocks the back of the car. "We still need our picture."

I sigh. "To commemorate getting run off the road by some redneck piece of shit and then nearly falling to my death in the gorge?"

"Yep," Jennifer says smiling. "Get your camera."

Digging through my black duffel bag, I pull out a smaller camera bag and grab my Canon EOS Rebel 2000. The feel of the smooth leather grip in my hand dissolves all the lingering adrenaline from my trip down the mountain. After I find the little cordless remote, I scout a set up spot.

"Dana, can you pull the car out a little? Just to here?" I motion with my arm.

Dana climbs into the driver's seat without question. One thing I appreciate is this group believes in my vision for a photo; I don't have to waste time explaining it. When it comes to photos, they trust me.

Once the car is in position, I set the camera up on a mini tripod then place it on the hood and angle it down. I arrange the group kneeling with one knee down, one up. Lauren sits criss-cross applesauce on the ground in the middle.

I start snapping with my little remote then instruct, "Okay, everyone look up and say, *Fuck You!*"

They all laugh and yell, fuck you—Jennifer with surprising gusto.

Gabe

A bustle of fabric swishing, beads clacking, and flip-flops smacking announces the arrival of the girls, such a sharp contrast to the peaceful afternoon we'd been having that I wince.

"Sorry, sorry. We're here," Dana says, throwing her dark-brown hair behind her shoulder. Her silky tank top and shiny lipstick make her look like a little girl playing dress up. Or maybe just to me. I see the gangly thirteen-year-old who used to come over to our house in too short of plaid skirts asking for Ben. She heads straight to Joe and kisses him on the cheek.

Joe smiles, but it seems forced. Or maybe I'm projecting.

Jennifer comes into view next. I try not to stare as she slides a hand on the back of my brother's neck and gives him a kiss on the mouth. I can't look away. Her golden hair falls over both of them, blocking my view of their faces, but not of her tight wedding-white cut offs straining to contain her pert ass as she bends over.

Taking a long sip of beer, I force my eyes away, catching the girl with the anti-establishment haircut, a camera hanging around her neck, staring at me. Or rather she catches me staring at Jennifer.

She purses her lips, rolls her eyes, and takes an empty seat. "Does this place serve liquor? I'd kill for a whiskey."

"What happened to you guys?" Ben asks. "We were getting really worried."

Dana lets out a long breath. "Well—"

"Long story," Jennifer cuts in, "it'll sound better by the campfire."

The other girl with furry boots despite the heat is reading the menu, looking like she sucked on a lemon. "They only serve beer here."

"It is a brewery," Nick says and takes a swig of his drink.

"Yeah, but I thought they'd have wine too," she whines as the waitress places food in front of all the dudes at the table. Except the one they brought with tattoos covering his forearms sitting by the whiskey drinker.

Dana places a hand on Joe's arm. "You guys ordered?"

"We were hungry." Nick picks up a fry. "We thought you all stopped to shop or something."

Joe just shrugs.

"Hey, man, I'm Ben." My always friendly brother leans over the table to shake hands with the tattooed stranger.

"Eric," the kid says, shaking hands.

We all make introductions around the table. The girls order beers, most of them begrudgingly, and I sink my teeth into my burger. Bloody. Just the way I like it.

Lauren leans toward me. "What do you do, Gabe?"

I hold up my finger and point to my mouth, hoping she'll lose interest, but she just waits. After I swallow my bite I say, "I'm in advertising."

"Oh my god, like Jennifer," Lauren says. "Do you two ever work together or cross paths?"

I'm quick to say, "No."

But Jennifer is also quick. "Occasionally."

Dana's face wrinkles between her very plucked brows. She knows something. What has Jennifer told her?

"Well, I live in Austin, but I guess." I fake reaching back into my mind for some distant memory—not one I've played over and over again. "There was that one conference we both ended up at. Where was it?"

"San Fran." Jennifer smiles, mischief dancing in her eyes. She's enjoying this.

"Oh, that's cool." Dana sips her beer, and I wonder again if she knows more than she should.

Eric leans forward in his chair. "How do you all know each other?"

"College," Allie and Lauren say in unison.

"But some of us have known each other longer than that. Nick, Ben, and I all went to high school together." Dana fiddles with a coaster, her long nails clacking on the metal table as she does. "And Gabe, but he was a few years ahead. He's Ben's brother."

Eric squints at me. "Ahh, I see the resemblance."

I smile tightly. I've heard it my whole life. We have similar noses, and face shape, but I've always hated the comments about it. When we were kids, people would ask if we were twins even though I was always three or four inches taller. Still am.

Ben's Nokia vibrates obnoxiously on the wire table. Must be getting service now. He picks it up, puts a hand to his ear, and stalks off to the railing.

"I sort of miss the days where we didn't have cell phones, you know. Where you could just sit and have a beer and no one could talk to you but the people that were actually there," Allie says to no one in particular, twirling her beer around on the table.

Jennifer's tapping away on the tiny keyboard of her phone, "You're going to love Lost Lake then. There's no service up there, so all these fancy things won't even work."

She closes her phone and puts it in her bag.

My thigh vibrates, my phone in my pocket coming to life. I look at Jennifer, but she won't catch my eye.

Ben rejoins the table. "The bus is almost here. They just stopped for gas."

"Great!" Jennifer downs the rest of her beer in three long swigs.

"Whoo!" Dana cheers. "Get it, girl."

She slams down the beer—the clang of the metal making my jaw clench—wipes her mouth with the back of her hand, and looks me right in the eye.

I get up. "I'm going to hit the head before we get on the road."

"Yeah." Ben nods. "We all should, it's still a ways to the campsite."

Fuck. I want a moment alone. To get my thoughts together. To check my phone. But now it's a group pissing party.

I reach the bathroom first, followed closely by Nick, Ben, Joe, and Eric.

Nick talks the whole way. The dude never shuts up. "It's been so long since we all hung out. Lauren looks good. What's with Allie's hair, though?"

The bathroom is too full. I leave, heading straight for the front door. In the parking lot, I pull my phone out and open it. One message. I take a deep breath and click on the little envelope to open it.

We need to talk. L8tr.

It's from Jennifer. I let go of the breath I didn't realize I was holding and put the phone back in my pocket.

Fuck me.

The school bus rumbles through the lot. Taking the speed bumps as ungracefully as a drunk man trying to eat a bowl of ramen. I'm not sure why my brother thought it would be a good idea to trade in comfortable cars for vinyl bucket seats.

A loud exhale behind me makes me turn around.

"Sorry, was that out loud?" Allie runs a hand through her hair and looks around. "I'm going to go run over to that store before we get on the bus. Can you let the others know?"

"Sure," I say and watch as she walks across the parking lot, the back of her jean shorts covered in dirt for some reason.

"Where is she going?" Jennifer asks behind me.

I turn. To my disappointment, she's not alone.

"That store," I say, trying to sound casual. Trying to sound like a platonic soon-to-be brother-in-law.

"Ahh, that's not a bad idea."

Dana claps. "Ooh let's go. Maybe there are souvenirs."

Jennifer and Lauren laugh.

Ben comes running out of the brewery and picks Jennifer up from behind. She squeals, the sound making all the little hairs on the back of my neck stand at attention.

"Put me down."

Ben obeys quickly.

Jennifer tugs down her tank top that rode up the slightest bit on her lower stomach. "We're going to the store."

"Babe." Ben sighs. "The bus is stocked with road beverages and snacks. We have everything else we need at the campsite."

"Girl stuff," Jennifer says.

"Souvenirs!" Dana lifts a fist in the air as if leading the charge. Lauren and Jennifer giggle, the sound cutting through the humid day and lightening it.

"Whatever. I'm getting on the bus and cracking open a beer." Ben kisses her on the cheek.

"Have fun," Joe says to Dana.

Dana's face falls. "You're not coming?"

He shakes his head.

"What about you, Gabe?" Jennifer looks at me with those light-blue, almost green eyes.

"How can I pass up souvenirs?"

Jennifer turns her dazzling smile on me, and something in my chest loosens. "Let's go then."

@JustVeronica

534 likes 18 comments 155 saves 122 shares

Video posted July 20th, 2024 1:17pm PST.

The screen shows a blonde woman, her hair pushed back with a fluffy pink headband. She's dabbing foundation under her eyes.

"Get ready with me to go to a double shift at work.

"Okay so as you all know, I am a huge true crime nut and today on my very favorite show, *Murder? What Murder?*—they are covering a case I have a personal connection to. It's actually what got me into true crime in the first place. It's so surreal, having met them all. My friends are sick of hearing me talk about it. So you get to. Yay.

"It's The Lost Lake Murders. I was working at a brewery at the time. It was fine. Busy. The tips were good and mostly people kept their shit together. And one day on the lunch shift a typical group of late twenty-somethings came in for food and some flights.

"Overall, they were chill. Kind of more chill than I would've expected for a wedding party. Not much laughter came from

44

their table. Every time I passed the conversation seemed... What's the word I'm looking for? Stilted.

"For a bunch of friends, they seemed guarded with each other. But maybe I'm just projecting since I know what happened later. They drank a lot. Like a shit ton really. All of them were pretty tipsy by the time they left. All of them except the blonde woman, who I now know was the bride, Jennifer.

"She wasn't drinking. I've had friends question me about this. They say, but it was her wedding. Wouldn't she be partying? But I am one hundred percent certain. With what happened after—with Wyatt James and everything—that whole week is burned into my memory. She had a beer in front of her, but she didn't touch it. I offered to get her a soda, and she declined. It even looked like she was pretending to take sips."

"It was odd, but not enough to spark huge alarm bells or anything. After I saw what happened, I felt terrible. I shouldn't have served them that last round. I should've cut them off.

"Not that it would've saved any of them.

"I'm going to link this foundation below, see what it did for my under-eye bags. They're gone. Like literally."

#GRWM #Lostlakemurders #Murder?WhatMurder?

Allie

The sliding doors open and goosebumps ripple on my arms as the blast of air conditioning hits my skin, still sticky with dirt and sweat. I take a big gulp of the cool air, enjoying the fluorescent lights and brightly colored products.

I wander the aisles looking for the liquor. My nerves are still a little shot from my trek down the hill; a swig or two should soothe them. I stroll the magazine aisle and pick up an activity book. It's a jumbo one, the kind with all sorts of different puzzles, just like one I had as a kid. I flip through the pages until I find what I was looking for, a logic puzzle.

My grandmother, who (lucky for me) hated children, raised me. She hated everything really, except good gossip and a dry martini. She didn't have any toys or video games. Her home wasn't child friendly—the shelves filled with more things I wasn't allowed to touch than things I was. So, I'd pass the time reading pilfered Stephen King novels and pouring over these logic puzzles. You're given a set of clues, then you use the grid provided to eliminate suspects until you find the answer. I got so good at them I started making them harder by covering clues or timing myself.

Taking the book with me, I continue my search. I'm about to turn the corner to the next aisle when I stop short. At the end of the shelves, near the body wash, Jennifer and Gabe are whispering. They're standing close together, too close. I hide back on the end cap.

Shit. I thought Gabe was lusting after Jennifer's ass when we got to the brewery.

My finger itches for the trigger on my camera. This would fit in perfectly with what I've been working on. Stolen moments, somewhere between voyeurism and surveillance. I bring my camera to my eye, focusing on Jennifer and Gabe together through the viewfinder, her hips point toward him, his hands hang reluctantly at his sides, and their faces intense. But I put my camera down. They'd hear the shutter, wouldn't they? Even if they didn't, how could I ever use the photos?

I move to turn the other way, but my foot hits the shelf, knocking over several cans of Pringles with a loud clatter.

Jennifer suddenly appears, without Gabe. "Oh my god, Allie. What happened?"

"My foot hit the edge." I kneel and pick up the stray cans.

Jennifer bends to help. "Are you drunk already?"

No, I was startled by you standing oddly close to your brother-in-law.

Instead, I say, "Nope, not hardly. I was actually hoping to get a little whiskey for the bus ride...for everyone."

Jennifer wrinkles her pert little nose. "We have beer and wine on the bus. I don't think we need whiskey. Besides, I don't think they sell liquor here. But have you looked in the back? There's a whole antique store."

"Whoa? Really?"

"Let's go check it out. I think I saw Lauren and Dana head back there."

"Do you need to get something, though?" I ask.

She shakes her head, holding up a brown paper bag already in her hands. She must've known exactly what she wanted when we came in.

"Already got it. Just needed some girl stuff."

Girl stuff? What girl stuff? There's no way perfect 28 day cycle Jennifer would plan her wedding when she has her period.

We wander to the back. A mannequin guards the entrance wearing a bright-yellow sundress with giant green flowers straight out of the seventies. Next to her is a shopping cart with books stacked inside.

I can't tell if it's two businesses or one; there's a small open door between them. Lauren and Dana find us just as I'm holding out the dress on the mannequin. I can feel Dana watching me, and I wish she'd just give it a rest. She's going to say something snarky, then I'm going to say something back, Jennifer is going to play peacemaker, and the rest of the afternoon will be so awkward. Why do I keep subjecting myself to this?

Gabe

Out the sliding glass doors, I'm immediately met with a blast of the afternoon heat like a stiff slap in the face. Just what I need. I walk down the road, trying to clear my head. I'm not ready to get on the bus yet.

Why couldn't Sheila have just come with me? I'm not an idiot. I know why. She's an intern at a law firm working on a big case. Either way, it was unfair of me to ask her to come just to be my emotional beard. We've only been dating a few months.

Is that right? Only a couple of months? Wait, we met in October. So, it's been almost a year. How did that happen?

The sun glints on the windows as I pass boutique wineries and antique shops, ending up at a small park with a bench facing the water and pulling out a pack of cigarettes. One of my New Year's resolutions this year was to quit. It's only July, so there's still time. Today is definitely not the day to give up my vices. This one at least.

Twirling the white paper stick between my fingers, like I learned to do in high school, I pull out my lighter, put the cigarette to my lips, and inhale deeply, watching the river rush by.

How long can I hide here before someone comes looking for me? Once the heat from my cigarette starts to warm the insides of my fingers, I stub it out.

I'm just snagging another cigarette when a voice startles me.

"Mind if I bum one of those?" A girl with short red hair and pointy collarbones jutting out of her white tank top asks, holding out an arm covered in knotted hemp bracelets.

I eye her. "You old enough to smoke?"

"Shit, man. I'm nineteen. I just look young because I'm small."

I smile. "Nineteen is young."

"But old enough to smoke." She sits down on the bench next to me. "I'll trade you for one. I'm no freeloader."

I hand over a cigarette and shake my head, uncomfortable out here alone in a park with a teenager while I'm pushing thirty. "You can have one. I don't need anything from you."

"Let me trade you. It's not weird, I'm not going to offer to suck your dick or anything."

I scoot a little away.

She laughs, a shrill sound that makes my ears buzz. "Come on. Light me, please." She leans in, the cigarette to her lips, and I flick my lighter, cupping my other hand to block the wind.

On her exhale, she says, "I'll read your palm. I'm really good. I learned when I was thirteen from this old lady that used to be my neighbor. Come on, it'll be fun."

She smiles, and a warm summer breeze blows through the park.

"Okay. Sure." I hold out my palm.

The girl takes it in her small hand and traces her pointer fingers on the lines, her nail bitten to the quick, black nail polish chipping off. "You have air hands."

"Air hands?"

"It means you're curious by nature."

I give her a wry smile. "Aren't we all?"

"No." She laughs, that high-pitched din that sets my teeth on edge. "You'd be surprised how many people choose ignorance. There's a reason 'bury your head in the sand' is a saying."

She traces her finger on a groove near the top of my palm. "This is your heart line. You have a tendency to be restless in relationships, but when you're really in love, you wear your heart on your sleeve."

I nod, suddenly very invested.

"This is your head line." She giggles. "You have a lot to learn."

"That's the truth."

"This small cross here shows you're a hit with the ladies." She wiggles her eyebrows, her cigarette hanging out of her mouth, reminiscent of Groucho Marx.

I laugh and feel some of the intensity of the moment evaporate.

She traces a finger on a crease in the middle of my palm that intersects to two lines and lets out a huff. "This is your stress line. It's kind of big."

"That's what she said." The joke is out of my mouth before I really consider the appropriateness.

She just rolls her eyes. "Big stress line means big trauma."

The truth of this sinks into my bones. I was an angry kid, and an even angrier teenager. It didn't help that Ben was always so easygoing. Sunshine to my clouds. A day never passed without my mother remarking on it. *Ben mowed the lawn without even being asked, isn't that lovely? Ben got an A in Algebra, maybe he can tutor you? Ben got another badge today at Scouts, do you want to give it another try? I'm sure they'd take you back if you apologize.*

By the time I was sixteen, I'd had enough. I ran away. My father tracked me down after about a week at an abandoned house that local kids used to fuck in and junkies used to shoot up. I was dirty and drunk on forties of OE, but at least I didn't try smack. I could've easily, and I've often wondered what would've happened if I did. My *Butterfly Effect* moment, I guess.

I've always felt solid, righteous even, in my ability to refuse. Mom didn't see it that way. She didn't speak to me for a month after I got home. Maybe that's what this girl sees in my palm. Can the broken lines of my hands really show my fractured relationship with my mother?

"Is it in the future or in the past?"

She shakes her head. "It doesn't work like that. This is your life line." She squints at it then lightly runs her fingertip from the top of my palm to the curved groove near my thumb. "How old are you?"

"Twenty-nine."

She drops my hand and takes the cigarette out of her mouth, exhaling a huge plume of smoke. "I'm not that good at it yet."

My phone vibrates in my pocket as if on cue.

"Did you see something?"

She gazes off at the river, then at her own palm, then throws her cigarette. "I probably shouldn't smoke. My life line says I'm going to live a long, long time. Probably til I'm ninety. It'd be a shame not to be able to breathe on my own at the end."

Holding out her palm face up to me, she traces a long line to the base of her hand. "Take care of yourself, mister."

She stands and walks away. I examine what she called my life line—a deep red groove that cuts off abruptly.

"Hey," I call after her. "Should I quit smoking?"

She stops and turns. A shiver rushes through me as she shrugs. "Smoke 'em if you got 'em."

She strolls away, waving over her shoulder.

I stand, brushing ash off my legs and trying to shake off the interaction. It's silly, listening to this girl. Palm reading. Come on. Am I really that desperate for direction in my life that I'm going to put stock into a random teenager at a park?

I need a real drink.

@DelilahAbbot | What UpDog?
60.3K likes 1.9K comments 6.6K saves 3.7K shares

Video posted July 20th, 2024 1:30pm PST.

Gorgeous amber light fills the screen. It shows a close-up of a red-haired woman sitting in a studio with hardwood floors and mirrored walls. She's wearing a matching beige crop top and leggings, both of which are linked in the shop.

"So, most of you know me as a yogi, a mom, a human. I'm all about positive living and treating others with kindness. But I wasn't always like that. I used to be lost. And I'm sitting here watching the *Murder? What Murder?* livestream, getting ready for my two o'clock vinyasa class and I realized I've never shared this story of what led me to be the person I am today. I met Gabe Ramirez.

"I ran into him. Total chance. The Universe had to have been behind it. And I read his palm. I don't even know why. Something in me wanted to save him. As soon as his hand touched mine though, I got bad vibes. Really bad. This might sound really weird, but talking to him felt like staring death in the face. If I hadn't been so addicted to nicotine at the time, I

54

would've left. I would've dropped his hand and walked away. But I really wanted a smoke, and for an older guy, Gabe was pretty hot.

"All the death and chaos was right there in the lines of his palm. It wasn't until *years* later that I found out what really happened, though. After I talked to Gabe in the park, I had this heavy feeling of dread in my chest, and it just wouldn't go away. So, I hitched my way down to California, took a free yoga class, and it changed my life. As you all know.

"But my interaction with Gabe has haunted me. Not all the time. You know me, most of the time I'm up. I'm in the flow. I'm happy. But sometimes when I'm on a walk, or holding a long pigeon pose, or making a smoothie in my Samurai blender (it's linked in the shop)... sometimes I've found myself back on that sunny day in the park. I wonder if there's something I could've done. Or said. I know there's not.

"It's just astounding how awful people can be."
#Mystory #Lostlakemurders #Murder?WhatMurder?

Dana

Allie holds out the dress from the mannequin form. It looks like it's about her size—tiny. It's also an absolutely hideous color, somewhere between canary and baby food.

"That would look really cute on you, Allie!" Jennifer squeals, Lauren nodding behind her.

"You think?" I look at the dress again. The pattern is awful. "I'm not sure about the yellow with her complexion."

Jennifer tilts her head to the side. "You'd look great in yellow with your dark hair."

I suppress a sigh. Jennifer always does this around Allie. Usually, Jennifer and I agree on everything. We like the same foods, we shop at the same stores, we even have the same taste in guys—both of us have a massive crush on Ryan Gosling at the moment. We've seen *The Notebook* in the theater twice already. But around Allie, she suddenly becomes very contrary. I think it's so Allie feels more included, or something.

"Some color might be nice," Lauren says as she walks back into the store.

Allie lets go of the dress. "I don't know if it's really me. I might've worn something like it a couple of years ago."

She follows Lauren inside.

"Of course. Because we don't know who she is, right?" I whisper to Jennifer. I think her problem is that we see her too well.

Jennifer rolls her eyes. "You know Allie, she always has to be different."

Jennifer walks inside, and I follow. A strong smell of dust, with a subtle vanilla undertone, permeates the store. Random stuff lines every corner—ceramic horses, enamel pins, a brass sign spelling out *love* in cursive script. Overflowing shelves, cluttered tables. There's even knickknacks hanging from the ceiling. On any trip we've ever taken, we always stop at antique stores we pass. It's a thing. I pick up a burgundy eel skin pocket book, the leather soft as butter but leaving a light covering of dust on my hands. I throw it back on the table and vow not to touch anything else. Honestly, I prefer it when we stop at the cleaner gift shops.

I wish Joe had joined us.

It is nice to see him getting along with the other boys so well now. When Joe and I went on a double date with Ben and Jennifer a couple weeks ago, the atmosphere felt a bit frosty. We went to cocktails together and then dinner at Montage. The night was fun, we even shared an appetizer called Gator Bites that was actual alligator. But I got the feeling that Ben really didn't like Joe very much. Joe felt the same and said later that he thought Ben was jealous. Which is silly. I explained it wasn't like that.

Ben and I have been friends since we were in middle school. We briefly "dated." Not a lot to write home about. We went to a dance, held hands while watching *The Mask*, and shared a truly terrible kiss. There were braces involved. It was a disaster. At the time, I never wanted to do it again. Then, we decided being friends was better, or I convinced him of that anyway.

Sometimes I wonder...what if I hadn't? Once Ben lost the braces and got a couple inches taller, he didn't even resemble that awkward teen. He was handsome, confident, and now he's extremely successful. It could be my wedding this weekend.

But that's a silly thought.

Ben's dated loads of girls since then, some of my friends from cheerleading. Then we went to the same college, Portland State University. I was surprised he didn't go to a school on the East Coast, but he went on and on about the finance program at PSU. I could see when I introduced him to Jennifer, he was a goner. He got this glazed look in his eyes. You could just tell it was love at first sight.

I find Lauren and Jennifer giggling, trying on sunglasses, both with ridiculously massive sun hats on.

"Yes! I love it!" Jennifer grabs a bright-yellow floppy canvas sun hat and puts it on my head.

"Nope." But I can't help smiling as I catch a glimpse of the hat in the mirror. It's kind of cute.

Jennifer places a straw hat on her head and suddenly makes it look effortlessly cool. I toss the yellow parasail back on the shelf, and something gold and shiny catches my eye in the display case next to the hats. Looking closer, I can hardly believe it.

"Look, girls!"

Eric

When I'm done with the bathroom, no one is at the table. I make my way outside, and everyone is gone.

So far, this isn't the romantic trip I'd imagined. I can't figure out why Allie ditched me. You know those things you can get for your keys where you whistle twice and it beeps? I feel like one of those would be really useful on Allie.

Something about her is not quite right. Like when she jumped over the railing. I tried to grab her, to pull her back up, but she moved so fast. I'm not going to lie, it was badass, but also really dumb. She could've slipped all the way down in a heartbeat.

I'm known for not looking before I leap, but this was a-whole-nother level.

It's like her self-preservation switch is turned off. But maybe that's a good thing. What was it that Jack Kerouac said? Something about how the best people are the mad ones, the ones that burn, burn, burn like spiders across the stars. Something like that.

Allie definitely burns bright, that's for sure.

Heading down the sidewalk, I try to figure out where she would go. The streets feel empty. Where are all the people in this town? Despite the intense heat of the afternoon, a chill passes through me like a shadow.

I saw an episode of *Unsolved Mysteries* once when I was probably too young to be watching it, where a group of people went camping and then completely vanished. All their camping gear and shit were found at the campsite, but there was absolutely no trace of them.

I've always wondered if they vanished all at once or if they went one by one.

This line of thinking is dangerous. I wipe my palm off on my jeans. I just need to find Allie.

Down the road, I come across a bar that puts the capital D in dive. It has a beat up old sandwich board out front with what looks like a cartoon cowboy boot that, based on its red eyes, is either high or drunk. Painted in swirly black cursive it says *Last Chance*. This is where I'll find her, probably having a whiskey.

Last Chance is dark; the only light spilling in is from the propped open door, dingy windows and neon beer sign over the bar. A standing fan sits off to the side, but it feels like it's blowing in hot air from outside. There's a pool table in the corner where a couple of guys in leather vests with matching patches knock some balls around. To the side of the pool table is a jukebox, one of those newer ones with flashing lights and too many buttons, playing "Walkin' After Midnight." We have one just like it at the Bonfire.

No one from the party is here, and again those missing campers come to mind. I wasn't in the bathroom that long. Where did they all go? Did they leave me here? I glance around the bar again.

If they left me, I'll be fine. I've gotten myself out of worse places. I pull up a stool at the worn wood bar. The news is playing on a small television in the corner. The anchor woman, wearing a blue suit, walks in front of a white van.

"Wyatt James was riding in a van just like this one." She motions to the vehicle. "He was being transported to his hearing, when there was a terrible accident. The van ran off the road, flipping multiple times. The driver and guard were tragically killed, but James fled the scene on foot and is still at large.

"Wyatt James is on trial for the murder of five women horrendously slaughtered between 1995-2001. The victims, all from the Portland area, were between the ages of sixteen and twenty-five. Only during the trial did the full story emerge."

The screen flashes to an old sun-faded photograph of a young woman in a swimsuit with long dark hair. Then scrolls to another similar-looking woman playing in the snow. It keeps scrolling through family snapshots, showing the victims during happier times. They all have dark hair and big brown doe eyes with thick lashes, just like Allie.

"Usual cuts marked each woman's body. Shapes, diamonds to be exact, were meticulously carved into their skin before they were stabbed in the heart and left for dead."

The screen flashes back to the reporter. "Wyatt James has always maintained his innocence. Since his initial arrest late last year, there have been two more murders of young women with the same shapes carved into their bodies. Could it be a copycat? Or is Wyatt James innocent after all?

"Police are looking for any help in locating Wyatt..."

I run my hands along the beveled edge of the bar, grounding myself back in the present. Even on vacation, there's no escaping the ugliness that humanity is capable of. It's at once comforting and disheartening.

Holding my hand up to the bartender, I order a Pabst.

Allie

I slowly make my way through the room, looking at the eight tracks and mushroom-shaped cookie jars. Maybe this trip won't be so bad. Dana will be Dana, but we can all still have fun. I just need to relax.

I nearly stumble on the perfect pair of deep reddish brown cowboy boots, with a small heel and white top stitching. I slip off my shoe and try one on. It fits perfectly. I carry the other one and go in search of a mirror.

Dana's pointing out something in one of the display cases to Lauren and Jennifer.

I hurry over, my barefoot on tiptoe to compensate for the heeled boot on the other foot. "I want to see!"

Dana looks me up and down, the judgment on her face almost as thick as her foundation. Her gaze lingers on the cowboy boot. I know it's not her style. We've never shared the same taste in clothes, or music, or much, really.

Jennifer was my assigned roommate in the dorms. Her half of the room was already fully decorated when I got there—her Dave Mathew's tie-dyed tapestry hanging on the wall. I vowed to myself if she played "Crash into Me" more than once a week,

I'd move out. Or better yet, burn that tapestry and hide her CDs.

I was sure we'd hate each other, or at best get along only enough to cohabitate. But then I met her. She walked in wearing cut off shorts and an old Mickey Mouse T-shirt, her long golden hair loose at her shoulders. Jennifer is magnetic, she was even then, and as the years have passed, her pull has only gotten stronger. She has an easy smile and when you talk, she looks at you, really looks, and listens with her whole body, leaning in, nodding, like what you're saying is meaningful. Like you are the most important person. When she first turned her attention on me that day in the dorm, it felt like sitting in the sun on the first warm day of summer. We wandered campus together and got ice cream at the quad. It was the first time in a long time I made a real friend.

Jennifer met Dana and Lauren in her Intro to Philosophy course. After a year all together at the dorms, we got a house off campus together, Dana convincing us all it was the best decision. Despite being roommates for nearly two years, I never felt the same closeness with Lauren or Dana. For all the countless nights we spent together drinking wine, doing face masks, and watching *Sex in the City*, at the end of the day they're Jennifer's friends.

"What did you find?" I ask, not in the mood for any criticism on my fashion choices.

Lauren points at the display case. "Look."

I follow the line of her finger to the most amazing knife I've ever seen. It has a dull metal handle with gold patches not yet worn off. It's shaped like a naked woman. With a delicate smile on her face, she covers her crotch with her hands while her breasts are on full display. Ornate waves mark the base that lead to a six-inch blade. More of a dagger than a knife.

"Holy shit." It's amazing.

"Guys, look at this!" Jennifer calls out from a nearby stall. Dana and Lauren hurry off, but I stay a bit longer to admire the dagger.

I track down an attendant, and they ring up my purchases. Jennifer finds me as I'm taking the brown paper bag. "Let's go!"

We all head back through the drugstore.

"I'll be right there," Dana says as we get to the door. "I just need to grab some shampoo. I'll meet you all on the bus."

Outside, the heat wafts off the asphalt in waves. I follow Jennifer and Lauren across the street.

The bright-white school bus trembles under the weight of the heavy bass.

Jennifer climbs the stairs first, swaying her hips then, obeying Snoop's instructions, she drops it like it's hot in the narrow grooved space between the vinyl seats. Ben lets out a low wolf whistle, while Lauren starts dancing with Jennifer. I bring up the rear, shimmying my shoulders despite myself. It isn't really my jam, but even I can admit it's catchy.

A champagne cork pops, and a whoop escapes me that I didn't even know was coming. Nick climbs over the bucket seats to bring me a glass and grabs my hips as the song changes to "Toxic." His hands are strong, but I have absolutely no interest in dancing with Nick. I move away in time to the music and sip the cold, fizzy elixir, looking around the bus for Eric.

A crackled voice comes over the speaker. "Folks. Listen up, the music is all right, but y'all need to sit down when the bus gets moving."

I nearly spit out my champagne, laughing. "Oh my god. It really *is* just like summer camp."

Jennifer nods and smiles, a devilish twinkle in her eyes. "Of course, sir. We're just waiting for one more girl."

"No problem," the gruff-looking older man says with a small salute. He's wearing a black leather biker vest, his white hair slicked back and thinning a bit on top. He reminds me of my bus driver from grade school, well minus the biker vest.

"Do we need to get our bags?" I ask.

"They're already loaded," Nick calls out, raising his beer. "They're in the back."

I raise my solo cup of champagne back to him.

"Oh no, are you all just waiting on me?" Dana says as she climbs the bus stairs.

"It's cool. We're not in a hurry. The campsites should all be set up, so it won't matter if we get there after dark," Jennifer says brightly as she takes a seat next to Ben.

Ben half stands in the bucket seat, pointing at each of us. "Hey, hold up. Where's Gabe?"

I do my own count. "And Eric?"

Gabe

own the road, I find a place and walk inside, my eyes adjusting to the dark. Two bikers playing pool freeze as I enter, watching my every move. This is not a bar for tourists or any old passersby. This is a bar for locals, and the sooner I leave, the better. I'll just have one drink.

That kid Eric is perched on a stool, his elbows leaned against the long wooden counter. I really want to be alone. But it's not like I can ignore Eric. Can I?

I approach. "Mind if I sit?"

If Eric is surprised to see me, he doesn't show it. "Knock yourself out."

The bartender slides a frosty can of beer to Eric, and he catches it mid-slide.

The bartender is smiling, but when he turns to me, his face is stern as he asks what I want. Maybe he likes Eric because of his tattoos. They're all black ink. Lots of random pictures. Some look professional, but some are definitely homemade. It reminds me of this kid I knew in middle school who would sit in fifth period English with a broken Bic pen and a sewing needle, poking away until he had yet another pointy Stussy S.

There's a cassette tape on Eric's forearm with a band name scrawled on it. I lean in a little closer, and he holds out his arm so I can get a better look.

"Got any?"

Sitting up straighter, I take a sip of my whiskey, trying to wash away my embarrassment for being caught staring at his arms. "No. Thought about it a couple times. I even had a friend draw up a design for me, I just never committed."

Eric nods like he understands, but clearly, he doesn't. Over-thinking doesn't seem to be a problem for Eric. Maybe he doesn't understand the magnitude of permanence, or maybe he understands in a way I never could.

A loud laugh busts through the door.

"There you two are." Allie struts over, her cowboy boots thumping against the wood floor.

"Hey, boots." Eric smiles at her in a way that feels familiar and also so foreign. When was the last time I looked at anyone like that? I know the exact day, but now it's all gone to shit.

Allie lifts one leg and twirls like a ballerina, drawing the attention of the bikers playing pool. "Aren't they amazing? I had to get them. Everyone's waiting for you two on the bus."

Allie sits at the bar and calls to the bartender. "Can I get a shot of Maker's quick? And their tabs?"

The bartender salutes.

"We have to go. Jennifer's pissed."

I can picture her, arms crossed, lips tight.

The bartender hands her the drink. She winks at him then downs it in one go.

We all file out, the bikers watching us in that lazy menacing way a snake watches a mouse when it's full. Lagging behind, I pull my phone out of my pocket. Two bars of service and one text from Ben.

We ready 2 go!

I send a quick text, but not to Ben.

Music blaring from the bus reaches me before we even step foot in the parking lot. I take a big inhale like I would before diving into a pool and trudge up the steps.

"Gabe! Gabe!" Ben and Nick are chanting.

"Gabe! Gabe!" The girls join in, clapping now as well. "Gabe! Gabe!"

"Okay, okay. I'm here! Enough!"

"Driver!" Ben says.

Jennifer swats him on the arm. "His name is Rusty."

Ben gives Jennifer a kiss on the cheek, murmuring something in her ear. When he pulls back, he says, "Rusty, my good man, let's go."

The engine rumbles to life with spurts and chugs, and we're off.

About an hour into the drive, the party vibes die down. Light music plays over the stereo, something Lauren picked out. What little civilization is left fades away, houses and churches replaced with trees and more trees. The road goes up and then starts to wind. Corkscrew after corkscrew. The bus slows to a snail's pace to make the turns. I pull out my phone. No reply and no service. I glance over my shoulder, toward the back of the bus. Jennifer's sitting close to Ben, holding hands, looking out the window.

I don't know why I sent the text.

That's not true. I know why. I just can't help myself.

Allie groans. "Oh man, I think I might be sick."

"Look out the windshield," Dana says and goes to sit behind Allie, rubbing her back. "If your brain can anticipate the turns, it'll make you feel less nauseous."

Allie moves quickly to the front, and Dana's hand hangs in the air for a moment. They're odd friends, those two. They act more like me and Ben.

The road narrows, the curves more frequent and the trees thicker. All the blood rushes to my toes and gasps surround me as we go around a sharp turn coming bus to face with a raccoon running across the road. The school bus lurches to the side, teetering precariously for a moment on two wheels, getting dangerously close to the steep cliff, then righting itself with a thud. It's a miracle we didn't tumble right over the side. The cliff looks bottomless. Rocks skid over the side, tumbling out of sight into the abyss.

The bus returns to the paved part of the road.

"Everyone okay?" the driver asks.

Yeses are softly spoken.

"I think so," Ben says. "We're nearly there, right?"

"Not sure. I haven't driven up this way before," the driver says, his eyes fixed on the road.

I turn to Ben. "Haven't you been up here a million times?"

He shakes his head. "Just once. But we loved it." Ben puts an arm around Jennifer. "I'm pretty sure we're close to the campground."

Nick chimes in. "It's about a mile further."

The road only stays paved for another half mile before the whole thing turns into gravel. We bump painfully along. What the fuck are we doing? Ben loves camping. But Jennifer has never struck me as the outdoorsy type. Maybe I don't know her as well as I think I do.

On the right, there's a small glossy wooden sign with the words *Lost Lake* carved into it. The bus pulls into a large circular lot and parks.

Allie's the first one off the bus, practically throwing herself at the doors before we fully stop. I exit at a more measured pace.

The air smells clean, like dirt and trees and sunlight. There's a small boat ramp at the far end of the circular lot leading to deep blue water, Mt. Hood towering behind it proudly. The sun's already starting to dip behind the massive mountain in the distance, the sky taking on that pearly gray hue that happens before the real sunset. I inhale deeply, feeling the heaviness in my chest loosen, the muscles in my upper shoulders ease.

Ben slaps me on the back. "It's something, huh? Wait till you see the set up."

I look around. "Where are we staying?"

Ben points to a small dirt trail. "We have to trek in just a bit."

Rusty's loading the bags into a small green wire wagon.

We rejoin the group. Rusty hands the wagon handle over to Nick. "You kids going to be, okay? You have everything you need?"

Ben says. "Yep, everything should be all ready for us. Thank you, Rusty. We'll see you in a couple days."

Rusty salutes and gets on the bus, honking the horn as he drives away. The tightness returns in my chest as the reality of the plan hits me.

We're out here in the middle of nowhere with no vehicle.

Sober Bikers Unite

Rusty L. Smith Posted on Facebook July
28 2014

Just a quick intro. Sobriety date- 3/18/2004. Started riding shortly after. Riding became my new addiction. Longtime member of the group, first time poster.

Today is a hard day for me. Ten years ago I dropped off a group of kids out at Lost Lake. I worked for a driving company at the time. Later I became a bus driver for school, it was better for my sobriety. Less party buses. But ten years ago, I took a wedding party out to Lost Lake by Hood River. Most of them drunk as skunks.

That day tested me. All that booze on the bus. I felt funny dropping them off in the woods, way out up on the mountain with no way home, but it was their plan. And I needed to get to a meeting, so I closed the doors and sped away. Turns out those were the kids from the Lost Lake Massacre. I heard it all on the news. I shouldn't have left them up there. I've had to live with that guilt.

Allie

As soon as the bus comes to a stop, I run out the squeaky doors gulping fresh air, my stomach roiling. I'm never the best on long drives, but all those twists and turns, I gag just thinking about it.

A warm hand lands on my shoulder, and I spin around.

Eric moves, backs up. "I didn't mean to scare you. I just wanted to see if you're okay."

I let out a breath. "I'm fine. Just got a little car sick, or bus sick, I guess."

Eric nods then moves his gaze from me to the lake. It's post-card perfect, with the still blue water in front and the mountain looming in the background basked in golden light.

"It's beautiful. But I know you won't want to take a picture."

I laugh. I feel better now that I'm not in a rickety metal death trap.

"Come on!" Dana claps from the opening of the small dirt trail. "Let's go see the campground!"

Enormous pine trees covered in hanging moss tower on either side of the narrow trail. There's a gnarled one with branches hanging over the path that is particularly menacing. It reminds me of my grandmother.

When I was a kid, the neighbor lady used to watch me every Sunday. She smelled like moth balls, but she always made muffins or cookies or brownies, so I didn't mind going over there, but I hated leaving. I hated the walk back to our house, my grandmother's house, really—in all my years there, it never felt like mine. There was a long line of trees dividing our yards. I was always scared of those trees, like they were standing guard. I thought they were angry with me specifically. When the wind would blow, it was like they were waving their angry arms. The loud rustle of the leaves their livid cries. I wanted to run. To be as far away from the trees as I could get as fast as possible. But then the trees would know that I knew they were more than trees.

So, I would walk, as calmly and casually as I could muster, while my heart was beating out of my chest, my knuckles white, fingernails digging into my palms. On one very blustery day, I told my grandmother about the trees, and she said between sips of her gin martini, "Smart girl. Never tip your hand. Just keep walking by, cool as a cucumber."

I shake myself out of the memory. Beyond the trees, there's a view of the lake, a light breeze causing ripples, but not one boat out in the water.

It's so quiet, just the muffled sound of our footsteps crossing over the pine needles and dirt. As the trees get thicker, the path gets darker, and the late day sun dips below the tree line. There's a little wooden bridge over a creek covered in large bulb twinkle lights.

The first campsite is on the other side of the bridge, a massive white canvas tent already set up. Hanging from the enormous tree near the tent is a colorful hammock filled with throw pillows. Red canvas camping chairs surround the fire.

"Wow," I say walking into the site. In the tent, there's a large bed covered in a pillowy soft white comforter, with a pink fur blanket thrown on top and about twenty throw pillows. There's a Pendleton patterned rug partially covering the floor in shades of dusty pinks and grays. The top of the tent goes up into a point, giving it a high ceiling feel, and a chandelier with glass cups filled with votive candles hangs from the middle support pole. A fucking camping chandelier.

On the bedside table there's a gift basket with all sorts of fancy snacks and packets of flavored drinks. There's a rust-brown beanie with the words *Ben and Jennifer* 2004 embroidered on it, and I immediately put it on with a laugh. I pick up the next party favor, a pink 10 inch Maglite style flashlight with my name engraved on it. The weight of it surprises me.

"Nice hat," Jennifer says behind me. I model it for her with a little twirl. "I thought this could be your tent—yours and Eric's. Is there enough room for both of you?"

She's pissed I brought him—her tone is laced with it. "There's more than enough room." I smile. "Are all the sites like this?"

"Pretty much. This is actually the smallest site." She frowns. "I feel bad. If we'd known Eric was coming, we would've had a flashlight made for him too and put you in one of the larger tents with more space."

Mine's always the smallest. It would've been even if they knew he was coming. I'm used to it by now with this crew. I put the flashlight back. "It's fine, really."

"We have another site for hanging out. During the planning, we were calling it Central Perk. You know, like from *Friends*. Come on. I'll show you."

We all follow Jennifer to the next site. There's another huge canvas tent, but inside instead of a bed is a couch, furry bean bag chairs, two larger chairs, and a fully stocked bar cart. Outside there are multiple coolers and a grill.

Camping chairs draped with blankets surround the fire pit; a boom box rests on the table nearby. They've thought of everything, as usual.

The site is much bigger than mine, almost three times the size. At the very edge is a small staircase that leads to the lake. I walk down it, leaving the rest of the group to fawn over the fancy set up. At the bottom of the wood and dirt stairs, there's a little trail that keeps going into the thick darkness of trees. Does it circle the entire lake?

I kick off my shoes and cross the cold dirt trail, the grass cool on my feet, a welcome change from being barefoot in leather cowboy boots. Not my most solid plan for sure.

This nature stuff might not be so bad.

I sit down and put my feet in the lake, gasping at the swift shock of cold water. Instinctively, I yank them out, but then I ease them in again, this time kicking as I go, splashing the water.

I'm still sweaty and dirty from my trip down the hill. Fuck it. I take off my shirt, wriggle out of my shorts, and jump in the lake. The cold steals my breath for a moment, goosebumps covering my skin. I arch my arms and swim hard into the lake, hoping the movement will warm me up, and it does. The water surrounds, me and a surprising calm washes over me.

Once my arms burn from the effort, I make my way back to the shore, sitting on the side of the lake in the grass. The air's still warm, and the grass soft. The lake is quiet, just the faint sound of birds singing in the distance and my feet splashing in and out of the water. It's weird knowing we're the only ones out here.

But then I notice movement through the trees across the lake.

Dana

Honestly, this is exquisite. Exactly how we planned it—actually, it's even better than we imagined. Central Perk is amazing. Jennifer and Ben really went all out with the booze too. There's some serious top-shelf stuff on the bar cart. I smile when I see the case of Tempranillo. It's the exact brand Jennifer, Lauren, and I drank what seemed like gallons of on a trip to Puerto Rico. They served it cold at the hotel we stayed at, which was unexpectedly refreshing. Taking one of the bottles by the neck, I go to put it in the cooler for later but stop when I see Allie's little friend over there getting a beer. I'll chill some later. I grab a glass instead and undo the screw top, pouring myself a little nip.

For the life of me, I can't remember why Allie hadn't come with on that trip. Money probably. She's always been a bit of a penny pincher, and she's so weird when Jennifer offers to pay for her.

"Gimme, gimme." Lauren snags a glass and holds it out to me.

I splash some in then pour myself a little more. It's an occasion after all. This year's been so hard, I deserve to let my hair down. Cut loose.

Lauren takes a large gulp. "Ooh, just like Vieques."

Jennifer hurries over to us. "You're drinking one of my surprises!"

"Sorry, not sorry." I wink at her. "Want a glass?"

"Later. I'm still feeling buzzed from the brewery."

Of course she is. Jennifer's just as small as Allie. Yet somehow Allie can pound drinks all day—well, until she can't. Hopefully she won't get like that on this trip.

Jennifer bounces up and down on her heels. "So, what do you think?"

"It's perfect," Lauren says.

It is. I'd just been thinking how wonderful it all turned out. But now, standing here in front of Jennifer, with her shiny hair, still looking completely put together after hours in a car and bus, I don't want to admit it. I nod instead and take another sip of the tart red wine so I won't say a snarky remark like too bad the rugs are knock offs.

It's ridiculous that I even want to say something like that to my best friend, especially since I was there when we selected the rugs. It's just sometimes when I'm near Jennifer, despite being a size six to her two, I feel small. I've always had issues with comparing myself to others. There was that girl in high school...what a mess.

I take another sip of wine. That was a lifetime ago. And I've grown. I didn't say the bitchy thing, and I'm smiling. We're having a great time.

Joe joins our little group. I put my arm around his back, snuggling into him. His body feels stiff, like any normal adult that's been on a literal school bus for hours. I lean my head on his shoulder, trying to soften him. This time next year, this might be our wedding. Except I do *not* want to get married somewhere quite so *wild*.

Don't get me wrong, I love nature, and Jennifer's photos are going to be amazing, but I wouldn't want my dress to be soiled. I think we'll get married at The Heathman at Christmastime—they have such a nice tree there. Or if we want to do a summer wedding, maybe at a winery. I went to a wedding last year at a winery in Brush Prairie and it was stunning. Although the reception was on a paved platform, it still felt like being in nature, surrounded by lush greenery, but no heels sunk into the ground.

There's no way I'm getting married in flats.

"This is sweet," Joe says.

"Thanks. I couldn't have done it without my girls." Jennifer hip bumps Lauren.

"And the wedding planner," I say, keeping my voice sweet but reminding Jennifer of how much of this she had no part in.

"Well, yeah," Lauren says in the most agreeable tone. "We're not masochists."

Joe laughs a little too loud.

"Let me go tell Ben where we're going, then I'll show you your tents." Jennifer smiles. "There's more gifts."

Gabe

Ben smirks at me. "Crazy, huh?"

Crazy is an understatement. Sitting on a fluffy bean bag chair covered in faux pink fur, I take in the massive tent. I've lived in apartments smaller than this. "How'd you get all this stuff out here?"

Ben shrugs. "The wedding planner arranged it all. Apparently, these upscale camping weddings are all the rage in the UK. Drink?"

I nod.

"Jennifer saw pictures from the planner's portfolio and fell in love with the idea."

Jen's idea?

Ben pours some whiskey into two crystal glasses then hands one to me, clinking his on the way.

"Cheers," I say, looking at the blankets on the chairs by the fire pit. I motion my head that way as Ben takes a seat on the couch. When he plops down, I can hear the air in it shift. Must be inflatable. "Hopefully it doesn't rain."

Ben makes a face somewhere between a grimace and a frown. "Watching the weather is our new hobby. It's rained more in this area this year than it has since 1943. But it's just stuff. If it rains, it'll get wet, then it'll dry out. The forecast said it's supposed to be dry while we're here, but..." He shrugs. "Either way, it'll be fine."

Jennifer slinks into the tent. "We won't have any rain."

"Of course we won't." Ben stands and takes Jennifer's hand. "As usual, the universe will bend to your will." He kisses the back of her hand, and I clench my fist reflexively, thinking about the odd palm reading in the park.

She smiles. "Damn straight."

Ben returns to his seat on the couch.

"We're going to keep exploring the sites."

Ben smiles but makes no move to get up.

Jennifer turns to me. "Your tent is next door to the left if you're facing the lake. We'll all meet back here in an hour or so to make dinner."

I try to say thank you, but the words die in my throat as Jennifer gives Ben a chaste kiss.

"Our site is three over," she says practically into Ben's mouth.

Ben whispers something I can't hear. She walks off, and the noises of the group fade.

Inhaling the fresh lake air and the strong scent of whiskey, I take out my phone. I don't have any bars of service.

Ben laughs as I hold up the phone. "Those are completely useless out here. No service."

"Anywhere?"

He shakes his head. "When we came to check the place out, as far as I could tell, there was nothing."

A slick of unease settles in my gut at the thought of not only no vehicle, but also no cell service, as I put my phone back in my pocket.

"Is Sheila coming with the rest of the guests on Saturday?"

"That was the plan. She had some work she needed to finish, so she was going to fly out Friday night and rent a car. But I missed a call from her." I sigh. "I should've checked the message before we got up here."

Ben laughs, again. Everything is so fucking funny to him. I grit my teeth and take a sip of whiskey. Of course he's laughing. He's happy. It's his goddamn wedding party.

"You probably should've. How long have you guys been dating again?"

"A while." I met Sheila at a bar right after I got Ben and Jennifer's save the date card in the mail. I walked right up to her sitting alone sipping a white wine and flipping through a large file. I asked if I could buy her a drink, and then another, and at the end of the night I asked very politely if I could take her home and lick her pussy.

The sex is good. Sheila's hot, with long brown hair and even longer legs. She's smart. Too smart for me. It's quite possible she's not here now because she's already seen through my bullshit.

I shrug. "I'm sure it's all fine. I'm going to get settled." I pour a little more whiskey in the glass and head to the site next door.

The set up looks the same as the other campsite, but with no hammock. I lie on the bed for a while, staring at the ceiling, but I'm restless. Heading down the stairs toward the lake, I pull out a cigarette. The sky's getting darker and the water along with it. I light my cigarette and take a deep inhale. A splash in the water draws my attention. It's Allie in a bikini, dangling her feet into the lake.

"Hey." I walk over. Once I get closer, I realize it's not a bikini, but her underwear. I avert my eyes, instead focusing on a nearby fern. "Sorry."

She hardly glances my way, her focus fixed on the dense trees across the lake. "It's fine, really. Look over there."

I follow her pointed finger. Even squinting, I can't see anything besides the landscape. "What? What is it?"

"A couple minutes ago, I saw movement." She's scanning the trees still, her eyes darting back and forth.

"Could be a deer or something." I smile wide, trying to lighten the mood. "Maybe Bigfoot."

"Ha-fucking-ha. Do you think there's a camping site on that side?" Her normally smooth brow has a large worried crease in the middle.

I shrug. "I'm not sure. But it's all the way on the other side of the lake. I wouldn't worry."

She looks at the trail behind me. "Do you think this trail goes all the way around?"

"Probably." I sip my whiskey, considering. It stands to reason there'd be a path. Most lakes, especially ones with camp-sites, have them. Allie's expression remains strained.

"What do you do? Back in Portland?" I ask, more to distract her than any real interest on my part.

"I'm a bartender, mostly."

Now I'm interested. "Mostly?"

"I also make stuff."

"Like what stuff?"

"Art. I'm an artist. I just don't like the way it sounds when I say it. I sound like a dick." She puts on a fancy accent and raises her pinky in the air. "I'm an *artist*."

I laugh. She's funny. And not like Ben's other friends. What is she doing here with them? "I see your point. What kind of stuff do you make?"

"Photographs mostly."

"That's pretty broad. Of what?"

I jump as a deep voice says, "I brought you these."

Eric stands behind us, a beer and a towel held out to Allie.

"Sorry, man, I didn't know you were down here. I can grab you a beer too."

He turns his head back in the direction of the campsite. My throat goes dry as I notice the black stick and poke diamond tattoos on his neck, sprawling down below the neckline of his shirt. There has to be at least ten in various sizes, just that I can see. I let out a long exhale of smoke.

Murder? What murder? Episode 189 July 20, 2024

"**B**efore we get into Wyatt's story... I need some answers."

"Ha, Jules, you always do. Fire way."

"So, let me get this straight. Our little group of hotties went out to this super remote place in the woods on a school bus. And then they let the bus leave?"

"Yes, Jules, that's exactly what they did. Like they had never seen a scary movie in their entire lives."

"I can't believe it. Only I can because I would've totally done something like that in my early twenties."

"One hundred percent, me too."

"So, what was the plan exactly?"

"The plan was for the wedding party to camp and have some time to chill before the big day. So, the rest of the guests were coming just for the wedding and the reception on Saturday. At that point, they'd ride one of the buses back with the guests and stay at a hotel in Hood River."

"So, the wedding was Saturday, but they got there Wednesday?"

"Yes. Nine of them got there Wednesday. The bride-to-be

Jennifer, the groom Ben, his brother Gabe, and then there were the bridesmaids, Dana, Lauren, and Allie. There was the best man, Nick. Then there was Joe, who was Dana's date, and Eric, who was Allie's coworker."

"I got it. I think. Wait, hold up. Her coworker?"

"Yeah, Eric had just started working with Allie at the Bonfire."

"Oh my god. The Bonfire on Stark Street, right? I loved that bar!"

"Me too! But get this, the weird thing was Eric had literally just started. The night before they went on this trip was his first day, or I guess night, on the job."

"What? Did they know each other before?"

"No. Not as far as anyone knew."

"So, Allie basically invited a stranger into the woods."

"Yes."

"Oh boy."

"You can say that again."

Eric

Allie reaches for the beer, and I place the towel around her shoulders. While I was exploring the sites, I saw Allie jump into the lake in nothing but her sexy black underwear. I got two beers and tracked down a couple towels. These are not camping towels. They are fancy hotel style towels, heavy in my hand and soft under my fingers. I don't even own towels this nice. After seeing Allie's house, I doubt she does either. How do they all stay friends and why?

Fire creeped through my veins when I saw her talking to that Gabe guy. I don't like him. He's a walking rain cloud, just his presence immediately brings the mood down. Anywhere else, I would tell him to fuck off, but I don't want Allie to think I'm an asshole, because despite what some people might say, I'm really not.

"He's...interesting," I say as I watch Gabe leave. "He keeps giving me weird looks. I don't know, maybe it's in my head."

"Something's up with him for sure."

"Does he have a thing for you?" I smile, trying not to sound as jealous as I feel.

She laughs. Ahh that noise. If I had a cell phone, I'd make it my ringtone.

"No." She lowers her voice to a whisper. It's so sexy, a shiver zips through me. "I think he might actually have a thing for Jennifer."

I match her whisper, leaning in closer. "Is that the bossy one with the purple shirt?"

"No, that one is Dana. Jennifer is the bride."

"Oh shit."

She nods.

"Glad it's not our mess. Salut." I hold my beer out to hers. She cracks hers open, holding it away so the small spray of beer doesn't get us, then knocks it against mine and takes several gulps.

An eagle soars through the empty sky. It makes a large arc and circles around, keeping its wings completely stiff. Allie follows my gaze.

My grandmother's voice rings loud in my head before I say, "It's an ideal day to be bold."

Allie

"Ideal, huh?" What a funny thing to say. Eric's full of surprises.

His cheeks turn an adorable shade of pink. "It's something my grandma always used to say. We'd go on nature walks—they were hikes, really—but she called them nature walks. Whenever we saw an eagle, she'd stop and say, 'It's an ideal day to be bold.' I can't see an eagle now without thinking about it." He shrugs. "Were you close with your grandma?"

I pause, considering the question. My grandmother raised me. My mother was a migrating butterfly, always flitting in and out of the picture looking for a sunnier place to be. So, proximity-wise my grandmother and I were very close, but emotionally she was a hard woman to get to know.

Taking a sip of my beer, I'm still unsure of how to answer, when out of nowhere the eagle dives, talons first, almost cartoon-like, and snatches a fish from the lake. I'm so surprised that beer sputters from my mouth. I wipe it away. "Holy shit! Did you see that?"

Eric's lips curl up slowly. It's a knee-weakening smile. He reaches out and swipes at a drop of beer left on my mouth. Heat unfurls through me as his finger lingers on my lip. I take it in my mouth and suck lightly, watching his pupils double in size.

He pulls his finger back gently, lifting me up to stand and bringing me close to his body, close enough for me to feel how excited he is. "Wanna check out the tent?"

I nod, locking my eyes with his.

He grabs my hand, and we run up the stairs. Stopping by the picnic table of our site, he turns to me and puts his large hand on my cheek. His blue eyes glisten with heat. I kiss him hard, wrapping my arms around his neck, careful not to spill my beer all over him. His lips are soft and wet.

A tingling sensation spreads through me as his hands find my hips. He hoists me to sit on the picnic table. I let out a squeal, surprised at this new take charge side of Eric.

But I like to be the one in charge.

Setting down my beer, I pull up the bottom of his shirt. He helps tug it the rest of the way off, throwing it over his shoulder, revealing a washboard stomach and so many tattoos. The largest is of three skeletons dancing under his ribs. I run my fingertips on the inked bones, feeling his goosebumps as I do.

He leans in and kisses my neck right under my jawbone. I let out a moan, his soft touch sending an electric pulse straight between my thighs.

His lips increase their pressure on my neck while he unhooks my bra. His hands make their way around to my breasts, giving both a hard squeeze. Then, lightening his grip, he rubs his thumb back and forth over my nipple.

Another moan escapes me, and his hands respond, squeezing my breasts. I shrug off the rest of my bra and relish the cool breeze on my bare skin. Eric bends his head and kisses my right breast, lightly teasing with his tongue. I squeeze my legs around his waist and feel how hard he is through his jeans.

A piercing crack echoes through the trees, and all the blood rushes to my toes. It sounded like the earth itself opened up. I pull back. "What was that?"

Eric looks around. As he moves, there's a flash of color through the trees. Was it a person?

"Probably just something at one of the other sites. Maybe they're breaking branches for firewood."

Eric turns his attention back to my breasts. But I'm still searching the trees behind him for color, movement, anything that shouldn't be here. I'm not sure what I'm looking for.

There's a faint sound far off, like a low rumble. Then another loud crack.

"Did you hear that?"

Eric stops and stands straight, looking like a prairie dog.

Music comes from the site next door.

"The music, maybe? Do you want to go in the tent?"

I pick up my beer and sip it, considering. "Maybe we could pick this up again later?"

Eric's face falls, but he says, "Sure. Yeah. I'm getting pretty hungry."

I pull the towel over my shoulders. Eric grabs his shirt, shaking off the dirt before putting it back on.

Sighing, I wonder if I'm being paranoid. Should I have just taken this beautiful man into the tent? The smell of burgers wafts over from the neighboring site. I smile and hop off the table. There's plenty of time.

"Let's go check out the food." I go to the tent and put on a dry tank top, leaving the still wet bra on the table. Wriggling on my shorts, I dig out my favorite oversized cardigan that hangs to my knees. As I get my Van's from the antique store bag, the dagger falls onto the ground.

Eric picks it up, turning it over in his hand. "Whoa! What's this?"

"It's rad, huh?" I slip the shoes on my feet and hold my hand out for the dagger. Eric's gripping the handle tight, and I instinctively take a step back.

"It's..." He pauses, thinking, then says, "intense."

He hands the dagger back to me.

The woman on the handle smiles serenely at me. "She is. She just looked so lonely sitting in the display case, I couldn't leave her there. Anyway, I thought it might come in handy camping."

I put the dagger on the side table by the bed. Right next to the large gift basket. "Let's go eat."

Eric says, "I'm just going to find the bathroom. I'll meet you over there."

I give him a kiss that leaves no doubt that I want to pick this up later and go to the hangout campsite one spot over. The sites are hidden from each other by big clusters of trees, so I can't see who all is there until I walk into the site. Nick's standing at the grill, beer in one hand, spatula in the other. He catches my eye as I approach and gives me a look I can't read. I break our staring contest quickly, not sure what his gaze meant, but not liking it all the same. Nick's always given me an odd feeling. Not like full-on creeps, but he's definitely one of *those* guys. If someone asked him my eye color, he'd probably have no idea. Now if someone asked him my cup size, I'm sure he'd have a pretty good guess.

The picnic table is set with plates, potato chips, watermelon, macaroni salad, and a boom box playing "Float On." I suppress a groan. I'm a huge fan of Modest Mouse, but not this new album. It's so clean, so poppy. Give me *Lonesome Crowded West* any day over this top forty bullshit.

Dana and Lauren sit in chairs by the small fire, drinks in hand laughing and chatting. All the others are nowhere to be seen.

Gabe

My heart pounds heavily in my chest as I continue down the dirt trail. I pull my cigarettes from my pocket and light up. Just because this Eric kid has diamonds on his neck doesn't mean anything. A small voice in the back of my head won't stop. It must be the news reports about Wyatt James getting into my head. But what if he really was innocent and whoever was responsible was never found?

Ridiculous. Lots of people have weird tattoos. The other day at a bar in my neighborhood, a dude had a Mrs. Doubtfire tattoo, for Christ's sake.

My heart rate starts to match the pace of my footsteps. I take a deep breath of fresh mountain air, then inhale an even larger breath of sweet, sweet nicotine.

I pull out my phone, and there's still no service. I hold it up, moving it this way and that, but no bars appear.

"Damn."

Should've just listened to the message from Sheila before coming out into no man's land. I shove the phone back in my pocket.

I walk for so long that it seems faster to just keep going and come around the other side. There are a couple of empty camping sites along the way. It's eerie being the only group at a big camping spot like this. This definitely isn't what I would've chosen for my wedding. Not that I'm dying to get married, but I'd be a liar if I said I hadn't been thinking about it more and more.

It might be nice to settle down. Start a family. I may not have a choice in the matter on that front. That thought makes my head swirl, so I pick up my pace again and focus on my surroundings.

The shadows are getting long. Sweat drips from my brow. The trail opens up, and there's a large lodge with big windows and an A-frame roof. There might be a phone.

The wooden steps of the porch creak under my boots. I try the door. Locked. Figures. The porch wraps around the building, so I follow it around, searching for a way in. In the back are sliding doors, but they're locked as well.

I check my phone again. Still no service. Why didn't I just answer the phone when she called? I know why.

Jennifer.

Shoving my phone back in my pocket, I notice there's a trail on the backside of the lodge. I follow it, and it leads to the parking lot where the bus pulled in. I take the upper trail and am just about to go into the bathroom, when someone grabs my arm and pulls me into the trees.

"What the—"

I whip around, ready to slug Nick for one of his stupid pranks, when my words catch in my throat. It's Jennifer. Her blonde hair framing her flushed cheeks. I reach out and tuck a strand behind her ear.

She moves away. It's minuscule, but I notice.

What the fuck? She's the one that pulled me into the trees,

not the other way around. Then our talk in the Walgreens comes back to me in a whoosh.

I say, "Did you...?"

"Yes." She locks on me with those pale-blue eyes. What is that Lou Reed song? "Pale Blue Eyes." Everything I've had and couldn't keep. That's not quite it, but the feeling is the same. Sometimes the tune reverberates in my head when I look at her and a profound wave of sadness passes over me, followed always by a swift kick of anger.

I have to look away, and it's a good thing I do, because Ben's striding down the path, straight toward us.

"I'm pretty sure he can't see us from back here," Jennifer says.

But I'm not so sure. I jump out onto the path. "Hey, man."

Ben's face shifts, like a shadow passes in front of it. He has his phone out. Does he get service out here?

"What are you doing behind the bathrooms?" he asks, his brow wrinkled.

I plead with Jennifer in my head to go the other way, hide behind a tree, anything but what she does, which is step out on the path and tuck her shirt in. Why does she need to tuck her shirt in right at this moment?

Ben's eyes shift back and forth between me and Jennifer until they land solidly on me with an almost audible thunk.

"What are you two doing?"

I hesitate for a beat that feels like an hour.

The leaves blow in slow motion.

A cricket chirps so loud it feels like it's in my ear.

Jennifer speaks, and the world returns to normal speed. "Gabe found a deer. It ran back that way through the woods. I only got to see a glimpse, but it was stunning."

She smiles, and my little brother melts right before my eyes.

"It's a woodland paradise, just like you wanted."

Paradise. Right. "I'm going to head back."

"Okay, Nick's already grilling."

I make my way toward the communal campsite.

Nick's at the grill, beer in hand, his eyes firmly locked on Lauren's ass as she bends over the fire to fiddle with the placement of logs. There's a small stereo on the picnic table playing The Strokes. The sun's well behind the tree level now, and the temperature is dropping with it. Allie's messing with the liquor bottles in the tent. Lauren sits next to Dana near the fire, picking back up her wine. They lean their heads close together, whispering.

Dana sees me approach and calls out, "Gabe, the babe."

I grit my teeth. I hate that fucking nickname. Her and all the other cheerleaders used to call me that.

"Beer's in the red cooler," Nick says. "Burgers'll be ready in a bit."

I grab a beer, trying not to imagine what Jennifer was about to say.

Allie

I pour myself a good measure of whiskey. Lauren and Dana are whispering, most likely about me. Why did I agree to come here? I don't have anything in common with these girls anymore. At least when we all lived together, we had school. We all had classes to go to, finals, professors, some of the same ones even, but now there's nothing.

I bring my whiskey back to the fire. Booze will make it better. Gabe's joined us, but all the others are still gone, including Eric. Maybe he's pissed I cut off our make-out session. Hopefully not, but if he is, fuck him. I'm here to be with my friends, not get nailed on a picnic table. But if he plays his cards right, it could be both.

"Burgers are ready," Nick calls out.

He comes and sits by the fire with a beer in one hand and a plate piled high with food in the other.

"Whoa, carb loading?" Lauren laughs.

"Hard no. Did I tell you I ran a half marathon last weekend? Trained for three months and PRed. This weekend I intend to sit on my ass and drink lots of these." He raises up his beer.

Dana shakes her head. "You're going to need the energy for the games tomorrow."

Games? Of course, Dana organized games. Because she doesn't play enough of them in her day-to-day interactions.

Eric bounds down the steps like a little boy at the fair. He has a flashlight in one hand.

"This place is amazing," he says, his eyes lit up. "I saw a mama deer with two babies. They had the little white spots and everything, just like Bambi."

I swear when he says it, Gabe flinches. Honest to God flinches. Does he not like deer? Even I can appreciate how cool deer are. I'm about to ask him about it when Lauren speaks up.

"That's magical. Where did you see them?"

Eric looks left, then right. "It was that way, I think. I got a little twisted. I don't have the best sense of direction."

Gabe turns his face toward Eric, his eyes reflecting the flames from the campfire. "Did you take a shower?"

"There's a shower?" Eric says as he grabs a plate of food. "This place is so cool."

Jennifer and Ben wander in next, get some food, and take a seat next to each other by the fire. I might be imagining it, but it seems like there's a fizzle of tension between them.

Joe's the last one to join the party. He brings his full plate of food over. The burgers must be cold. I didn't have one. They smell off somehow.

Dana runs her nails on Joe's arm. "I was just about to go look for you. What happened?"

"Fell asleep there for a minute. But I'm good now." He cracks open a beer. "What have y'all been up to?"

"Nothing." Lauren groans. "I'm so bored."

"I can think of a few things we could do..." Nick says with a little wink.

Lauren throws a pine cone at him.

"Should we tell ghost stories?" Joe sets down his burger.

"No," Ben and Jennifer say in unison.

Joe holds both hands up, balancing his plate on his knees. "Alright. Maybe we could play a game?"

Dana smiles. "Oooh, what game?"

Lauren leans in, her ample cleavage threatening to spill out of her shirt. A quick glance around tells me I'm not the only one to notice. Nick is practically drooling.

She licks her lips and says, "Two truths and a lie."

"Yes! Let's play." Jennifer is staring at Gabe when she says it but quickly turns to Ben. "You go first."

Ben rubs his hand on his chin. "Let's see."

I jiggle my empty glass. I'm going to need more whiskey for this. "Anyone else need a refill?"

Gabe takes the cigarette he was about to light out of his mouth. "Bring the bottle."

Finally, someone has a reasonable plan. I walk over to the tent, Ben droning on behind me. "I've ran three marathons, I'm afraid of spiders, and once I scored a touchdown from our own forty yard line."

Is that good? I know nothing about football. It must be if he's bringing it up. Ben is a golden boy, 4.0 GPA in college, good job, well groomed, stays in shape. And dull as white crew socks on a summer day. When Jennifer started dating him, I gave him two weeks tops. But here we are almost three years later at their fucking wedding.

Gabe blows a huge plume of smoke out as I hand him the bottle. "The spiders one is a lie. You're not afraid of anything."

"That's not true," Ben says. "But I'm not afraid of spiders."

Dana adjusts her posture and smooths her hair. "I'll go next." Her brown eyes go skyward as if she's searching the stars for answers. "I went to summer camp every summer as a kid. I am excellent in bed. And I was almost a Dallas Cowboy's cheerleader."

Lauren laughs. "Too easy. You're not excellent in bed."

Dana sticks her tongue out at her.

Lauren holds up a hand. "Kidding. I'm sure you are insatiable, and we all know you were nearly a pro-cheerleader. You never shut up about the insane try-out process. It has to be the summer camp one? But that can't be right. You definitely went to summer camp, you told me about that girl—"

Dana cuts her off. "I did, but just that one summer. I'm not even sure why I brought it up. I hated that place. Ben and Nick are the ones that went year after year. "

Nick raises his beer to Ben and they clink, the cans making a dull thud.

Dana smiles, but it doesn't reach her eyes. It looks downright painful. "Okay, smarty pants, your turn then."

Lauren sits back. "Hmm. My favorite color is gold. I've been to forty of the, how many..." She snaps. "Fifty states. And when I was a kid, I got stuck in a dryer for hours."

There's a moment's silence, then Jennifer says, "The dryer one."

Lauren shakes her head, her eyes wide. "That really happened. I was little, maybe four or five, and went on a bear hunt. It was one of my favorite games. I was pretending it was the bear's cave. I got in and pulled the door behind me."

"That's awful," Jennifer says, her pristine face pinched. "I didn't know that happened."

Dana speaks, her eyes firmly fixed on the fire. "The states one. You haven't been anywhere."

She looks at Lauren, and something passes between them that doesn't look entirely friendly.

Lauren looks away first and sighs. "I know. I'd love to travel more. I'd really love to see Montana, there's this place, Going-to-the-Sun Road in Glacier National Park that looks magical."

Joe leans in. "That road is amazing."

Dana sits up in her camping chair, blocking Joe's view of Lauren somewhat. "Allie, it's your turn."

I don't want to play. But I also don't want to argue or get Dana's death glare. She already seems to be in a mood. Not wanting to fight wins out. I take a breath and, on my exhale, say, "Fine. I hate tequila. *Rear Window* is my favorite movie. And I once met Peter Falk at Universal Studios."

Jennifer plays with her hair, piling it on top of her head and letting it fall before saying, "You love tequila. You love all liquor."

I hold up my tumbler in a cheers. "Busted. Your turn, Jennifer."

She waves a hand in front of her. "Too many girls in a row. It's Joe's turn."

Joe rubs a hand over his chin. "How would any of you know if I was telling the truth or not? None of you know me."

"I do." Dana smiles.

Joe doesn't smile back. "This game has no stakes. Let's play truth or dare. Groom goes first. Truth or dare, Benny boy?"

Ben looks at Joe, and I know what he's going to say before he says it. "Truth."

As long as I've known him, Ben has never picked dare.

"How many women have you slept with?" Joe asks, his face distorted with long shadows from the campfire.

"Oooh, spicy." Dana rubs her hands together.

Ben's cheeks turn a rosy pink in the firelight. He whispers in Jennifer's ear. Her eyebrows shoot up. "Really?"

He shrugs.

Joe says, "That's not fair. You have to tell the group."

"What's it matter? I'm the only one that cares." Jennifer puts an arm on Ben. "It's your turn."

Ben smiles and asks Jennifer right back. "Truth or Dare?"

"Dare."

Ben rubs his chin. "Hmmm."

"Dare her to give you head," Nick says and takes a big swig from his beer.

Lauren wrinkles her nose. "Ew, gross."

"I dare you..." Ben pauses and begins again. "I dare you to show us the last person you texted."

Murder? What murder? Episode 189 July 20, 2024

"Barbara, how does Wyatt James figure into all of this?"

"First you have to know a little about his case. What do you already know about Wyatt James?"

"Assume I know nothing. It's always a safe assumption."

"Ha. Okay, fair enough. It all started at summer camp."

"That's the story of my first kiss."

"For Sarah Novak, it was her last."

"Tell me more."

"Just outside of Portland in August of 1995, a girl named Sarah went missing. Do you remember that at all?"

"It doesn't ring a bell. But I would've been pretty young at the time."

"Yes, yes. Don't rub it in. Anyway, Sarah Novak was seventeen and gorgeous. She had long dark hair, freckles, and a button nose. She was bubbly. The kind of girl that's nice to everyone. She was working for the summer as a camp counselor and everyone loved her. Her boss said she was always the first up making coffee and the last to bed helping to clean up, checking on her campers. But some of the other counselors said that wasn't the real reason she was last to bed."

"Ooh summer love."

"Love is debatable. But her co-counselor, Mary, said Sarah was meeting someone after everyone went to bed. She was almost positive she was going to see a boyfriend, but Sarah would never confirm or deny. So, Mary was not surprised when on the last night of camp, after all the campers went to sleep, Sarah left their cabin being careful not to slam the screen door. She was surprised, however, to find Sarah's bed still empty in the morning."

"Fuck."

"Yeah. At first, Mary thought maybe Sarah slept over in her 'boyfriend's' cabin, but she had no idea who it could be. She didn't want to get Sarah in trouble, so she didn't say anything. Then the morning got going and, well, you remember what the last day of camp is like."

"Oh man, it's chaos. Trying to pack everything, getting everyone to sign your shirt, ah, so many tears."

"So many tears. And Mary and Sarah were in charge of the middle school girls, so just imagine trying to help, comfort, and get the kids the fuck out of there all by yourself."

"Nightmare."

"Totally. Mary put her head down, she did what she needed to do. All the girls were safe and accounted for when they left on the bus after lunch. All but Sarah.

"It was around this time Mary really started to worry. She went to the head of camp and told him Sarah was missing. They split up into pairs and searched the nearby woods, but Sarah was nowhere to be found."

"No."

"They called local authorities, who also searched. Still absolutely no sign of Sarah. It wasn't until two months later in October that Portland police received a map in the mail of the campground with a red diamond drawn on it."

"A red diamond? Like drawn on the map?"

"Yes, in an unidentifiable substance. At first, the cops didn't do anything with it. For an entire month it just sat in some file."

"You've got to be kidding?"

"Well, the map didn't say anything. There was no note. Just a red diamond. But then a young officer made a connection of the location to the Sarah Novak missing person case. They teamed up with the forest department to widen the search. On the second day, rain fell in heavy sheets as a forest ranger found Sarah's body in a small cave a little ways off one of the main trails. She had been stabbed, repeatedly. And upon closer inspection, they weren't just stab wounds. Tiny diamonds were carved into her flesh, over and over again. Around fifty of them. Sarah Novak was murdered, and she was just the first."

Gabe

My heart stops.

Jennifer gives me the briefest glance. She's a rabbit caught in a trap. We're fucked.

Then she turns on her thousand watt smile.

"Sure." She pulls out her phone from her back pocket and flips it open. "Oh wait. It died." She shows the gray unlit screen, and my heart starts beating again. "But I can tell you it was Melanie the wedding planner."

Ben laughs. "I knew it. Who will you text after we're married? You'll have so much free time."

Jennifer swats at Ben then swivels to Dana. "Your turn."

Dana faces Joe, her expression getting very serious. "Truth or Dare?"

Joe doesn't hesitate. "Truth."

"Wuss," Nick says.

"Have you ever been in love?" Dana asks.

I cringe inside. Five more minutes. I'll finish my beer, and then I can go to my tent without looking like the grumpy old man I am.

"Yes. Deeply," Joe says without any effort to elaborate more. He turns to Lauren. "Truth or Dare?"

It's odd he didn't ask Dana back. Dana must think so, too, because she starts packing up the food on the table.

Lauren looks at Dana. "Umm, dare, I guess."

"I dare you to—"

"Flash us!" Nick says, and Lauren makes a sour face at him.

"Hmm," Joe says. "That's not a bad idea."

Lauren rolls her eyes. And in one swift move, she stands and lifts her shirt while sticking her tongue out at Nick and Joe.

"Happy?"

Nick smiles wide. "Very."

Joe holds up a finger. "But I didn't actually say the dare, so technically..."

"Oh, come on, Joe. She showed you her tits. Challenge complete," Dana says, settling back with a fresh glass of wine. "Gabe, it's your turn. Nick has forfeited his turn by influencing other players."

I finish my beer in three large gulps and stand. "No. I'm going to hit the hay. Have fun, you crazy kids."

"Wait a second," Jennifer says. "You don't have to ask anyone, but someone has to ask you. It's only fair since you got to watch us bare our souls."

"And our tits," Dana says bitterly.

Lauren crosses her arms over her chest.

"Ask away." I swallow hard and squeeze the empty can in my hand.

Jennifer smiles. "Truth or Dare?"

"Dare."

"I dare you to jump into the lake, right now. Naked."

Really? A skinny dip. That seems a little tame for Jennifer. I don't trust it. I'm almost positive it's a trap. I go to take a sip of my beer to bide time but then remember it's empty.

Lauren whistles. "Take it off. Take it off."

I haven't moved, still trying to figure out Jennifer's angle, when Allie sets her glass down with an exaggerated sigh.

"Don't be such a pussy. I'll do it." Allie shoots up out of her seat then immediately crumples to the ground like a popped balloon.

Dana

Lauren yelps in my ear as Allie lands precariously close to the fire with a thud. For a second, it looked like she was going to fall straight into the flames. Then what would we do? How would we get help? We planned this wedding for nearly a year—why did we never think of what to do in an emergency? We have no car, no phone; we're stranded.

Why hadn't I thought of that? I think of everything. How has this never occurred to me?

Jennifer's by Allie's side first. She rolls her over, so her face is up, and gives her some light pats on the cheek.

"Allie, wake up."

"Is she okay?" Lauren puts a hand over her mouth.

Allie's eyes are rolled in the back of her head, just the whites gleaming in the light of the fire. She looks dead.

Thinking on my feet, I seize a bottle of water from the cooler, unscrew the cap and splash a bit in Allie's face. Some of the group cries out around me.

Allie's eyes shoot to Jennifer's face. I'm so relieved my muscles turn to jelly and I take a large swig of the water in my hand.

Allie exhales heavily. "That was weird."

My relief is swiftly replaced by white-hot anger. Allie couldn't pace herself, just this once? She has absolutely no self-control.

Allie moves to her elbows, but Jennifer holds her shoulders. "Wait. Just lie there for a minute. Ben, hand us some water."

Why wouldn't she ask me? I have a bottle right here. I'm the one who woke her up in the first place. I go sit back down.

Ben quickly fetches another water from the cooler.

"What happened?" Nick says through a mouthful of chips.

I shrug. "She just passed out."

"I didn't pass out. I ..." Allie sighs. "Shit, just got all fuzzy for a second." She pushes herself up to sit. "I'm fine now. See."

Jennifer's face is strained, but she nods. Allie's drunk. We all know it.

"I just need to eat, that's all."

Allie gets back in her chair by the fire with Jennifer holding her by the arm.

"I'll get you a burger," Jennifer says, letting go of Allie's arm once she's sure she'll sit up on her own.

Allie smiles. "And macaroni salad."

Jennifer laughs, and they all join in, nervously at first, but then it seems like the mood truly lightens. I don't laugh. Allie's always sliding by, getting away with being irresponsible. I'm not going to make her feel better about it.

"But I'm serious," Allie says. "Don't skimp on the sides."

"Yes, bitch! And macaroni salad."

Jennifer passes me on the way to the picnic table, and I hear her whisper to Gabe but can't quite hear what she says.

Murder? What murder? Episode 189 July 20, 2024

"Things quieted down for a while. They had no leads on Sarah Novak's case. They questioned her teachers where she went to high school, everyone she worked with at the summer camp. Nothing. No one knew who she might've been meeting night after night. Then two years later, in Portland in October of 1997, a girl named Wendy Robinson went missing. Do you remember that at all?"

"Oh my god. Yes. There were posters everywhere. There was a rumor at my school that our janitor, who was this very creepy old guy with super long fingers, took her and had her in his basement."

"Did Wendy go to your school?"

"No. But that didn't make it any less plausible. I'm telling you, the guy was super menacing. Not run-of-the-mill, but like Freddy Krueger scary."

"Yeah, every school hired that janitor. And as it turns out, just about every school in the Portland area had similar rumors. See, that was the thing about all these cases, and especially Wendy's, they were swarmed in rumors. If you get one bee sting, you're probably going to be fine."

"Unless you're allergic like Macaulay Culkin in *My Girl*."

"Yes. Unless you're allergic. But one bee sting if you're not allergic you will survive. But if you get a thousand, you're not walking out of there."

"So, wait. She died from bee stings?"

"No. It was a metaphor. I'm getting ahead of myself. Let me just tell you her story before we get into the rumors. Wendy was a sophomore and going to Lincoln High. She was gorgeous. Long brown hair, big brown eyes. And she was nice, popular, everyone loved her—teachers, peers, everyone. She was just a fucking good person you know? She even volunteered at an old folks home, and they all loved her too."

"And those are some cranky motherfuckers."

"You'd be cranky too if you had no teeth."

"True."

"So, Tuesday, October 20, Wendy went to school. From all accounts it was a normal day. She was worried about a math test she had and spent the night before studying for with friends. They all said she seemed like her normal perky self, except being worried about this test. After school, she went to cheerleading practice but left early because she wasn't feeling well. There's some debate here over the real reason Wendy left early, but we'll get to that. She walked home. It was about a fifteen-minute walk, and she did it almost every school day. But on this day, she never made it home."

"Dun, dun, dun."

"Yeah. Her family thought maybe she went out with friends, so they didn't really start to worry until she still wasn't home at 11 p.m."

"When I was in high school, I'm not totally sure my parents would've worried until the next day."

"Yes! Exactly, Jules. It was the nineties, it was a different time. But Wendy's parents were concerned, so they called some of her friends. They all had the same story—she walked home after cheerleading practice.

"So, now they're really anxious and they call the cops. The police tell them, and this is a quote, 'She's probably with her secret boyfriend.'"

"What? That's supposed to be comforting?"

"I'm not sure. So, the cops tell them to call back if she hasn't turned up by the next night. She didn't. They called back and the search started.

"Her parents and younger brother posted missing flyers all over town. They turned their home phone into a tip line. They set up search parties. And nothing."

"No tips even?"

"Oh no, tons of tips. That was my point with the bees. The cops and her family were completely swamped in tips and taken in by all these rumors that were flying around her school. Kids were saying she was dating an older guy. Some other kids said that was just vicious gossip going around school and had been for weeks. One of her best friends, a fellow cheerleader, said she left early that day because her school photo had been glued to a pretty graphic page ripped from a porn magazine. Her face was put in place over a woman enjoying some quality time with a man, if you get my drift, and the word *SLUT* was scrawled next to it in red sharpie."

"Whoa. High school fucking sucks."

"Yeah. You're telling me. But none of the other girls on the team could confirm this, and they could never find the photo. So the cops didn't take it seriously. Any of it. They thought she just ran away."

"Was she dating someone?"

"If she was, they never came forward. The cops were clueless, until they literally received a clue in the mail on October 30. A cream envelope was delivered with no return address. Just like the one they got with the Novak case. Inside was a map of Forest Park with a small red diamond on it.

"The cops went to the spot on the map and found Wendy just off the trail. She was in just her bra and panties. Her neck, sternum, and stomach were covered in dried blood. Diamonds were etched into her skin, around twenty of them. The post-mortem showed some drugs in her system too."

"Drugs, what drugs? Did she do drugs?"

"No. Wendy didn't even drink the occasional Boones farm like her friends. They found Lorazepam in her system, quite a lot of it."

"Isn't that for anxiety?"

"Yep, Jules, that's one of the main uses. The stab wound to her heart is what killed her, though. Wendy Robinson was the youngest victim, just two weeks away from her sixteenth birthday. And the killings didn't stop there."

Allie
Thursday, July 21, 2004

When I wake up, my head throbs from where I hit the ground. The white tent is almost glowing in the morning light. Last night was so weird. Everything just went black. One second, I was sitting by the fire, and the next, I was lying in the dirt. I didn't think I had that much to drink, well, I mean, I had. But I've had more before and been fine. Maybe I didn't drink enough water?

Taking a deep breath, I raise my hands above my head and feel the soft comforter. Everyone probably thought it was just because I was hammered, again. I sigh.

But what do I care what they think? After this wedding, we'll go back to our respective corners of the city, me in SE and them in NW. We'll go back to calling once in a while, getting brunch every few months. Anything that happens this weekend doesn't really affect my real life. I reach over in the bed expecting to find Eric, but it's empty.

I sit up. Where the fuck is Eric? My fingers shake as I throw off the comforter.

Shit. I must've done something really stupid last night. I put on fresh clothes then down the rest of the water that's sitting on the bedside table. Ahh, sweet water. I pick up my phone and flip it open. No bars, no power, nothing. It's deader than a door-nail. I put it back on the table and notice there's nothing else there. The gift basket and, more importantly, the knife I put there the day before are gone. I search the floor and around the bed.

There's the toppled over gift basket, but no knife.

Maybe I put it away. I strain to remember, but nothing comes and my head throbs with the effort. I'll look for it later. I probably stuffed it in my bag. I'll have to dump the whole thing out to find it without cutting myself.

I slip on my Vans. Brown specks cover the toes. They're pretty beat up anyway. The stains could be from work, and I just hadn't noticed yesterday. I grab my camera and hang it around my neck.

Cool mountain air slaps my cheeks as I emerge from the tent. It's the kind of day that starts out with a little nip but will heat up fast. Like the tiniest bubbles in water before the roiling boil comes. I can almost see the appeal of all this nature.

The hammock is swinging slightly in the breeze. I run over, hoping to find Eric there, but it's empty. My stomach drops. He probably slept somewhere else. When I find him, I'll apologize for whatever I did this time.

I let out a long, low breath, trying to ease the pounding in my temples. Coffee. I need coffee. I walk over to the site next door, expecting to smell bacon and see people up, but it's also empty. There's a loud buzzing coming from a nearby tree. Flies and a few bees congregate around a black garbage bag, loosely closed, some of the trash spilling out. Clearly no one else is concerned about bears.

A flash from last night comes to me, of the trash can outside the bathroom knocked over. Was that real?

I open the cooler, hoping for an ice coffee or even a Diet

Coke. But my choices are Pabst or water. I grab some water and chug half of it. Satisfied that I'm sufficiently hydrated, I snatch a Pabst. We're camping after all. I pop in a Simon and Garfunkel CD and hum along to "Baby Driver" while making a pot of coffee on the small camping stove.

The French press is steeping, and I make an attempt at cleaning up the mess of trash. When I get back to Portland, I'm going on a cleanse, one of those green juice, cayenne pepper serious cleanses. And I'll start running. Not late night running to the next bar before last call, but proper, in the daytime, get in shorts, pull my hair back, three times a week running. Maybe I'll even get a sweatband. A cute vintage one with matching wrist bands. I'll finish the art project I'm working on and get a show at the Froelick Gallery downtown.

I nod at my plans while sipping my beer when engine noises come on in the song and I'm struck by such a strong sense of déjà vu I have to take a seat on the picnic bench.

There was a car last night, or the sound of one, anyway. I woke up Eric and told him about it. After that, it's all still fuzzy. I scour the corners of my mind, but it's like chasing a mouse—once you get a glimpse, it's gone so fast you start questioning if you even saw it at all.

There's another memory from last night. I went to the bathroom and two people were whispering in the dark. Who was that? Did that really happen?

My heart leaps in my throat as sirens blare. There's a crackle and Dana's unmistakable voice as if through a loudspeaker. "Wakey, wakey, bitches. It's time to get up. Circle Up is in ten minutes at Central Perk."

Can I leave? Can I hide? I have zero interest in whatever games she has planned. Dana always wins. Even when you somehow manage to beat her, she'll find a way to come out on top.

Dana walks up the stairs in micro pink terry cloth shorts with white piping, tall striped American Apparel socks, and a white tank with gold lettering that reads Team Bride. She looks like she stepped right out of *Dazed and Confused*. She has a bullhorn in one hand.

"You made coffee?" she asks with shock written all over her face.

My defenses immediately rise. "Yes. And? What's with the costume?"

She puts down the bullhorn and clangs some metal coffee cups together. "It's a summer camp themed wedding, Allie. Lighten up." Then she looks down at my black tank top. It's not the same one I wore yesterday, it's similar, but not the same.

"What?" I say looking down at my own shirt. "It's clean."

"Where is your *Team Bride* shirt?"

My what? "I don't know what you're talking about."

"I gave you one at the bachelorette party last month." She huffs and opens one of the coolers, getting out a pack of bacon. "Forget it. Clearly you already did."

I search my memory. Did she give me a shirt at the bachelorette party? I had a lot of champagne that night, but I wasn't that drunk. I would've remembered if Dana gave me a shirt and told me to bring it on the trip. The beer that's still in my hand is suddenly heavy, like it's full of stones.

Dana's always pulling shit like this. Subtly doing things to leave me out. I want to scream at her. But what good will that do? I take a deep breath.

When I was a kid, I used to go to an art school for a month in the summer. It was in this old Victorian house that creaked at night. My first year there, I was so scared it felt like my chest was cracking open. One of my teachers told me there was no reason to be frightened, but that it was okay to feel that way. They were all about embracing all your feelings. I think she actually thought I was homesick, but she couldn't have been more wrong. I just didn't want some creepy Victorian ghost sucking my soul through my eye sockets. Either way, she didn't want me to miss out on all the fun stuff we were doing. She told me about the magic box. She instructed me to imagine a box then asked me lots of questions about it. What color was the box? How big was it? What did it smell like? Once I had the box solidified in my mind, she told me to take all the hard, messy feelings I had and put them in, close it, and put the box on the shelf. She assured me all the feelings would still be there later.

I picture my box now, unchanged from when I was a kid, purple with pink sparkles and a faint smell of cinnamon rolls. I put all my complicated feelings about Dana in, pour a large swig of beer on it, and close it tight.

Lauren runs up the stairs, her high ponytail bouncing and, of course, wearing a *Team Bride* shirt.

"Mmm, coffee." She pours herself a mug oblivious to the tension in the air.

Gabe

In no hurry to get to whatever-the-fuck they have planned for today, I head to the bathhouse and step right into the shower.

When the water turns cold, I get out and dry off. I cringe as I hold the shirt in my hands. *Team Groom.* There's no way I could feel like more of a fraud. It's like buying a Nirvana shirt from Hot Topic and wearing it not being able to name one song, only so much worse.

Not wanting to even catch a glimpse of myself in it, I turn away from the mirror as I put it on. I wish I could get coffee without having to talk to anyone. I rack my brain. Nope. There's no way. Time to bite the bullet.

Everyone's in various states of hungover as I walk into camp. Except Dana. She flits around, checking her clipboard, acting like she's been up for hours and is on her third cup of coffee. Or something stronger. Does she have coke?

Hmm. That might be interesting.

Allie and Eric are in the tent having a hushed conversation. Allie looks a little green.

Ben's sitting with a steaming cup of coffee but isn't touching it. Jennifer has a bottle of water. She looks healthy and happy, her rosy cheeks glowing in the morning light.

I force myself to look away.

Dana checks her watch again and lets out a huff. "That's it. I gave him ten extra minutes." She slams down the clipboard and holds up ten fingers for emphasis. "I'm going to go get him up."

Nick must be avoiding this shit show this morning, too.

Jennifer laughs. "Damn straight. I'll come, too."

When they leave, I can breathe. I sit with my cup of coffee and a strip of bacon and actually enjoy the chit chat between Lauren and Joe about the last season of *The Wire*.

After a few minutes, Dana and Jennifer come back.

"He's not there." Jennifer's voice wavers with concern

"We're starting without him," Dana declares, tucking her hair behind her ears and grabbing her clipboard again.

"But where is he?" Allie says.

Ben stands. "Last night he said he might go for a hike this morning."

Jennifer has a scowl on her face. "This is so typical Nick. He has to make everything about him. He can't just go along with the plan for a couple days. For our wedding."

She practically stomps her foot, and I picture the handful she must've been as a teenager. I nearly laugh out loud but catch myself.

Ben shrugs. "It's fine. We can play without him."

Jennifer puts her arms out in a wide gesture. "The teams won't be even."

This is so stupid. Teams? Teams for what?

Dana's scribbling on her clipboard. "Actually. Without Nick, the teams are even."

"Huh?" Jennifer goes to look over Dana's shoulder. "How's that work?"

"When we planned it, we didn't know Eric was coming." They both give a pointed look toward Allie.

"He makes it even, without Nick."

"Perfect." Jennifer smiles. "Let's go."

Dana leads the way to a row of kayaks laid out in the grass near the edge of the water. Toward the other side of the lake, tied to two buoys, is a checkered ribbon that says *finish* across it.

Just what I need, a race.

Fuck.

I want to go back to the tent with the whiskey. Did Ben tell Jennifer about all our races as kids?

Dana jumps up and down. "It's a kayak race. Whoever is first across the finish line wins two points for their team. Boys are on Team Groom and girls are on Team Bride."

Joe laughs, and it's so deep it makes the hairs on my arm stand on end. "It hardly seems fair. A man is obviously going to win."

Jennifer pokes at Allie. "Have you seen this girl's arms? I wouldn't count your chickens."

Dana says, "While Allie's arms are Linda Hamilton in T2 amazing, I did think of that. The girls team gets a one minute head start."

Joe crosses his arms across his chest. "Seems fair."

"What's with the points?" Eric asks. He's been quiet all morning. Quieter. I'm pretty sure he and Allie are fighting.

"Great question. Each event is worth a certain number of points, the team with the most at the end of the day wins."

Joe raises his eyebrows. "What do we win?"

"It's a surprise."

"What are the other events?" Eric asks.

"Another surprise. Come on, let's go. I'm ready for our first win."

My heart's beating fast. I wish I hadn't drunk so much last night.

I don't give a flying fuck about winning points for Team Groom.

What I care about is beating my little brother.

I'm in good shape, go to the gym a couple of times a week, go climbing with buddies every couple months. Ben's tying some ropes on his red kayak. He picked red and I picked blue, just like when we were kids. My arms are definitely bigger than his. I got this.

The girls get their kayaks in a line in front of the boys. Dana lifts her bullhorn.

"I'm going to sound the siren, and then we're going to start. Wait a full minute before you guys go."

Ben holds up a thumb in the air and looks at me with a smirk. It's a good thing Eric's kayak is between us, or I might smack that smile right off his face.

The siren blares, and I clutch my paddle tighter. I hold it up so I can see my watch. 9:34. I'm waiting until 9:35. Come on numbers. Turn. Out of the corner of my eye, Ben's kayak inches forward. He's going. It's only been thirty seconds, tops, and that little shit is going.

I plunge my paddle into the water and take off, quickly finding a rhythm. Joe and Eric are still near the starting line as I pass Lauren on her left.

"Hey," she whines as I pick up my tempo, my heart thundering in my chest.

Jennifer's the next boat I pass. Her face is pure grit and determination, but her spindly arms are no match for me. I watch up ahead as Ben passes Dana, then Allie.

It's just me and Ben left, and we're nearly at the finish.

I'm so close I can taste it.

Sweat drips down my back as I paddle faster. The nose of my kayak is almost to the ribbon. I ease up on my grip. In my head, I've already glided into the finish. Out of the corner of my eye, Ben comes into view, that shit eating grin plastered on his face.

Eric

I pride myself on my innate understanding of people. It's an essential skill for a writer. And that's what I'd like to be someday—an author, just like Jack Kerouac or Thomas Pynchon. But I don't understand these people.

Especially Gabe. He just kept going. The race was over, but he kept paddling like a man possessed. I was nowhere in the running. I saw something move in the water and stopped to see what it was. It was large, but when I looked again, it was gone.

Allie actually came pretty close to winning. But Ben passed her at the last minute. You could tell Ben had it. And the only two left were boys, so they could've chilled out, glided into the finish line. Or Gabe could've let Ben win, seeing as it's his wedding and all. Instead, Gabe doubled down, charging ahead. Ben won, and Gabe paddled all the way to the other side of the lake. He threw his paddle against a tree when he got out.

Brother stuff. My sister and I would never act like that. We were always looking out for one another.

Until we weren't.

Shaking my head, like I can physically shake the thoughts out, I get two beers out of the cooler. Stay in the present. It's a beautiful day, at a beautiful lake, with a gorgeous girl. I wait at the bank for Allie to paddle in. I've been getting the feeling she's still pissed at me for last night.

I give her a hand out of her kayak and hand her a beer. "To the almost winner."

She takes it, her brown eyes warm. Things may have thawed between us, hopefully. "Thanks. That was...intense."

I wave it away, having already decided not to delve any deeper into Gabe's mind than necessary.

Our fingers brush lightly as we head over to a group of picnic tables where everything is set up with drinks, snacks, and a long white Tupperware container. It almost looks like a tackle box. Maybe the next competition is fishing.

"Team Groom wins that round," Dana says, marking her clipboard. She yells over to Ben, who's standing by the shore with Jennifer having a whispered conversation. "Congrats, Ben."

"Next event is friendship bracelet making." Dana shakes the tackle box.

My chest feels light. I can actually win this one.

"Yes!" Lauren says. "I'm super good at making bracelets. What are we talking about here, hemp with beads or embroidery floss?"

Joe laughs that booming laugh he has. I think he tries to make it deeper than it actually is. "I don't get how that is a competition."

Lauren looks at him like he's nuts. "Prettiest one wins, duh."

Joe says, "Prettiest to who? Who judges?"

Dana points to Ben and Jennifer, still standing a little ways off, heads close together. "The bride and groom will. Obvs."

Joe shakes his head. "This event seems biased."

Dana opens the Tupperware to reveal neat little cubes of different colored strings and beads. "Stop whining."

I jump right in, grabbing a few colors of string and a safety pin. "I'm not half bad at making friendship bracelets. Went to summer camp six times as a kid."

Allie nudges me with her hip. "Six summers, huh?"

"Yep," I say. "From fifth grade all the way until I was a junior. Started out as a camper, became a counselor."

Allie looks impressed, her dark eyebrows rising, the sun kissing the side of her cheek. "Wow. So, you must know a lot of outdoorsy stuff."

I laugh. "From your technical jargon you're using there, I'm assuming you don't."

"No. Not really."

Jennifer and Ben walk over, a dark cloud following them. When I get married, I don't think I'll be as gloomy as these two are. Maybe they're having second thoughts about the wedding. With the way Jennifer looks at Gabe, I wouldn't be surprised. But maybe I just think that because of what Allie said.

Ben clears his throat. "We're going to check the sites again for Nick."

"I'll come too," Allie says, and my heart sinks. We were having a nice time, finally getting back to the snappy back and forth we had the night we met, and now we're going on a wild goose chase.

I put down my bracelet stuff to join them. If Allie's going, I'm going.

"Should someone check on Gabe?" Lauren asks.

"He'll be fine," Ben says. "He just needs to blow off some steam."

Ben, Jennifer, Allie, and I leave down the trail. I walk close to Allie, making sure our fingers touch every now and then. The third time it happens, it might be my imagination, but I think Allie moves a little farther away. It's possible she's still fuming about last night. But what else could I have done?

We walk straight to Nick's tent, led by Jennifer. I still can't quite tell all the tents apart, and I don't think Allie can either. But Jennifer knew exactly where she was going.

There are two blue canvas camping chairs by the fire, both completely empty. I walk over to the large white tent. There's no sign of Nick anywhere.

And that's when I see it sitting right next to the bed.

Allie

ennifer wasn't kidding when she said I had the smallest spot. Nick didn't plan on bringing a guest either and his tent is almost twice the size as mine.

Ben and Jennifer are looking around his cooler, and I'm wandering around the edges of his site. There are so many trees, all snarled and close together. Anything could be out there, and how would we even know with all these massive trees to hide it or them?

Eric calls out from inside the tent.

I run to him. "What is it?"

Eric points to the side of the bed.

I tiptoe over, and the black ball of anger in my gut grows. Not only does Nick have an enormous bed, he also has a small sitting area and a little bar cart, a bottle of top-shelf whiskey sitting right there among other liquors. Do all the other tents have a fully stocked bar?

Nick's suitcase is open on the other side of the bed. I make my way around and nearly trip on a pair of boots. I pick one up. They're hiking boots, the bottoms caked in dried mud.

"Why would Nick go hiking without his boots?" Eric asks.

"Jennifer," I yell. What are they doing out there anyway?

Jennifer and Ben rush into the tent, and I show them the boot. "Nick wouldn't go hiking without his boots."

Jennifer puts a hand to her mouth. A fat tear rolls down her cheek, her face red and blotchy like she's already been crying.

Ben paces around the tent, making it feel cramped.

I cross over to the bedside table, nearly bumping into Ben as I do. There's a glass a fourth full of whiskey and a gift basket just like mine, only something about it seems different. I riffle through the single-serving gourmet coffee packets and the bespoke spiced nuts. It's missing the flashlight.

I dump out the basket onto the table, shaking my head. It's also missing the beanie. "He must've gone somewhere last night."

Jennifer moves her hand from her mouth. "We have to call for help."

Ben stops pacing and goes to Jennifer, wrapping his arms around her. "I'm telling you, he does this kind of stuff all the time. He's probably..." He looks around the tent and points to the glass of whiskey on the table. "See. He was drinking. I'm sure he got a crazy idea and went for a hike in his sneakers. Or he might have brought his trail running shoes. He knows this area really well."

What he says makes logical sense, but in my gut it doesn't feel right.

"Sure," I say, "he might've done all that. But shouldn't he be back by now? What if he's hurt?"

Ben and Jennifer stare at each other for a long moment, so long I ache for my camera. Can a lens capture whatever is passing between them?

"Okay," Ben says, breaking the moment. "Let's go figure out what to do."

We hurry back to the group. They're still messing with colored bits of string.

Lauren pops up and rushes to Jennifer. "Oh, what happened?"

Jennifer's face crumples. She walks away with Lauren at her side. Dana hurries to them. Should I go? It's not that I don't want to comfort her, but I don't want it to look like I'm doing it just because Lauren and Dana are. So, I stand still, feeling like a dick.

"What's wrong?" Joe asks.

Ben's face is tense, jaw clenched. "Nick's not back. She's... We're worried. I keep trying to tell them he does this kind of thing all the time."

Jennifer, Dana, and Lauren come back over to the group.

Ben turns to Jennifer. "I'm sure he's just out on the trails. He loves long hikes."

I shake my head. "How is he hiking without his boots?"

Lauren says, "He's not on a hike. I know it."

Murder? What murder? Episode 189 July 20, 2024

"After Wendy's body, there was nothing for a long while again. The next girl went missing two years later in October of 1999."

"Around Halloween again, creepy."

"Very. Jessica Porter was a student at Portland State University living in the dorms. She was majoring in English and wanted to be a writer. She was gorgeous like Wendy. Long brown hair, big brown eyes. And like Wendy, everyone loved her."

"Jeez, do you think he has a type?"

"Totally, but it had been so long since Wendy, and even longer since the first murder. When Jessica went missing on October 30 people didn't immediately assume someone was targeting young women with long dark hair. But clearly that is what was going on. Get this, too, when Jessica was last seen, she was at a Halloween house party. Guess what she was dressed as?"

"Ummm, let's see. Trinity from the Matrix?"

"Jules! That's such a good guess. That movie was so hot in 1999."

"Yeah. So, I got it?'

"No, you're wrong, I'm just impressed with your stunning knowledge of pop culture. Jessica was last seen dressed as a bloody cheerleader."

"Shitttttt. Was she supposed to be Wendy Robinson?"

"I think it was more generic than that. I hope."

"Who reported her missing?"

"Her roommate in the dorms. They were both freshmen, both from the Midwest. She was immediately concerned because Jessica had never slept anywhere but their dorm room. She didn't have any family in town. All her friends lived in the dorms too. So, in the morning when Jessica didn't show up to breakfast and no one had seen her since the party, her roommate called the cops."

"And they started the search."

"No."

"What do you mean no?"

"Jessica wasn't a minor. They said she was probably staying at boyfriend's or something."

"You're joking."

"I am not, Jules."

"That's fucking ridiculous. What about the first 48 and all that bullshit?"

"It was a different time. But her roommate and other girls in her dorm started putting up fliers around campus that day. One of the girls was a journalism major and she called the news."

"Fuck yeah she did."

"They're the ones that initially made the comparison to Jill and Wendy, then it was a panic. Girls were moving out of the dorms. The university' instated a school-wide curfew of 8 p.m. Night classes were canceled. People were losing it."

"Yeah, I would've been, too, and I'm blonde."

"Two weeks went by with nothing. No leads. Her roommate thought she had been dating someone but hadn't met him. He wasn't at the party they went to that she knew of. She told the cops, but they had nothing to go on with so little info."

"More secret boyfriends? Ladies, if you are dating someone let your friends know all the details, including their full name. Actually, dudes too. It's good advice for everyone. Don't date in secret."

"Totally, there is a difference between privacy and secrecy. Then the cops got another envelope in the mail."

"No."

"Another map, this one of Tyron Creek State Park with a diamond drawn over Bunk Bridge—"

"Bunk bridge?"

"Apparently that's what it's called. It's a pretty low to the ground bridge that goes over a small creek. Before they got there, though, a couple of hikers were crossing it and saw an arm jutting out from the rocks below, a bright-red diamond carved into the wrist."

Gabe

I knew they were watching me when I threw that paddle, acting out like a sullen teenager, but I don't care. I storm down the trail, white-hot rage flaring in my chest. I was so close. How did he beat me again?

Ever since we were kids, we've been competitive.

"I'll race you to the corner."

"Last one there is a rotten egg."

Being the older brother, I usually won. Until one day I didn't.

We were racing these circular metal sleds down a large hill by our grandparents' place. I was in the lead, barely, and then Ben swerved. He ran into me, and I slid off the course. The sled hit a rock with a clang I felt in my bones. I went flying, headfirst, into a tree. Ben was down at the bottom of the hill celebrating, and I was lying on the ground—not passed out but not all there—bleeding into the snow. Later he said he didn't mean to run into me. He said he hit a bump. After that day, though, it was anybody's game. He knew he could win and that changed everything.

I kick a rock into the bushes nearby, it hits a tree with a satisfying thwack, chunks of bark flying. It feels good, so I kick another one, but this time there's no thwack, just a rustle as it sails through the bushes.

Then a clang.

A clang so loud, so sharp it has to be from the rock hitting something metal.

Following the invisible path of the rock, I find a car.

It's on the edge of a small open area, another campsite, but not one of ours, there's no fancy white tent, no fancy booze, no fancy chandelier. There is, however, a four door dark blue car almost hidden in the trees.

What's a car doing here? How did it even drive in?

I turn toward the site. There's nothing set up, no camping chairs, no gear. I put my hand on the hood of the car. Is it my imagination, or is it still slightly warm? I follow the tire tracks. They lead to the trail, just wide enough for the small sedan.

I make my voice an octave deeper as I say, "Is anybody there?"

Silence replies.

Returning to the car, I cup my hands over the window and peer in. It's dark inside the vehicle, but I can just make out a black suitcase on the backseat. No camping gear.

I go back to the campsite. There're a few cigarette butts by the fire pit, but other than that, it's clean. I kneel to pick one up, my left knee popping as I do. It's a Marlboro light, the logo so faded it's hardly visible. I let out a long slow breath and throw the butt in the fire pit.

The sky's turning. Clouds blocking out the sun. I brush off my jeans and head back on the trail, all my anger having incinerated like a piece of kindling in a raging bonfire. Singed to nothing.

Who's car is it? It might be the car of whoever set all the

campsites up. Someone had to fluff all those pillows and hang the hammocks. Furs and frills in the woods.

I make my way back to the group, clocking the somber expressions on everyone's faces. Are they all really that pissed I threw a stupid paddle? I should've just kept walking.

Bypassing their little picnic, I beeline for the cooler, grabbing a beer. Lauren's in the middle of saying something.

"He told us, and I quote, 'I'm going to sit on my ass all weekend and drink beer.' Why would he go on a super long hike—"

"With no boots," Allie says.

"Right." Lauren points at Allie. "Without his hiking boots, if he was exhausted from running some race."

Jennifer has her arms crossed tightly around her waist. "We need to call the police."

"How?" Joe gestures around. "None of our phones get service. Are we going to *Gilligan's Island* a tree phone?"

Ben points to the large log cabin. "There's a phone in the lodge."

I shake my head. "I just tried to get in there yesterday. It's locked."

"It's worth a shot anyway." Jennifer takes off at almost a run toward the lodge with Allie right behind her.

We all follow at a more reasonable pace, me and Ben bringing up the rear, with Joe on our heels. He catches up to us. "What's Nick's deal anyway?"

Ben's brow furrows. "Deal?"

"How'd you set all this up?" I ask Ben as Joe cracks open the beer in his hand. "I know you said the wedding planner, but did she hire people to put the tents up and stuff?"

Joe laughs. "Why are you so interested? Thinking about getting into the wedding planning business?"

I force a chuckle. I don't know why Joe's insisting on butting into this conversation. "No, I just found a car parked at a site just a little ways up. If the people that set up the tents and everything are still here, we should probably invite them for dinner tonight or something. I don't know, though, it was a little weird. The car was kind of parked in the trees, like someone was trying to hide it."

"A car?" Ben's eyes flash with what looks like fear to me. But it can't be. Ben's not afraid of anything. "There shouldn't be anyone else out here at all."

Dana

We approach the log cabin as a mob straight out of a black and white whodunnit movie.

This is silly.

Nick disappears all the time. But he always comes back. Sometimes drunk, sometimes with a new friend. Once when we were on a trip to Canada for Ben's nineteenth birthday, he wandered off down the strip and came back high as a kite on shrooms. This search is ridiculous.

Through a layer of grime on the windows, I can make out shelves holding canned food, sunglasses, inflatable balls, and beer. I make my way to the large wooden doors. Jennifer grabs a handle made from an antler and pulls.

The door opens easily.

Gabe must've been mistaken about it being locked. Something's definitely off about him lately.

Allie follows right after Jennifer. They're in a frenzy about Nick. They always do this too—hype each other up in all the wrong ways.

I've known Nick and Ben both since high school, and in all that time, Nick has done some really selfish things. He's forgotten birthdays. Or he'd cancel plans last minute. Once he went after a girl we all knew Ben had a crush on. That was all years ago, though. Nick has really grown up since school. It won't surprise me when he casually strolls out of the woods, unaware of all the fuss he's caused.

Jennifer and Allie head into the office. I keep walking down the hall to the back room. The walls are a dark forest green with walnut crown molding. There's a foosball table, the red plastic handles worn smooth. A large buck with jagged antlers that nearly touches the ceiling hangs above the pool table. It reminds me of home. Dad has a couple trophies in his den.

On the other side of the room from the games, there's a small step down, like a seventies style living room, that leads to a leather couch and loveseat arranged by a large stone fireplace with wingback chairs on either side. Nick isn't here, that's for sure.

I go back to the hall. The faint sound of giggles coming from the bathrooms piques my interest. I open the door to the women's room. It's a single use bathroom, completely dark and empty.

Behind me, Lauren emerges from the men's bathroom on the other side of the hall and quickly shuts the door.

"Dana! You scared me."

Her hair is disheveled. What was she laughing at by herself in there?

"I scared you? What are you doing coming out of the men's bathroom?"

"Huh?" Lauren seizes me by the arm and leads me down the hall. "I didn't even realize it was the men's room. Have you seen Nick?"

"No." We walk back into the game room. "He's not here. What were you laughing at?"

"When?"

"Just now. In the bathroom."

Lauren shakes her head, her eyes wide. "I don't know what you're talking about."

Joe comes in, flushed and out of breath.

"Where were you?" I ask.

"Checked the basement. It's freaky down there. I ran back upstairs once I saw it was empty. Nick isn't here."

Allie

I've had a sick, uneasy feeling ever since Nick didn't show up for breakfast this morning, which might partly be the hangover, but not entirely. They keep saying that it's *just like Nick*, but from what I remember from our college days, he's more thoughtful than that, when it comes to his friends anyway. Would he really ditch out on his best friend's wedding festivities? I know I thought about it.

Jennifer and I go straight to the office.

Inside, nothing looks out of place. A framed map of the campsite hangs on the wall. There're papers neatly stacked on an oak desk next to a mug that says *World's Best Grandpa* filled with pens. A large calendar, the tear off kind, hangs on the wall. Scrawled in red on today's date, it says *Ramirez bridal party*. There's no sign of a phone.

"Where's the phone?"

Jennifer walks behind the desk. "Walt, the guy that runs the campground, keeps it tucked away. He told us he doesn't like looking at it."

She opens a drawer, and all the color drains from her face.

An icy chill passes over me as she holds up a frayed phone cord. "It's not here. Someone cut the line."

"Why?" It's not a helpful question given the situation, but it's all I can think of. Why would anyone cut the phone line? Where did they put the phone?

Jennifer's still shaking her head as she opens other drawers in the desk. "I have no clue, Allie."

"Do you think it's a joke? Like would Nick joke around like this? Or Ben?"

Jennifer lets out a huff of air, slamming the last drawer. "No, Ben wouldn't. I'm not sure about Nick. He's harder to predict, but I don't see how anyone would think this is funny."

It isn't funny. Jennifer continues her frantic search of the office. I walk over to the wall with the framed map. Old cursive lettering across the top reads *Lost Lake Campground*. Each campsite is marked, all of them on the side of the lake we're on. Doing a quick count, I see there are only thirteen sites in all, each with a drawing of a tent. The lake is burly, taking up most of the map, illustrated with waves, a boat, and a little sea monster. It's charming—like something you would see in a children's book. Even the docks on the lake are marked. I wish I had my camera to take a picture, but I left it back at camp.

There's a smudge on the glass near one of the docks. I lift my arm to clean it with the cuff of my hoodie when I stop mid-air. It's not a run-of-the-mill smudge or a smashed bug as I originally thought.

It's a tiny red diamond.

"Come look at this."

Jennifer stops rifling through a bookcase and walks over. "What?"

I point to the small red shape.

"What?" Jennifer shrugs. "It's just some gunk. It's not going to help us call anyone, that's for sure."

"Do you think it's marking something?"

"No." Jennifer tries opening a file cabinet with no luck. "I think it's probably ketchup from one of Walt's extremely nutritious meals. You should've seen the size of the burger he was eating when we rented the site."

I shake my head. "I really don't think ketchup splatter lands in the perfect outline of a diamond."

"Guys, I found something," Gabe yells from across the hall. Jennifer and I lock eyes.

We bolt over to the little store.

Jennifer glances left and right, slowing as we enter the shop. "Gabe?"

"Back here."

We follow the sound of his voice. Gabe's kneeling in front of a cash register. Ben and Lauren appear behind us.

Jennifer looks at Ben with narrow eyes. "Where were you guys?"

"Checking out the game room. I thought there was a phone back there, too, but I didn't see one. Dana and Joe are still looking."

A short laugh escapes Lauren. "If by looking you mean playing pool."

Gabe holds up another frayed cord.

Ben walks over to inspect it. "What happened?"

Gabe says, "It looks like there was a phone here...once. Not anymore."

Icy tendrils of fear squeeze my heart. Who the fuck took all the phones?

Gabe turns to Jennifer. "How did you get in the building?"

Jennifer's face is an unnatural shade of white. Joe and Dana come bustling up behind us. Jennifer says, "The door was unlocked."

Joe holds up the frayed cord, his other hand holding a Pabst.

"Fuck. Someone took the phone? Do you think it has anything to do with the car you found?"

Jennifer flinches. "You saw a car? That's not possible." Jennifer shakes her head. "We rented the entire campsite, all of it. There shouldn't be a car. Where did you see it? I need you to take me there now."

Gabe

"No." My voice is hard even to my ears. But taking Jennifer to the site will only make her spiral more.

Jennifer's face is determined. I know there's nothing I can say to change her mind.

Lauren steps forward. "We'll all go. We can look for Nick along the way."

Everyone's staring at me expectantly. I let out a heavy breath, hoping to lighten the weight on my chest. No dice. "Fine."

I lead the way down the path, with the group trailing behind me. The clouds have burned off and the sun's hot until we get into the shade of the trees. The site with the car's farther away than I remember. Is the car gone? Did we pass it?

Stopping, I swing my head this way and that, trying to orient myself.

"What's wrong?" Jennifer asks. "Why did you stop?"

"I'm not sure where it is."

"They must've left," Dana offers. "They probably just got turned around."

"We would've heard the car," I say. Then I remember the

trail went down a little hill. We haven't come to the hill yet. "It's still up ahead."

I keep walking, Jennifer immediately behind me. After a few minutes, we come to the hill, and I spot the car right where it was when I saw it before. The site itself still empty.

"Part of me just thought you were messing with us." Jennifer covers her mouth.

I shake my head as we walk closer.

Joe leaps ahead and runs right up to the car.

"Wait," I call after him, but he doesn't listen.

"What?" Jennifer asks me.

I frown. "What if someone's in the car?"

Joe tries to open the driver's door.

"It doesn't look like it," Ben says and joins Joe.

"Was someone in there when you saw it before?" Jennifer asks me in a small voice.

"No." I don't know what I was thinking. A deep sense of unease settles in my chest.

"It's a rental car," Eric says from near the trunk.

I look at the pretty indistinct sedan. "How can you tell?"

Eric points at a sticker on the back window.

He's right. How did I miss that before?

"What?" Lauren says. "I don't get it."

Eric says, "Most rentals have these barcode stickers on the windows."

Lauren goes over to look. "How do you know that?"

Eric runs a hand on the back of his neck. "Everybody knows that."

Lauren turns away and rolls her eyes at Dana. I don't think Eric saw it because he's too busy peering in the back window. I still get a bad feeling about that guy. How did Allie even meet him? What are we doing out in the middle of the woods with a virtual stranger? I look around the group, suddenly feeling very alone. How well do I really know any of them?

Just about as well as they know me.

My attention drifts to Ben, guilt coating my stomach in bile. He's kicking at the cigarette butts near the fire pit. "Well, whoever drove the car up, they're not here now."

"What makes you say that?" Jen says.

Ben motions his arms out wide. "Because they would be here. They would be setting up a tent or making a fire, or swimming in the lake, and they're not. It's probably someone from Melanie's crew. They broke down and caught a ride back with someone else."

Jen shakes her head. "Why didn't she mention it then?"

Ben walks over and grabs her by the waist, pulling her close to him. "So, you wouldn't worry."

I look away, and for the millionth time since I landed at the airport, I regret coming here.

"Guys, I think I see something." Joe has one hand cupped over the windshield and the other shining a flashlight through the passenger side window.

Where did he get a flashlight? It's the middle of the day, why would he even think to bring one? It's one of those big metal Maglite's too that weighs a ton.

Lauren rushes over to the car.

"Look, the rental agreement is on the seat."

I walk over and peer through the driver's side. I can smell Jennifer approaching before I feel her presence at my side. A light vanilla scent. Sure enough, on the passenger seat is a yellow Hertz envelope, a small bit of the black and white paperwork hanging out the side. How did I miss that when I looked before? Was it there? It must've been. It must've been too dark to see without the flashlight.

Jennifer cups both hands to the glass. "Can you make out what it says on the contract?"

"Not really." Joe moves the flashlight this way and that.

"I can a little," Lauren says, and Joe moves over to give her a better view. "It only shows the last two letters. 'L.A,' I think." Lauren lets out a long breath.

Alarm bells ping in my head. L-A.

"Hmm, that's not very helpful," Joe says, backing up.

Allie, her brow creased like it was when she thought she saw movement across the lake, says, "Where did you get the flashlight? Was it in your gift basket?"

Joe shakes his head. "No. I mean, I have one in my basket, I just didn't bring it. This one was under the car."

Allie grabs it and turns it over in her hands. All the color drains from her face like a plug has been pulled, even the deep frown lines disappear.

I know what she's going to say before she says it.

She turns the light to show us the engraved side. "This is Nick's flashlight."

Ben squeezes Jennifer's hand and whispers in her ear.

Fuck.

Jennifer breaks free, and I recognize the look on her face. The half a beer and coffee in my stomach churn into an unpleasant mixed cocktail.

"We need to go get help," Jennifer says to the group.

"I think I know a way," I say. "There's two bikes leaning against the lodge, they look pretty rickety, but they should get us down the hill to a phone."

"I'll go," Jennifer says softly, her eyes a steel wall.

Jennifer wants to go? Really? I know she does spin class but come on. "No offense, but I'm going to take Joe or Eric."

Eric raises his hand. "I can go. I'm good on a bike."

Jennifer ignores him. "What? You think I can't keep up?"

Ben puts a hand on her arm. "Gabe and I will go check the bikes out, bring them back to camp, and make a plan. Okay?"

Ben makes eye contact with me.

I nod.

The bikes look fine. Run-of-the-mill, medium-sized mountain bikes. The tires could use a little air, but we can't find a pump around, so we'll have to make do.

We wheel them back to camp, coming to it through the top trail and leaving the bikes in the lot where the bus pulled in yesterday. Was it only yesterday? It feels like weeks ago. A lifetime ago.

The group's sitting silently in the camping chairs, like actors in a play waiting for the curtain to rise. Have they just been waiting this whole time? Everyone except Eric, who's lighting the grill.

Ben clears his throat. "So, we found two bikes. Gabe is going to ride to get help. Who would like to go with him?" Ben keeps glancing between Eric and Joe when he says it. I'm grateful Ben isn't insisting on coming. I don't think my guilt could handle that much alone time.

Eric raises a hand and is about to say something when Jennifer stands. "I'm going."

Ben sighs. "Babe..."

"Don't *babe* me. You're both being completely sexist. I go to spin class four times a week. Four."

I suppress a groan. I knew she was going to bring up the stupid spin classes. The only thing worse than being with Ben alone for that long is being alone with Jennifer for hours. And the only thing I want is to be alone with her for hours.

Fuck. I run a hand through my hair, tugging it slightly as I do.

"Fine, come. But I'm not going to wait for you to get up some of those hills."

Jennifer walks by me and whispers under her breath, "You'll wait for me."

Murder? What murder? Episode 189 July 20, 2024

"This is why I never go hiking. You can't unsee that."

"No, Jules, I don't think you can. This was the third body found with shapes carved all over it. The girls were similar in appearance, and they were all almost exactly two years apart. Nothing but that and their death and the fact they lived in Portland tied these three girls together, though. They went to different schools; they grew up in different neighborhoods. The cops were stumped."

"Not surprising."

"No. The news was all over it at this point. The cops didn't want the public to know about the diamonds and asked all the witnesses not to talk to the press at all."

"Why didn't they want the public to know?"

"I think it was in case of false confessions, or hoping when they finally had a suspect, they'd have a trick up their sleeve and trip them up or something.

"But the couple that found the second body were having financial troubles. Their coffee shop was about to go under. So, they accepted a very generous offer and spilled the beans."

"Whoa! The coffee beans, no less."

"Couldn't resist the dad joke. The press started calling it The Gem Cutter Killings."

"Oh shit! Now *that* I remember."

"Yeah, it was insane for a while. It was all over the news. People were coming forward left and right saying crazy stuff. That they'd run away from the Gem Cutter killer, that they'd seen him, they even had people saying they were the Gem Cutter killer."

"Someone confessed?"

"Multiple people confessed."

"How did they know that one of them didn't really do it?"

"Well, they were taking one of the confessions very seriously, but it turned out he had been in prison at the time of the first murder, so they were back to square one. Two years later, the next girl went missing."

"You mean the last girl went missing."

"Well, Jules, there's some debate about that..."

"Wait, what?!"

"We'll get to that later. But first, let's talk about Sophie Morris. Sophie was twenty-five years young. She worked at a co-op off of Alberta and she graduated from PSU."

"Ooh that's a connection."

"She had long brown hair."

"Another connection.

"And everyone loved her."

"Ding, ding, ding. We have a winner."

"She fit the bill, that's for sure. It was October. Sophie was working the closing shift at the co-op. She got off around 11 p.m. and was going to meet up with some friends, but she never showed up. Sophie lived with one roommate. When Sophie's work called looking for her the next day, Sophie's roommate got really worried and called the cops. Sophie was reported missing on October 28, 2001. The news was all over this case. Sophie was gorgeous and had always been a good kid. She volunteered at a cat shelter, for Pete's sake."

"Ahhh, a kitty shelter! Now I love her."

"Things started moving really quickly. Sophie was found at Laurelhurst Park three days after she went missing. There's a clump of trees toward the back near the horseshoes, do you know where I'm talking about?"

"Absolutely. I love playing horseshoes at Laurelhurst."

"Well, Sophie was found in her underwear tucked away in the trees by a group of friends that were there for a party."

"It wasn't a kid's party, was it?"

"No. No, it was adults, well sort of, it was twenty-two-year-olds drinking beer and playing horseshoes. One of them went into the trees to pee and stumbled on Sophie. He had a cell phone, so he called it in. I have the tape."

"No. Nope. I don't like dispatch tapes. I don't want to hear it."

"Jules, I know this about you. I never bring tapes on the show. But you're going to want to hear this one. And if you really don't want to, then put on your beats for a minute, our listeners need to hear this."

"Fine. Okay. I'm ready."

"*9 1 1 what seems to be the problem?*"

"*Uh yeah. I found a girl. A dead girl. I found a body.*"

"*Sir, did you just say you found a dead girl?*"

"*Yeah. At Laurelhurst Park.*"

"*Are you sure she's dead, sir?*"

"*Positive.*"

"*Okay. Please hold on the phone we're sending someone. What is your name, sir?*"

"*Wyatt James.*"

"Oh my god."

"I told you you'd want to hear it."

"Wait. Hold the fucking phone. Wyatt James found the last body?"

"Yes. He did. There was an envelope near the body with the map. It was addressed to the police and stamped but never sent. Wyatt's fingerprints were all over it. And it was his party at Laurelhurst Park. It was his twenty-third birthday, and it was Halloween."

"Oh no."

"Yep. Halloween 2000. The cops took Wyatt James in for questioning the next day."

"Why? Did they take the couple in for questioning when they found the other bodies? Or that guy camping?"

"I'm not sure. But there were a few reasons they took Wyatt. First, when they got to the crime scene Wyatt was sitting on a picnic table smoking a Marlboro light."

"Oh, so he'll only get light cancer."

"Ha. True, but you remember being twenty-three. You're invincible."

"Right. I do remember and then you turn twenty-nine and everything starts falling apart."

"Don't even talk to me, I'm a hundred years old. Anyway, they found Wyatt James sitting on a picnic table smoking, but no one else. He said they were having a party but there were only three empty cans in the trash nearby and three cans missing from the six-pack Wyatt had."

"So, there was *no* party."

"I don't know. But they could never confirm it. Wyatt wouldn't give the cops the names of the people with him because he didn't want any of them to get in trouble for drinking in public."

"He just found a murdered girl in a park, and he's worried about his friends getting a ticket?"

"Yeah. Weird, right? So, the cops start looking into him. It turns out he has quite a few connections to most of the victims."

"Oh really?"

"Oh yes. He worked as a stocker back at the co-op. He was working there when Sophie Morris went missing. That's the first connection they found. Connection number two, he took classes with Jessica Porter. Several. Then the third connection was his first job when he was a senior in high school."

"Oof, McDonald's?"

"Nope. He was a camp counselor with none other than Sarah Novak."

"Yikes."

"But the real nail in the coffin was his mom's job."

"His mom's job?"

"Yes. Wyatt James's mother worked as a math teacher and was the head cheerleading coach at Lincoln High School since 1993."

"Oh shit."

"Yes. Oh shit. She was Wendy Robinson's coach."

"But how old was Wyatt? Would he really have been that involved with his mom's job in 1997?"

"In 1997 Wyatt was eighteen just about to turn nineteen when Wendy Robinson went missing. He lived at home until he was twenty-one. His mom frequently held barbecues and little get-togethers for all the cheerleaders at her house."

"Oh no."

"Oh yes. Wyatt James knew Wendy Robinson. And that means he was connected in some way to all four victims."

"Shit."

"But here's the thing, he wasn't the only one connected to the victims."

"No?! Who?"

"Someone in the bridal party."

Allie

Eric speaks up. "I can go. I've mountain biked a lot."

If his rock hard abs are any indication it's probably true.

Ben smiles. "Great! Eric and Gabe will go."

Jennifer stares daggers at him. Ben whispers in her ear. They walk to the tent, whisper-yelling at each other. Just like the good old days. They've always been one of those couples. That fights loud and fucks even louder. We all pretend not to notice, but I'm having a hard time looking away. Why are they getting married?

A few minutes later, Jennifer storms away.

"This is ridiculous. Thank you for offering, Eric, but I'm going." She turns to Gabe. "I'll meet you by the bikes, I'm just going to change into better shoes."

"I'll pack some water and snacks." Gabe runs a hand over his face, looking about as tired as I feel. What I wouldn't give for a stiff drink by a cool pool, with concrete around it.

Ben's suddenly right by my side. "Can I talk to you?"

"You already are," I say.

"Do you think something weird is going on?" His brow is

furrowed so deeply, I suddenly feel really bad for him. He thought he was going to come out and finally marry the girl of his dreams.

"Ben." I put a hand on his arm and maybe I'm imaging it, but Eric stiffens. "There's a lot of weird stuff going on. Where do you want to start?"

Gabe zips up his backpack loudly and slings it over his back.

Ben shrugs off my hand. "I'm just going to see them off. I'll be right back."

Eric moves closer, acting like he wasn't eavesdropping. "How are you?"

I shake my head, unsure how to answer honestly. How am I? Bad. Scared. Tired. "This is all pretty fucked."

"Yeah." He lets out a long breath. "I really think I should've gone with Gabe."

"There's no arguing with Jen when she's like that." My eyes start to water.

And Eric looks like he sat on an ant hill, his hands fidgeting, his feet moving back and forth in the dirt.

"I'm too antsy to sit," he says, shaking out his hands. "I'm going to take a walk. Do you want to come with?"

I hesitate a moment. I did, kind of. But I need to talk to Ben, and it looks like Eric could use a little space to calm his nerves. "No, I'm okay."

"Alright."

Eric leaves looking more agitated than I've seen him before. Maybe I should've gone with him.

Lauren and Dana excuse themselves to go to the bathroom. I briefly entertain the idea of joining them. I'm not sure I really want to stay by myself with Joe. But they leave so quick I don't have time to tag along. It's fine. Ben said he'd be right back.

The little stereo on the picnic table is playing "Happiness is a Warm Gun" at a low volume. I grab a beer out of the cooler, pop the top, and take a swig.

Jumping back, I nearly spit out my beer when a deep voice from directly behind me says, "Can I get one of those?"

Joe's standing next to me. Uncomfortably close. I try to step back, but the cooler has me essentially trapped. My calf hits it painfully.

He holds up his hands and recedes a step. "I thought you heard me walking over. I didn't mean to startle you."

I get another beer out of the cooler and hand it to him.

We sit in camping chairs across the unlit fire from one another. I would feel better having a wall of flame between us.

He opens the can and takes a sip. One small trickle of beer escapes his mouth and rolls down his stubbled chin, and my stomach roils. The song on the stereo switches to "Martha My Dear."

"What?" he asks, wiping his mouth.

I shake my head. "Nothing."

Joe looks blankly at me, his brown eyes almost black. "I think Dana's mad at me. Her and Lauren have been whispering all morning."

"What about?" This is an odd thing to confide. Why tell me? And why with Nick missing and the phones gone is he worried about it?

"Not sure." Joe takes another sip of beer.

I sit back in my chair. What do we know about Joe? This is the first time I've ever met him. I didn't even know Dana was dating someone new, which with how close we are is not surprising. "I'm sure it's not you. They're probably just freaked out about the situation. How'd you and Dana meet?"

Joe narrows his eyes. "It hardly seems like the time to reminisce."

Holding up my beer, I smile. "It's hardly the time to drink beers and listen to *The White Album* either, but here we are."

He nods. "Fair point. We met at the farmer's market. She dropped some flowers, and I picked them up for her. We got to talking. Did you go to high school with them too?"

I shake my head and refrain from saying *and she never lets me forget it.*

"Has Dana ever talked about what happened back then? She talked to me about it once, but..."

I rack my brain, but for the life of me I have no idea what Joe means. "Happened?"

Joe sips his beer. "It's nothing. I just thought Dana mentioned going to school with a girl that died in the woods. It must be kind of hard being out here."

"What girl?" I don't think Dana's ever talked about anything like that to me. Ben or Nick either.

The slap of flip-flops echoes through the trees, followed by Dana and Lauren walking down the stairs from the upper trail.

"What are you two talking about?" Dana asks, running a hand along the back of Joe's neck.

"How we met?" Joe answers quickly.

Hmm, not about the girl that died, I guess. I nod.

"It was so sweet," Dana says. "He bought me a coffee. It turns out he went to PSU too. We actually were in the same Philosophy 101 class and never even met. Can you believe it? I can't believe I didn't see this handsome face." Dana runs a hand on Joe's cheek then heads over to the bar cart in the tent.

"So sweet," I say, trying not to sound sarcastic, but I'm pretty sure I failed. I quickly cover with a follow-up question. "When was that? The farmer's market not the class."

Lauren plops down in one of the camping chairs.

"Um, when was it?" Dana's brown eyes look up toward the

sky as if the clouds hold the answer. "Like three weeks ago, maybe a month?"

I swallow my beer hard. Three weeks? So, no one really knows Joe.

Joe says, "That sounds about right."

Dana brings Lauren a glass of wine and sits down.

"How long have you been dating Eric?" Lauren asks.

"Not long." But I'm a better judge of character than Dana. Once Dana dated an older guy for four months. He was smooth and elegant and smarmy as hell. I knew right away that he was no good, and I was right. It turned out he was on parole. I never got the details for what; I only heard about what happened from Jennifer.

Even so, they would be pissed if they found out I literally met Eric the night before I invited him on this trip. Something is still niggling in my brain about that. I wish I remembered the end of that night. God, I wish I could remember last night. I need to stop drinking so much.

I set my beer down and quickly change the subject. "What have you two been talking about all day?"

Lauren and Dana exchange a look. Lauren licks her lips then says, "Nick. We have a theory."

Gabe

Dread sits on my chest, making it hard to take a full breath. I check my watch. It's around three. With the bikes, we should get to somewhere we can use the phone in a little over an hour. I look over at Jennifer standing a little off the trail huddled with Ben, her thin arms crossed over her body. Maybe two hours.

It should be Eric and I going. We could do it so much faster. As much as I don't trust the guy, he looks fit as hell. Not that Jennifer isn't fit. My mind flashes to her taut stomach, her smooth legs, her... I grind my teeth.

This is not a good idea.

Ben and Jennifer walk over. Ben slaps me on the back. "Take care of her."

Ignoring Jennifer trying to catch my eye, I give a small salute. "I'll do my best. We should go."

Getting on the larger of the two bikes, I can't help but stare as Jennifer swings her long leg over the bike and settles onto the seat.

She tilts her chin up, a slow smile playing at the corner of her lips. "Let's go."

I ride out first and, after a few moments, hear the squeaky chain on Jennifer's bike behind me. The wind in my hair and the sun on my face makes everything almost feel normal. Like we're just out for an afternoon ride on a typical day camping. Like two phones haven't been cut, like there isn't a mystery rental car, and like the best man isn't missing. I pedal harder trying to push away the thoughts.

Jennifer calls out behind me, but I keep pedaling, even on the downhill slopes. After a few minutes, the only sound is the whoosh of the wind and the pounding of my own heart.

No squeak of the chain anymore.

I press the hand brakes, my tires squealing in protest. The bike comes to a stop a good ten feet from where I'd intended. Looking back, I don't see Jennifer anywhere.

I turn the bike around. "Jennifer!"

There's no response.

"Jen!"

A small voice calls out from the side of the road. Jennifer's lying in the dirt.

In a flash, I'm off the bike and by her side. "Oh fuck."

Her thigh's bleeding, rivers of red mixed with the dirt. I take off the thin long sleeve flannel I'm wearing over my T-shirt and press it to where the blood is gushing out. I try not to look at the wound, focusing instead on her unnaturally pale face. "What happened?"

Jennifer's eyes are wide. "The bike... I just couldn't steer all of a sudden."

The bike is abandoned on the side of the road, the front tire limp, all the air having already seeped out of it. "Are you okay?"

"A little shaky."

I nod and peek under the fabric I've been holding on her thigh. It's a mess of red. Unzipping my backpack I pull out a bottle of water and pour some over her thigh. A completely inappropriate rush of want passes over me like a chill. I ignore it.

"What? Why are you shaking your head?"

"It looks fine." I twirl my flannel around, making it into one long twisted piece of fabric, and tie it tight around her thigh. She gasps and again, desire pulses through me.

I swallow hard. "Can you walk?"

"I think so," she says in a Happy Birthday Mr. President voice.

I help her up and then let go so she can test out standing. She stumbles and falls into me, her hands on my chest. She looks up into my face, her pink lips wet and parted. Before my brain has a chance to stop me, I lean down, putting my lips to hers and kissing her hard.

Her mouth opens wider for my eager tongue. Her hands move down to my crotch. I pick her up, still kissing her, and press her up against a nearby tree. She gasps and gives my crotch a hard squeeze that's almost painful in how good it feels. An uncontrolled moan escapes me right into her mouth.

I move one hand from her ass to lightly tracing the hem of her barely there cut offs. Her nipples are so hard they look like they could rip through her black bra and tight white tank top. It makes me want her more. A feat I thought impossible.

Finding the hollow between her shorts and her thigh, I push my fingers through. She gasps as I grab the crotch of her shorts and yank them down, giving my fingers more room to play. She yelps and it's the most delicious sound ever.

Her hand makes its way under my jeans and strokes me hard and fast.

I put her down and turn her around, dragging down her shorts and underwear. She's holding on to the tree, her back arched, her perfect ass just waiting for me.

"Do you want it?" I ask, my voice hoarser than I expect.

"Yes," she breathes out, barely above a whisper.

We melt into each other as we always do, matching each other's wants and needs so perfectly, even our breath syncing.

It's over before it started, and I'm once again left panting and feeling like a piece of shit.

I let her go. "I didn't... We shouldn't have."

Jennifer pulls up her shorts. "Let's not do this. Okay? We have chemistry. This kind of thing is bound to happen every now and then."

And now the fury is back.

"What the fuck, Jennifer? Do you really plan on marrying my brother and then just fucking me every now and then to release the tension?"

"Ben never has to know."

How does she think we can get away with this?

She rolls her eyes. "Don't act like you're innocent in all this."

I walk away. I have to. Because she's right. After a few long minutes of staring at the completely deserted road, I head back to where Jennifer is waiting under the shade of a tree.

"We should head back. We're not too far."

"What about going to get help?"

"I'll take you back then head back out again. If we go now, there should be time before it gets dark."

Dana

I lean in like we're sharing late night secrets, not that Allie and I ever did that much. "We think Nick is in love with Jennifer and he can't bear to see her marry his best friend, so he left."

Allie sputters into a coughing fit for a few minutes. When she stops, she looks at us like we were little biddies that have been watching too much *Days of our Lives*.

"Why do you think that?"

Ben walks back into camp. "What are you guys talking about?"

We're all silent. I'm fairly confident in my theory. Nick always has a thing for any girl Ben has an interest in, or maybe they just have the same taste. There was that girl in college right before he met Jennifer, Marissa or Melissa. I can't remember. And of course, none of us could ever forget Wendy. But I really don't see the good in sharing my theory with Ben. His wedding is already shaping up to be a disaster, he doesn't need to know his best friend emotionally betrayed him, again.

I can at least protect him from that.

"Nothing," I say. "Just passing the time."

There's another tense silence. I'm positive Ben doesn't believe me. But then he busies himself around camp, and I do mean busies. Ben can't stop moving. He sits in one of the camping chairs then gets up. Fiddles with the cooler and eventually grabs a water. He heats up the water on the stove. Then grinds some beans in a hand crank and loads them in the French press. While that's steeping, he straightens all the dishes.

I'm exhausted just watching him. Plus, he's organized the dishes in a weird haphazard way, large plates, stacked on small ones. I walk over to the picnic table as he's pouring himself a cup of the freshly brewed coffee and fix it quietly. "Ben, it's going to be okay."

He nods but doesn't say anything.

"You're the one that keeps saying Nick is probably just on a hike. Do you think something happened now?"

Ben sighs. "No. I'm sure Nick is fine... I shouldn't have let Jennifer go get help. What if something happens? I should go after them."

Jennifer. Of course this is all about Jennifer. I force myself to keep my gaze level, my tone light.

"They took the only two bikes."

Ben lets out a long huff. "Right."

Eric walks into camp, straight past us, and my muscles tighten as he does. It's a reflex. A defense mechanism. I will my shoulders to ease down. Eric sits next to Allie by the fire pit.

Allie was awfully evasive when we asked how long they've been dating. And when I picked her up yesterday morning, I could've sworn she said his name was Ernie. How well can they really know each other if she called him the wrong name just yesterday? And where does he keep disappearing to?

Allie

Flashes of our time here scroll through my mind. I wrack my brain, trying to remember if Nick said or did anything to make Dana and Lauren think he's in love with Jennifer. Or if he mentioned that he was going for a hike. But all I keep coming back to is that tiny diamond on the map in the lodge.

Jennifer was convinced it was just a smudge, but it's too perfect. It had to be drawn by someone. Is it marking something?

Eric leans in, his breath hot on my ear as he whispers, "Are you still pissed at me?"

What's he talking about? *Still pissed?* "Huh?"

"Last night, when I was trying to help you into bed, you got mad. You said you wanted me to leave you alone. So, I've been trying to give you a little space, more than I would, anyway."

I have absolutely no memory at all of Eric helping me into bed, or me yelling at him. But it sounds like something I'd do. In fact, I've done it to almost everyone on this trip before. I groan, feeling that familiar guilt bloom deep in the pit of my stomach. "No, I'm not mad. The mix of booze must've hit me wrong."

Eric tries to hide a smile. "I'm sure it was just the mix, nothing at all to do with the quantity."

"Hey." I swat him on the arm then go over to the cooler and pop open a fresh beer as if to prove a point—the diamond still lingering in the back of my mind. It's right over the dock on the pointy end of the oblong shape of the lake. Not super close to where we are, but not terribly far either.

Eric's staring off into the woods, his strong jaw clenched. Maybe he can help. I grab another beer and toss it to him. He catches it smooth as silk.

"Up for another walk?"

Eric says, "Sure."

I yell at the group, "We're just going to check out the lake."

With narrowed eyes fixed on nothing, Ben gives an abrupt nod. What was it he wanted to talk to me about? It'll have to wait. Eric and I head to the lower trail.

"Where are we going?"

"I just want to check out this thing. Come on, let's run." I don't want any of the others deciding to tag along.

My lungs burn, and my beer sloshes over my hand. The sun's shining directly into my eyes. I fucking hate running. What am I doing? Every now and then, my Vans slip on the trail and I nearly eat shit. The third time it happens, I slow to a walk. I don't even know anything will be at the dock. There's no reason we have to get there at top speed, for Christ's sake. I don't know what I was thinking earlier about taking up running. Maybe I'll do yoga instead. I can still get a sweat band.

Eric slows to a walk next to me. "Where are we going?"

I shrug. I don't want to explain about the diamond on the map. He'll probably think I'm being paranoid. "I thought I saw something over here earlier."

"What?"

"I'm not sure. Probably nothing, but what else are we going

to do? Just sit around and wait for Jennifer and Gabe to get back. Or Nick to miraculously show up?"

"Good point."

The sun sparkles on the water, and my heart rate spikes. It should be a calm, peaceful sight, but it's like looking in a funhouse mirror. Everything's slightly off, just distorted enough to be grotesque.

Deep breath in, slow breath out. I'm being silly. It's just hangover anxiety.

I jump nearly out of my skin and into Eric as a rabbit hops over the trail, startling me. It's like the universe is proving my point. There's nothing to be scared of.

Eric puts a hand on my back. "It's only a bunny."

The rabbit freezes for a moment, looking at me with its beady little eyes, then off like a shot, it bounds away. I don't know why people insist bunnies are so cute. They look like fat rats to me.

The trail curves, the trees getting thicker as it does. I take another sip of beer, the cold liquid slipping easily down my throat, and keep walking. The trail narrows as the trees get even thicker.

I draw in a sharp breath and spin around at the sound of a twig snapping. I don't see anything through the dense trees and ferns. Probably just another stupid bunny. I gulp my beer.

"Are you okay? I know Nick being gone is weird, but..." Eric trails off.

Am I overreacting? I can't have a panic attack at every stray noise. But I don't think Nick is on a hike. How would his flashlight get under the car? Why wouldn't he wear his *hiking* boots on a hike? I turn my focus back to the lake, glittering in the late afternoon sun. There's a small trail through the weeds that leads toward the water—that must be the way to the dock.

"It's this way."

The ground gets squishier the closer we get to the water, but my shoes are already trashed, so I don't care. The trail leads to a small wooden dock, with a couple of planks missing. I make my way to the end, peering through the gaps as I step over them.

Nothing is here.

Eric walks to the end of the dock and sits crisscross, sipping his beer and head turned toward the water. I bounce up and down a few times on the balls of my feet. Once I'm sure the old wood will hold both our weights, I slip off my shoes and gingerly sit at the end of the dock next to him.

I'm being crazy. It probably isn't even a diamond on the map. Note to self, don't marathon *Dateline* right before a trip to the woods.

"Did you find what you were looking for?"

I shake my head. "I'm not sure what I was looking for. This is going to sound crazy, but I thought there was a diamond on the map in the office, in the lodge. It was drawn directly onto the dock."

I dip my feet into the cool water, moving them back and forth. Small ripples from the motion radiate outward into the lake.

"A diamond?"

"Yeah. Like I don't know if you followed the Wyatt James case, but he used to send the cops maps marking where he left his victims."

Eric's face turns almost green, and his eyebrows shoot up to his hairline. "Are you sure?"

Am I sure? Jennifer didn't think it was; she thought it was ketchup.

I laugh. "No. I'm totally paranoid. It's just I heard all those news reports on the way up about Wyatt James escaping and..."

I cock my foot all the way back to make an extra-large ripple when my stomach churns and all my blood runs cold as something brushes against my foot.

It feels different than a plant, or seaweed, or whatever would grow in a lake. It tangles on my ankle as I try to pull it away from the dock. As I reach down to pry it off, salvia fills my mouth in a great gush.

Long black strands of hair circle my ankle. Someone's under the dock.

Murder? What murder? Episode 189 July 20, 2024

"So, after a *long* investigation, they arrest Wyatt James."

"It is pretty crazy that he knew all four victims."

"Yes, it didn't look too good for old Wyatt. They found some other evidence, too, like some journals he had where he wrote about and to Wendy Robinson. He wrote her poetry."

"Oh shit. Nope. That's a red flag right there."

"Agreed."

"Plus, ew! How old was he?"

"He was nineteen and she was fifteen. But here's the weird thing—"

"Weirder than writing poetry to a fifteen-year-old girl at the ripe old age of nineteen?"

"Yes, weirder. Wyatt James is in custody, awaiting trial. The judge denied his bail. Then in August of 2003 another girl went missing."

"Oh shit."

"Shelby Michaels was twenty-two. She worked at a coffee shop in the Pearl District."

"Let me guess, she had long brown hair?"

"It's like you're psychic. Shelby had long brown hair. One night she went to the Basement Pub with some of her coworkers. They had a trivia team and went for every trivia night. They drank for a couple hours more after the game was over, celebrating their victory. Her coworkers said Shelby had been drinking a lot, her and her boyfriend had recently broken up and she was drowning her sorrows, but they said she wasn't drunk drunk. Shelby got on her bike and rode to her apartment in NE off Flanders where she lived alone."

"Oh no."

"Shelby had the next two days off. She was supposed to meet a friend for brunch the next day but never showed up. Her friend didn't think much of it though because she said Shelby was kind of flaky. She'd often forget plans or claim she forgot."

"That's me too. I love people and I make all these plans and then when it comes time to actually leave my house, I don't want to do it."

"Same. But Shelby didn't show up to work Friday. Her boss tried to call, but she wasn't answering her phone. At the end of the day when they still hadn't heard from her, they called the cops. The cops went to her apartment and the door was unlocked. They went inside and found Shelby, in her underwear covered in diamonds. She was dead."

"Hang on. In her apartment? Weren't all the other girls found outside."

"Yes, Jules. Every other girl was found outside, usually somewhere naturey."

"One of the many reasons nature is not my bag."

"Agreed. There were some other differences too. There was no map anywhere. Also, there was a difference in the diamonds."

"In the diamonds carved on her?"

"Yep. The diamonds on Shelby were much smaller and there were a lot less of them."

"So, it wasn't Wyatt James that did it."

"Well, it couldn't have been Wyatt because he was locked up."

"Oh no."

"Exactly. So, it's one of three possibilities. One—they had the wrong guy. Two—there was a copycat killer. Or three—Wyatt James was working with a partner."

Gabe

Jennifer's bike is completely useless at this point. The front tire is flat, and the rim's so bent it's a struggle to even push it. So, we leave it on the road.

I bring the bike I was riding, though, pushing it while Jennifer limps her way down the road. She can walk, but not fast.

She winces. "How far do you think it is back to camp?"

"We probably rode about a mile or two. At this pace, it'll probably take us an hour."

It's hot, the late afternoon sun beating down on us from above and bouncing back in our faces from the road. Sweat soaks underneath the arms of my shirt. The scenery is a monotonous line of trees, each looks the same as the last. My mind keeps wandering back to Jennifer bent over pushing into the tree. I shake my head as if I can physically shake the memories out of my brain.

The longer we walk, the more my pulse pounds at the side of my neck in the rhythm of my relentless thoughts.

What are we doing?

I didn't know Jennifer and Ben were together when I met her.

Fuck.

That's not true. What is true is I didn't know they were serious.

We were at a conference in San Francisco. One of those schmoozy things. Lots of drinks, not much work. Jennifer came up to me at the welcome happy hour and asked if I knew Ben. She recognized me from some of his pictures. After she said that, I recognized her too from Ben's MySpace posts. I offered to buy her a free drink, because that's the kind of stand-up guy I am. When we went up to my room, I told myself at the time it was all very innocent, just getting to know my brother's friend. But I'd be lying if I said I didn't know we were going to sleep together. And after a shared bottle of champagne, we did. Then we did again. We hardly left my suite at all until Sunday.

We missed all the events, except one. We made it to the keynote speaker in the large auditorium at the convention center across the street. She wore a short black skirt, professional but young and fresh. When she uncrossed her legs, I couldn't help but put a hand on her thigh. She never took her eyes off the stage as she moved my hand up her skirt and put my fingers where she wanted them.

We exchanged numbers but agreed that what we did was a mistake. We would never do it again, never speak of it. One week later, I opened my phone to a dark grainy picture of Jennifer's stomach. We've been texting ever since. Over a year now. Blurred low-res photos, so bad if you zoomed in, all you see are pixels of brown and gray. But what the photos lack we make up for in hyper-detailed descriptions of what we would do to each other if we were in the same state, in the same room, in the same bed. Until I got the invitation in the mail. Then the texts stopped.

After about thirty minutes of walking, I can't take the silence anymore. "Look, I know I'm not innocent in any of this. I know that. But do you think we should tell Ben?"

Jennifer spins to face me, and I flinch. "No."

"No?" I pause for her to respond, but she doesn't. "That's it? No."

"What good would it do, Gabe? If you're uncomfortable with what we've been doing, then we can stop. I thought we had stopped before this weekend. But telling Ben would be selfish and pointless. I'm still going to marry him."

"Why? We could've told him right away. When we first met. You and I could've been together for real." Even as I say it, I wonder if it's true. If we had come clean, would I have really wanted to be with Jennifer?

As if reading my mind, Jennifer says, "You wouldn't want to be with me"—she makes air quotes—"'for real.' And I don't want to be with you. It's just sex. It's meaningless. I want a future and a family. No offense, but you're not really the guy you marry." Jennifer turns around and keeps walking.

What the hell? I wipe sweat off my brow, trying to wipe away the pain, the pounding headache, the sick feeling in the pit of my stomach—but it's all too much.

"I'm not the kind of guy you marry because no one has ever given me a chance to be." I take a shaky breath and lower my voice. "Jennifer, I think I might love you."

What am I saying? Do I love Jennifer, or am I fishing to see if I can get her to love me?

She stops walking and looks at me with those crystal-blue eyes. And then laughs, a genuine deep from her gut laugh.

My anger rises up my neck to my face like a rash.

Jennifer covers her mouth. Once she's regained control, she says, "I'm sorry. I shouldn't laugh. That's very sweet. But you don't love me. I'm not even sure you like me. If I wasn't with Ben, I don't even think you'd want to fuck me."

Each word is a slap in the face. She can't tell me how I feel. But a small part of me, a sane, calm part of me, knows she's right. There're a million things I want to say to turn it all around on her, but she's right.

I'm a piece of shit.

My anger withers, blowing away on the humid afternoon breeze.

She puts a hand on my arm. "I'm not mad. We both messed up. Let's just move on."

I shrug her off.

"Look, my leg is fine." Jennifer kicks a little to demonstrate. "Really, I might need stitches but I'll live. I can head back on my own and you can ride your bike for help. Okay? Otherwise, I don't think you'll make it before dark."

I shouldn't let her walk alone, injured and out here in the wilderness. But I'm done arguing. Getting on the bike without another word, I ride down the hill.

I lean into the wind, the cool breeze in my face a relief. I try to focus on the road, the push down of each pedal, the blood pumping through me, anything but Jennifer.

I ride for a good while, not slowing my pace, letting the exertion exhaust me into a calm state. Speeding around a blind curve, I slam on the brakes.

The bike screeches in protest. My knuckles white. I can't squeeze the hand brakes any harder. Finally, the bike comes to a stop about three feet from a massive landslide.

A mountain of dirt, rocks, and broken trees cover any trace of road. It looks like the hill has shifted itself over completely. I search for a way around, but as soon as I put a foot up on the dirt, rocks shift. If I try to climb this, I could end up under another massive pile of the earth. Or skittering off the edge like all those tiny rocks.

There's no way out.

We're stuck.

I pace, scanning the mess for a way over, a way out.

There's none.

The lump in my throat won't go away, no matter how many times I swallow. I get back on the bike. All my energy is gone. It's like I'm pedaling underwater. After what feels like an eternity, I come across Jennifer slowly walking up ahead. I stand up, pedaling harder. She turns as I hop off the bike and bend over, trying to catch my breath. I really need to quit smoking.

"Why are you back?"

I straighten, trying to get the words out, but my lungs can't take in enough air.

She grabs my arms, and despite everything, an electric current runs through me at the feel of her soft hands. "What is it?"

How can I tell her there's no way off this mountain?

Allie

"What is it?" Eric looks at me, beads of sweat speckling his brow.

I gag as I touch the wet hair, taking it off my ankle with the tips of my fingers, trying to feel it the least amount possible. Once my ankle is free, I peer over the side of the dock. Floating in the water, tucked underneath the planks, is a full head of dark hair attached to a half-naked girl, face down.

The piercing scream fills my ears before I realize it's me.

Eric holds my arms tight. "Allie, take a breath."

I cover my mouth with one hand, the feeling of the cool metal of my ring on my lips bringing me back to earth. Shaking my head, I point to the water.

Eric looks over the side, and his breathing changes. "What the fuck?"

Nick was my first thought, but it's clearly a woman. My mind floods with questions. Who is it? What happened? How long has the body been there?

Eric's eyes are wide. "What do we do?"

I gulp in a few large breaths, considering. What do we do? It calms me. We need to *do* something. "We have to pull her out."

Eric shakes his head. "We shouldn't touch anything. What about evidence and all that?"

"Evidence?" We have no idea what happened to the girl. Evidence of what? Plus, if the body just sits in the water, it won't help anything. I've seen *Forensic Files*, if we leave her, any "evidence" on her will likely be lost to the lake. "We have to pull her out. Do you want me to get Ben and Joe to help?"

"Where are we going to put..." Eric swallows hard and looks around. "It."

Somewhere protected from animals, but we can worry about that later. If I say all that to Eric, he might snap. His eyes have taken on a shifty quality, not quite focusing on anything. We'll just take it one step at a time.

"For now, let's just put her on the grass over there."

Eric's face is deathly pale, with an almost blue tinge.

"Do you want to go back to camp and send someone else to help?"

He shakes his head. "Let's just fucking do this."

I lean over the side of the dock, unsure how to get the body out. I don't want to tug on her hair, but I can't see anywhere else to reach for. I gingerly try pulling a long, wet strand.

"What are you doing?" Eric says suddenly at my side. "We can't pull them by the hair."

I let out a long steady breath. This isn't going to work. "You're right. I just don't think I can reach her any other way."

Eric pulls his shirt over his head, kicks his shoes to the side, and jumps in the lake.

Echoes of splashes travel through the air, but he still hasn't moved the body from under the dock.

"What's going on?" I ask as I pace back and forth on the dock. For someone who looked like he was about to faint a minute ago, he's sure comfortable in the water with a dead body.

"It's stuck." He swims toward the back and splashes around over there.

Finally, he strokes back to where I'm standing. "Do you have a knife?"

"No." My mind flashes to my missing dagger.

"Can you run and get one? Maybe one of the cooking knives? I think the body is tied to the dock."

I run.

A sharp pain pierces my foot. I really should've put on my shoes before I took off. But I want to get the knife quickly. I want to get this over with, get the person out of the water. I turn into the communal campsite, taking the stairs two at a time. Everyone spins to look at me.

Joe's sitting in a camping chair having a beer with Ben. Dana and Lauren are whispering together in the tent. Jennifer and Gabe aren't back yet, and there's still no sign of Nick.

"I need a knife."

Ben looks at me like I've lost my mind. "What?"

"Or something sharp. Scissors."

Dana comes over to me. "Don't you have that weird lady dagger you bought from the antique store?"

I ignore Dana. I don't want to explain to everyone that I don't know where it is. The picnic table with all the cooking stuff catches my eye. In the bag of silverware, I find a small steak knife. That'll work. Hopefully. I take off running again, holding the knife in one hand.

Dana runs after me. "Wait, where are you going? What's going on?"

Out of the corner of my eye, I see Ben come after both of us.

Dana quickly catches up to me. Of course. She's an actual runner.

I slow to a walk, my bare feet killing me. It would've taken all of two seconds to put on my shoes. Why don't I think things through? "You don't have to come. I don't think you want to see this."

"See what? Are you high? Did you two go off and eat shrooms or something?"

I wheel around to face her. "You really think I'd do that? Our friend is missing. There's a weirdo car half-hidden in the bushes, and you think I would go trip balls right now?" Dana snaps her mouth shut. "There's a body, an actual dead fucking body, in the lake."

Dana's eyes fill with tears. "What?"

Ben's jaw goes slack. "Oh my god. Is it Nick?"

"No. It's a woman. I don't know who it is. But we've got to get her out of the water."

Ben says, "Eric's over there?"

I nod.

We walk the rest of the way in silence. When we arrive, Eric's sitting on the dock, dripping wet and hugging his knees into his body. He looks destroyed. Eric turns to look as I make my way onto the dock, and there's something in his eye that makes me queasy.

"I brought the knife."

I hand it to him, and he hops back in the water. Ben rushes forward. "I'll help. You stay with Dana. We've got this. You can both head back."

"This isn't the fifties, Ben. Even though I'm a woman, I'm fully capable of helping."

Eric calls from the water. "I need a hand here."

Ben runs over, and I take Dana's arm, leading her to the grass.

I focus on anything but the dock as they hoist the body out of the water. The clouds are a stark puffy white against the darkening blue sky, like cartoon clouds. A perfect day. It's like the day doesn't know there's a girl lying dead.

They carry her off the dock to the muddy shallows and lay her on the grass.

I can't bring myself to look.

"I'm not sure where we should put her." Ben's searching the trees.

"Can't we leave her there?" Dana points to an open clearing.

Ben squints. "I don't think all the direct sun is good."

"It's not like she's going to get a sunburn, Ben," Dana quips. Then as if realizing what she's said, she covers her mouth, fresh tears watering her eyes.

Ben turns to Eric. "Do you think we can take her all the way to the lodge? I found a basement when we were searching. We could put her there. She'd be protected."

Eric shivers, like a wave ran through his skin, but he says, "Let's go."

They pick her up, and I finally can't stop myself from looking at the body. She's in a matching black bra and panties. She's almost gray, like stone. Starting near her navel and snaking up to her neck, diamonds cover her skin—cut right into her flesh.

No, it can't be. I count each one I can see. Thirteen. I shudder and start to feel dizzy.

Ben's commanding voice brings me back. "Go ahead to camp. We'll bring up the rear."

Looking him in the eyes, we share a moment of understanding. He doesn't want Dana to have to see. Doesn't want us to stare at the body as they carry it.

I follow his orders, and Dana and I make it back to camp quickly. Marching right to the tent, I pour a hefty measure of whiskey in two glasses. I hand one to Dana, who's sitting by the unlit fire pit, staring into the ashes. She takes it without speaking, and we both gulp.

Murder? What murder? Episode 189 July 20, 2024

"Let's get back to the bridal party. They heard reports of Wyatt James escape on the way to Hood River—"

"Oh my god. He escaped?"

"He did. To our twenty-somethings, it's just a passing news story really. Not anything that's going to affect them in real life, you know?"

"Like our stories."

"Yes, totally. So, our group of hotties—"

"There should be a name for a group of hotties like a bunch of flamingos are called a flamboyance or a murder of crows."

"It was a murder for sure. Anyway, our crew is out camping, and from what we know, they were having a pretty good time. Rusty the bus driver has been interviewed many times on various shows and he always said, they had a 'real party vibe.'"

"Party bus 2004."

"Ha. Exactly."

"Ok, hold up, Barb. I have questions."

"Yes, Jules, I figured you would."

"I usually do."

"One of the many things I love about you. Please ask away, I don't know if I'll be able to answer them, but I can try."

"Okay, so the hot people go camping, then find a dead body in the lake. Why don't they get the fuck out of there? I would leave."

"Well, they tried to, remember? But they couldn't because of the landslide."

"Wait. So that's real? I thought Gabe was lying. I mean he's sleeping with his brother's fiancée. How can you trust Gabe really?"

"I am not in any way shape or form defending Gabe. But there really was a landslide. Shortly after they arrived, a truck ran off the road and hit a tree. Normally this wouldn't be such a big deal, I mean it would be for the driver of the vehicle, but it wouldn't have caused the chain reaction it did. It had been an unusually rainy year, though. Like record-breaking rains all spring and into the summer. It made the hills out there unstable. So, when the car hit the tree, it caused a landslide."

"Incredible. This group had all the luck. A landslide?"

"A fucking landslide. The road was completely blocked."

"Holy shit, that's insane."

"If you think that's insane, just wait till you hear who was driving the truck."

Dana

Gabe and Jennifer walk into camp looking like they stumbled out of hell. And it may be uncharitable, but the only thing I can think is they fucked it up. They were supposed to get help, and here they are, back with absolutely nothing to show for it. Honestly, they should've sent me and Ben. We're the responsible ones.

Jennifer has a long trickle of blood running down her leg from a piece of fabric tied around her thigh. Ben immediately runs up to her. "What happened?"

"The bike got a flat and I fell. But I'm fine." Jennifer hugs Ben, and I swear Gabe looks away. "We have some bad news."

Worse than only coming back with one bike and no help?

Gabe clears his throat. "Let's all go sit."

Allie, Joe, and Lauren are all sitting by the fire drinking. After my glass of whiskey, I switched to water. I didn't want to get totally blitzed when Nick is missing and there's a dead girl in the lodge.

Allie obviously has other plans. She stands, not even a wobble in her step as she pours herself another whiskey. For someone so tiny, she sure can put them away. I'm always amazed by how much she can drink before she even seems drunk. She looks terrible, though, yet still compelling in that uniquely Allie way. Her face is pale, and there are dark circles under her eyes. After what we just saw, we probably all look a mess. I smooth my hair as I take a seat, shooing away a small mosquito.

Lauren asks, "Did you find help?"

"The road is blocked," Gabe says. "There was a landslide."

"Wait." Joe stands. "What? A landslide. As in a real landslide?"

He nods. "There was no way around it."

We're stuck? Like, actually not able to leave?

That's not possible.

The mosquito buzzes in my ear, and once again I shoo it away.

"Can we go the other way?" I ask, annoyed they haven't thought through all the possibilities before bringing this pronouncement to the group.

I'd expect this from Gabe. He always half-asses things. At least he did when we were kids, and from what I've seen of people, they don't tend to change. But Jennifer surprises me. She usually explores every angle.

Ben says, "There's only one road until you get to the fork toward the bottom. There is no other way."

Gabe ambles to the cooler, snatches a beer, and takes a long drink. He plops in one of the camping chairs as far away from anyone else as he can get.

Jennifer sits. "Can someone please tell me what's going on?"

No one speaks.

"Seriously, what the fuck is going on?" Jennifer yells, her small fists balled up. My poor friend. I move to sit next to her, taking one of her hands in mine. We planned the perfect wedding and look where all our plans got us.

Joe puts a hand up in a simmer down motion. In response, Jennifer's eyes shoot fire. For a second, I think she's going to smack his hand right off his arm.

"Give them a minute," he says in that baritone that sends tingles all the way down to my toes.

"A minute. No, I will not give them a minute. We're stuck here. Nick is missing. The phones are gone. And to top it all off, there is a fucking landslide that is going to ruin my wedding. I don't have any minutes to give."

Joe and Lauren exchange a look, just a small one, but I notice it. I let go of Jennifer's hand and take a sip of my water, the cool liquid chilling my insides. It's the water, I tell myself, not whatever that look might mean.

Ben sits down on the other side of Jennifer. "Allie found a body," he says in an even tone one might use to coax a cat into a carrier. "Under one of the docks."

The whole tale comes spilling out, the group taking turns, adding their parts. I stay silent. I have nothing valuable to add, so I just observe.

After the whole sordid story is out, everyone falls into a spent silence, like when the screaming stops at the end of a rollercoaster. I stare into the fire, watching a flame eat away at a charred log.

What are we going to do? We need a plan.

Jennifer shakes her head and mutters. "Of course, Allie found a body."

Allie coughs on her sip of whiskey. "What's that supposed to mean?"

Jennifer throws her hands in the air. "Just who else, really?"

She's so right. Allie is a magnet for chaos. I'm not saying she's responsible for the girl's death. It's just something about her that this kind of stuff happens—a lot. Although Ben, Nick, and I have had our fair amount of tragedy too. But that's completely different. It's like Allie goes looking for it.

Eric walks over from where he's been fiddling with stuff at the picnic table and sits by Allie.

"We thought you were going to your tent," I say to Allie. "Why did you go all the way out to the dock in the first place?"

Allie purses her lips. Her face is so raw, deep lines grooved between her brows, I almost feel bad for her. Her shoulders slump as she says, "What does it matter?"

"Can you tell what happened to the girl? Or how long she's been there?" Gabe asks. "Did she slip and hit her head or something?"

"No." Ben, Allie, and Eric all say at the same time.

"It wasn't an accident." Ben takes a sip of his drink then lets out a long sigh. "I know this sounds crazy, but I think Wyatt James killed her."

My stomach drops like a rock down a well so deep it takes eons for the faint splash. I thought we left all the Wyatt James stuff in the past.

Eric

Gabe's eyes are so wide he looks like a cartoon. He nearly spits out his drink. "Wyatt James, as in *the* Wyatt James, the serial killer?"

Ben looks Gabe in the eye. "Yes, as in the serial killer that just escaped." He turns to me, and my palms start sweating for some reason. "You saw the body. All those diamonds."

I did. There were diamonds carved all over the girl. But I'm not sure what it's supposed to mean or what the right thing to say would be.

"It's crazy." Allie uses her hands to explain, whiskey sloshing onto her arm.

She's already on her way to drunk. Not the smartest move with a psycho killer dumping bodies into the lake. But she's a wild one, part of what draws me to her.

She continues, "But what other explanation could there be? All the news reports said the Gem Cutter escaped custody early yesterday, right? And he was in this area. That would give him enough time to come up here. Maybe he brought the girl with him?"

It would be a more convincing argument if she didn't slur the word explanation.

Lauren pipes up, her tank top moving down even lower on her chest, a feat I didn't think possible. "Weren't his victims found at campgrounds?"

Joe points to Lauren. "Yeah, they were, I remember that. His first—"

Gabe shakes his head, cutting off Joe. "That's fucking ridiculous. So, what you're saying is that Wyatt James broke out of jail and decided to go camping, then happened to stumble upon some random girl and ritualistically murder her? Nope. That doesn't make a lick of sense."

I'm sick of Gabe. His attitude is shit, even before all the bad stuff started happening. Who is so grim at their own brother's wedding? I stand up. "What do you think happened then?"

Allie stands too and faces Gabe. I nearly laugh. Her tiny frame doesn't scream intimidation, but I appreciate the senti-ment. She's on my side, and despite the shitty circumstances, that feels pretty fucking good. With a clenched jaw, Gabe's eyes look wounded but angry.

Allie says, barely above a whisper, "You weren't there. You didn't see the girl. And there was a diamond on the map."

Gabe takes a step closer. "What map?"

Ben walks over to us. "Let's all just sit, okay?"

I look around the small group, all watching us like we're in an episode of *The Real World*.

Allie flops back in the chair. "The map of the campground in the office at the lodge."

Gabe backs up and sits, so I do too, feeling the heat of the moment evaporate. But it doesn't feel like it's over between me and Gabe.

Dana lets out a long, childish sigh, like she's been waiting for her latte at Starbucks for five minutes and is about to speak to the manager. "Where is Nick?"

Jennifer leans forward in her chair, her bright-blue eyes narrowed. "Yeah, where is Nick? Isn't it a little weird that he suggested this place and now, right before Allie finds a body, he disappears?"

Ben shrugs. "He does this. He gets a wild hare, disappears and comes back with a wild story."

"It just doesn't feel right," Jennifer says. "Why does he never have a girlfriend either, like a real girlfriend?"

Lauren picks up the bottle from where she put it by her chair and pours more wine in her glass. This group sure likes their booze. Don't get me wrong, my friends like to drink, but they also know when to abstain. Well, except Lenny. He drank his way into a full-body cast board sliding down a set of stairs after juicing it. And yet as soon as he was out of the hospital, he was back at the skate park with the OE, night train, and Kool aid. No sense to him.

If they aren't careful, they're all going to end up like Lenny.

Lauren says, "He dates."

"But he's never with the same girl for more than two weeks." Jennifer crosses her arms tightly, pulling her sweater closer to her body. "I think we should all slow down on the drinks. We have to figure out how to get out of here."

Ben looks at Jennifer like she's lost her mind. "You think Nick, my best man, my friend who I've known my whole life, is really a serial killer? Is that what you're saying?"

Jennifer sits back in her chair, her arms pulling in even tighter, like she's trying to hold herself together. "I just think something is off about him, that's all. And where is he?"

Plenty of people aren't into serious relationships, that doesn't make them serial killers. But from what I've seen of

Nick, he does give off major creep vibes. He always looks at the girls like they're meat. Mostly his attention lands on Lauren, but every now and then I've seen him look at Allie in the same wolfish way. It makes my skin boil.

Allie

We're fucked.

"Let's figure this out. We need to leave." Dana stands, her mouth etched in frown lines. "We don't have cars. Does anyone's cell phone get service?"

I shake my head, the action mirrored by the rest of the group. "Mine doesn't even have any battery power left, last time I checked."

"Okay," Dana says. "And there's no phone at the clubhouse?"

Jennifer says, "They're gone. We already checked. How is this helping?"

The frown lines on Dana's face etch deeper.

Joe turns to Ben. "Hey, did you ever rent those mountain bikes?"

Ben frowns. "Nick thought we wouldn't have time to use them."

Nick again. So, if I'm keeping score, Nick recommended the campsite, Nick suggested not getting an alternate form of transportation, and now Nick is missing and there's a dead body in the basement of the lodge. Maybe an escaped serial killer isn't the most logical answer. Maybe we don't really know Nick. He's always training. Going for long runs in the woods. What if that's not what he's really doing?

"So, what do we do?" Joe asks, still sipping his beer despite Jennifer's advice.

"It's Thursday, right?" Lauren says.

Dana nods and continues pacing behind the chairs. "Thursday is almost over."

Lauren points at her. "Exactly. So, all we have to do is make it through tonight and tomorrow night. The bus will be back Saturday with all the wedding guests, right?"

Jennifer says, "Melanie should be here first thing Saturday morning to make sure everything is all set up."

"Right. We just have to wait for her to come. She'll see the road is blocked and get help. We'll be fine," Lauren says with a clap of his hands like the matter is solved.

Gabe's still looking at me with his intense dark eyes. "Explain to me again how you found the body?"

I sigh. Is he drunk? "There's an enormous map of the campground in the office at the lodge. I noticed a small diamond drawn on it, and I went to look where it was."

"It was marked on the map?" Gabe stands, looking at me expectantly. "Show me."

"Fine." I turn my face to Eric and mouth, *Please come.*

Eric gives me a nod and says, "I'll come too."

Gabe wheels on Eric with fire shooting out of his eyes, so intense I instinctively back up. Eric puts both hands in the air. Gabe says, "What, you don't trust me?"

Eric slowly lowers his hands. "I don't know you, dude. I didn't mean anything by it. With all the shit going down, though, we should probably stay in groups."

Gabe keeps staring at Eric, his gaze sharp as a dagger.

"None of us really know you either. Where did you get your tattoos?"

"My tattoos?"

"Yeah, *dude*. Your tattoos. I couldn't help but notice you have an awful lot of diamonds."

Eric stands to his full height, a few inches taller than Gabe, anger radiating off him in almost visible waves, his mouth a firm line. It's so unexpected. Admittedly, I haven't known Eric that long, but he always seems so laid back. I've never seen him like this. He tears off his shirt, his abs flexed, his body covered in ink, and heat spreads through me despite the circumstances.

"These? Did you notice this too?" He points to a drawing on his rib of a girl flying encased by a diamond. The words *you are stardust* are tattooed below her. "It's an illustration from a children's book, motherfucker."

I stand and put a hand on Eric's chest, his skin hot to the touch. "Let's all calm down."

I look at Gabe.

Neither of the men are backing down.

"This isn't getting us anywhere," I say calmly.

Dana, still pacing, throws out, "You're being idiots. Knock it off."

"I'll go find it myself." Gabe stalks off toward the lodge.

Gabe

Who does that guy think he is? Ripping off his shirt like that? Although when I glanced at his tattoos, it clearly was a children's book illustration with the diamonds. I even remember that book from when I was a kid.

I'm definitely not feeling as certain that Eric has something to do with all this, but I'm not convinced he doesn't.

Either way, we have to find a way out of here.

The office must have a radio. For emergencies. They must have missed it looking for the phone or not known what they were looking at. I'll kill two birds with one stone—look at the map, find a radio. I throw my empty beer can in the bushes and pick up my pace.

The water reflects the clouds and the setting sun like a mirror. An eagle soars far overhead. I want to throw rocks at it. I make my way quickly to the lodge and go straight to the office.

The large frame takes up almost one entire wall. It's a gorgeous old stylized map of the campground, and just as Allie said, there's a small mark on the glass. I lean in closer and squint, the mark coming in and out of focus. Shit, do I need readers already?

Ben comes into the room, but I ignore him as I examine the map. There's a tiny red diamond on the dock where they found the body. It's extremely precise, no way it's just a smudge. Blood rushes to my head, making a roaring sound in my ears so loud I don't hear what Ben says.

I point to the mark. "She's right."

Ben gets closer as Jennifer slips in the room.

I tear through the desk, opening and slamming drawers. Nothing.

Jennifer says, "What are you looking for?"

I ignore her, scanning the room. Virtually every surface is covered in papers or knickknacks. Every surface, but one.

Behind the desk on the shelf facing the window is a large clear space. I walk over and run my hand along the wood. Not even a speck of dust. Something is missing.

I lean over the shelf to look behind it, but nothing is there either.

"Do you remember when you were here before?" I turn to Ben, then Jennifer. "Was there a radio back here? Or anywhere? Did anyone mention what to do in an emergency?"

Jennifer shakes her head. "Walt just said if we needed to use the phone it was in his desk."

Ben's frowning. "I think I remember seeing a radio, though. Back there." He points to the empty space behind the desk.

I nod.

Ben asks, "Will you come look at this?"

He points to a spot on the map on the other side of the lake in the trees, where we found the car.

Ben puts a hand on my arm. "Gabe."

"What?" I step back, and his hand falls. My nerves are live wires. I don't want him to touch me.

"We should go check this spot out again, right now. All three of us."

I can't believe him. Why? What would be the point? We didn't find anything useful there the first time.

My voice comes out as a roar. "We should get the fuck off this mountain."

"Why was Nick's flashlight there? What is the car even doing there? What if..." Ben swallows hard. "We really need to go look."

"Okay," I say. "If you need to look now, like right now, then I think we should split up. You two go check it out."

Jennifer puts a hand lightly on Ben's shoulder. "I don't think that's a good idea."

I hold up a hand. "I'm not going across the lake right now. It's getting dark. I don't think you should go either, but if you're insisting, then I get it. Go ahead."

Jennifer says, "He's right." Ben turns to face her. "We don't have our flashlights with us or anything. We can go in the morning."

Ben nods but looks disappointed.

I clear my throat. "I need you to show me the body."

Ben's face turns to stone, his jaw tight, and there's an almost unnatural tint of gray to it

"Or you can just point me in the direction of the basement." I lower my voice. "I just want to see, maybe it could've been an accident."

"There are literal diamonds cut into her. It wasn't an accident. You don't need to see it."

I brush my hands on my jeans. "I'll find it myself."

Ben sighs. "You're so goddamn stubborn. Fine. I'll show you."

He looks at Jennifer. "You need to stay here."

Jennifer crosses her arms tightly over her stomach but makes no attempt to follow us.

Ben leads the way down a narrow set of old wooden stairs. It's dark and just gets darker the further down we go.

Ben reaches overhead at the bottom and pulls a rope. A dim light shines on the basement. In the corner is a body, pale with long dark hair in black underwear and bra. She's lying on her side facing the wall. I touch her shoulder, it's cold but so familiar. I move her and spot the first diamond. As I turn the body so she's face up, panic rises in my throat accompanied by a wash of bile. I quickly turn my head to the side retching in the corner of the basement.

Ben walks slowly over to me. "I told you. You didn't need to see."

I look back to make sure I didn't imagine it. Lying, now face up, her face bloated, and an unnatural shade of blue is Sheila.

My Sheila.

Dead.

Not just dead but murdered.

Dana

Eric tugs back on his shirt but still looks angry, the muscles in his neck clenched uncomfortably tight. I have to say I don't blame Gabe for saying something. I totally understand his suspicions. There's something off about Eric, but I don't think he's an actual murderer. I think he's just an idiot.

Allie puts a hand on his arm. "Are you okay?"

"Everything is pretty fucking far from okay. I should've never come here. Stupidest idea I've ever had."

Alarm bells ring through my ears so loud I can almost feel the vibration in my fingertips.

I hold up a finger. "How was coming here *your* idea?"

"I..." He pauses and his limbs sag. "I'm going to take a walk."

"Are you sure?" Allie asks. "It'll be dark soon, and we don't know who's out there..."

It always surprises me how caring Allie is with virtually everyone else.

"I'll be fine. I'll take a light. I just need some fresh air."

She smiles. "We're camping. There's nothing but fresh air."

"Right. I'll be back."

Joe puts another log on the fire, and a swell of pride fills me. He's a good man. A solid guy.

Not at all like Eric.

What does he mean this was his idea? And who wants to be alone at a time like this? Although truth be told, I don't think we're in any real danger. I suspect that girl was there a while; the marks probably came from fish. It could've been an accident.

I turn to Lauren and whisper that there's no way Wyatt James is responsible for the girl in the lake.

It's too much of a coincidence.

"What are you two whispering about?" Allie snaps at us, proving my point that she's always nicer to people she doesn't know—people who don't really know her.

Lauren sits back, while I lean forward.

"We don't think Wyatt James had anything to do with it." I shake my head. "Why would he kill some random girl right after breaking out of prison. He wouldn't, right? He'd go try to get laid. Or get a slice of pecan pie like Ben Affleck in that movie."

Lauren says, "Plus, how would he get here? He'd have to have a car. Where is it?"

"Um, the car we found?" Allie gestures vaguely off into the woods.

"That has to be the girl's car," I point out. "How else would she get here?"

"I'm not convinced some escaped serial killer had something to do with the girl. I've always thought Wyatt James was innocent, honestly." Joe taps the top of his beer. "But playing Devil's advocate, what if Wyatt abducted the girl and they drove up here together?"

My blood runs cold. Even Joe thinks it's possible. There's just no way. Not after what happened before.

Gabe

Leaving Ben in the basement, I stumble up the stairs. He's talking, but I can't hear him over the whir in my ears. Jennifer follows me out the front door of the lodge. For once, I don't care what she's doing.

I trudge right into the lake with all my clothes on and fall to my knees in the water, shivering. It feels like I could cry at any moment, but my eyes are dry. I should cry. But when I squeeze my eyes shut, no tears come. My veins shake with adrenaline. I splash water on my face.

Jennifer stands at the shore. "Come on, Gabe. You're shivering. Let's get you in a warm shower."

I don't say anything. Don't nod. The most I can do is put one foot in front of the other. I stomp out of the water, watching each splash my feet make.

What is Sheila even doing out here?

The car. The rental car must be hers. She must've been able to fly out early after all. She rented a car, drove out here to meet us, when? And what the fuck happened between then and now? Why hadn't I picked up the phone when she called me?

Before I realize what's happening, we're in the bathroom

and Jennifer is unbuttoning my jeans. Her finger runs lightly down the side of my crotch as she unzips my pants. I look at her in horror. How can she think I want to have sex right now?

She grabs both sides of the waistband and pulls my pants and underwear down at the same time, exposing me.

When she drops to her knees, I stumble back as if she bit me.

I fumble for my wet boxers. "What are you doing?"

Jennifer puts a hand on my leg. "It'll help."

I can't believe what she's saying. "It's Sheila. The dead girl they found in the lake is Sheila. My girlfriend is dead. How will it possibly help to get a blowjob from my brother's fiancée?"

Her face is blank as she searches mine for answers. "What?"

"Sheila is dead."

She covers her mouth with her hands and runs out the door.

I step out of my wet jeans, grab a towel from the stack in the corner, and get in the shower. I hardly feel the warm water. I'm frozen solid. How long can I stay here? I lean my hand against the wall and shake out my hair.

The door to the bathhouse opens with a squeak. "Gabe?"

Shit. It's Ben.

"Gabe. You okay?"

"No."

"Okay. Can I do anything?"

"No."

One of the other showers turns on. Time to leave.

I didn't think it was possible for me to feel worse than when I turned Sheila over, but I do. How did I let things get so fucked?

Heading directly to my tent, I take a swig of whiskey straight from the bottle on the bar cart in the corner. The bed looks more welcoming than anything I've seen in the last few hours. After another giant swallow, I crawl under the covers.

My plan was to storm in there and prove it was an accident. In my head, the girl had slipped and hit her head. I'd point out the head wound, and Ben would clap me on the back and tell me of course I was right. But it was not an accident. Those diamonds are undeniable. And it isn't just some girl—it's my girl.

The thing that keeps popping up in my mind like a demented jack in the box is when? When was Sheila murdered? It had to be really recently because she called me when we were at the brewery. Oh my god. Was she calling for help?

The last thought scuttles past my brain like a nasty cockroach. Who put the diamond on the map?

@OliviawithanO | Content Creator

52.6K likes 4.9K comments 29.5K saves 5.2K shares

Video posted July 20th, 2024 2:12pm PST.

Screen shows a woman with long brown hair and shiny lips holding an iced matcha in a plant-filled room with subdued lighting and a sculptural lamp in the background. She's wearing a lush cream sweater linked in the shop.

"Hi. I'm Olivia Barry. Content Creator. And I'm sitting here watching *Murder? What Murder?* Like all the true crime girlies and I'm floored. They are talking about my best friend's murder. Sheila Tanner.

"Sheila was the best person. Such a hard worker. Like if you see me and you're like, that girl can hustle, it's all from what I learned from Sheila. She was an intern at a law firm here in Austin. She'd been dating Gabe for almost a year. And it was a disaster.

"Gabe was super hot, in this brooding Robert Pattinson kind of way. But he was a real dick. He didn't pay enough attention to Sheila. He never answered her texts. He always bailed on plans."

"In Sheila's own words: Fully interested when the clothes are off, then phone in front of his face when the clothes are on.

"Sheila loved a challenge, though. She was invested. On girls' nights she would talk about marriage and what their kids would look like. Gabe invited her on this trip. She saw it as a chance to meet his whole family. Her future family is what she said. I've never seen her that nervous. She couldn't get away from work for the whole camping portion of the trip, but she was planning on meeting them for the wedding.

"Then something really weird happened. On Tuesday, July 20th, twenty years ago today, she called in sick. This girl never called in sick a day in her life. NEVER.

"She told me she *had* to go on the trip. It was so unlike her. She wanted to be hired at that firm for real. Calling in was not a good look. When I pushed her on it, she snapped at me. Said I didn't know the whole story. I was like, girl, tell me. But she said she'd explain when she got back.

"She never came back.

"I should've never let her go. She kept saying there was something she needed to take care of. I dropped her off at the airport on Wednesday morning. She rented a car and called me from a coffee shop in Hood River. She was on her way to Lost Lake. That was in the afternoon; I'm not even sure how late, but the sun was still up. It was the last time I heard from her.

"Hug your friends, girls. Let them know you love them. And if they're dating someone you don't like, tell them."

#Mystory #Lostlakemurders #Murder?WhatMurder?

Allie

When Joe says Wyatt James could've kidnapped the girl and brought her here, Dana and Lauren's faces fall in tandem, like they choreographed it. I don't really understand why it's any better or worse if Wyatt James isn't involved.

By the time Ben and Jennifer walk back into camp, I'm dizzy from my swirling thoughts and no closer to an answer about any of it. One thing that's clear is I'm not going to figure anything out sitting in this chair drinking.

Ben looks like his shoulders carry the weight of the world. "There's something you all should know. The girl we found was Gabe's girlfriend, Sheila."

"What?" Lauren cries.

"No. She was only supposed to be here for the wedding. That's why I didn't get her a gift basket. Why would she come out here early and not tell anyone?" Dana says.

Ben shakes his head. "I'm not sure."

If we can just figure this out, then we'll all be safe. I want to try to find some answers, but it's gotten so dark. The kind of darkness that only happens out in the woods. We're swallowed up by it—like the night is a serpent and we are the mouse.

Eric walks into camp and sits by me. Gabe still hasn't returned from his tent. After twenty more minutes, Ben goes to check on him. They come back together, Gabe stumbling a little on the way up the stairs, losing the cigarette that's hanging out of his mouth.

Ben goes to Jennifer, messing with the food, threatening to make dinner, despite the fact that no one is hungry. Their heads bent close together. I strain to hear their whispering. They're too quiet, I can't hear anything but the light popping bubbles from my beer and the crackle of the fire. Gabe sits in a chair near me, looking like he drank a tumbler of whiskey. He pounds water and sparks another Marlboro Light.

Ben and Jennifer hold hands and take chairs next to each other by the fire, like a king and queen holding court. Jennifer clears her throat. "Now that we're all together, I think we need to *stay* together."

Eric gives me a quick, almost imperceptible side-eye. Lauren nods, and Dana says, "Okay."

Jennifer raises her voice. "I'm serious. Even if you have to go to the bathroom, go in pairs."

The muscles in my shoulders tighten at her tone. It's so high-handed, but in that *this is for your own good* way. It's not that I disagree, but none of us need orders barked at us right now.

Dana must feel the same way because she is downright scowling. She's usually the one making the plans, giving the orders. She says, "Sure mom."

Jennifer's face turns an unhealthy-looking color of red as she stands. "This isn't a joke. Wyatt James could be hiding out waiting to murder us all." She looks pointedly at Dana, lifting a long strand of her brown hair. "If I were you, I'd take this a little more seriously."

Jennifer drops the hair and stalks back to her chair.

Dana crosses her arms and crosses her legs as if her limbs can cocoon her, but for once, she doesn't say a word.

Eric

I fucked up. I don't think Allie heard it, or registered what it meant. I was just so pissed I wasn't thinking what I was saying.

Dana heard, though. That it was my idea to come here. And now she won't stop looking at me suspiciously.

Allie was so drunk, and she started talking about the wedding. Complaining, really. I jumped in. I told her the trip would be a lot more fun if she brought me. After a couple more beers and a few episodes of *Dateline* I think she agreed. She pretty much mumbled okay before she fell asleep.

Clearly, it wasn't my best idea.

But maybe I'm reading too much into Dana looking at me. Everyone is sneaking glances at each other. It's pretty obvious they don't trust each other. This isn't at all how I imagined this going.

Joe makes hot dogs, saying we'll all feel a little better if we eat. I doubt that very much.

Whiskey fumes waft off of Gabe in such rank waves I flinch every time he lights a cigarette. He clears his throat, and even that sounds slurred. "Look, I think it will be okay if everyone went back to their campsites to sleep—"

Jennifer opens her mouth and is about to speak.

But Gabe holds up his hand and continues, "In pairs or groups of three."

I scan the faces of the group, trying to gauge their reaction to this. There are a few nods, but Jennifer still looks unconvinced.

"That sounds reasonable," Dana says. "Good plan. I'll be with Joe."

Allie leans forward. "Lauren, do you want to bunk with me and Eric?"

No.

We need some alone time.

Jennifer shakes her head. "That will leave Gabe alone."

He stands, sways and sits right back down. "I don't mind. I'll be fine."

"I'll stay with Gabe," Lauren says. "Then we're all in pairs and I'm not a third wheel to anyone."

"Yeah, okay. That makes sense," Allie says, but her brow is furrowed. Is she worried about Lauren being alone with Gabe, or is she worried about being alone with me?

Joe puts the hot dogs on the table. "Food is ready."

We eat in silence. The stereo plays Dave Matthews Band quietly. I chew each bite carefully. As if the act of eating a hot dog can normalize everything. Look, I'm having a normal experience camping. Not that any of my experiences end up being typical. Why should this be any different? But like Kerouac said, "It's all a great strange dream."

Lauren throws away her plate. "So, what's the plan exactly? We're going to sleep in pairs, but then what?"

Ben pinches the bridge of his nose, like he could squeeze his thoughts out and somehow come up with a way to get us out of this. But there is no getting out of this.

"Like Jennifer said, our wedding planner is supposed to be here first thing Saturday morning. Unless someone else sees it first, she'll find the road blocked and get it cleared up."

"It'll probably take a while for them to clear that mess," Gabe says.

Ben nods. "So, help will probably arrive late Saturday or Sunday. We have plenty of food. If we stick together, we should be fine."

"Do you really think Wyatt James is out here?" Lauren asks.

Ben sinks in the chair, his shoulders slumped. "I don't know, but I'd like to go with a small group in the morning and check some things out."

Allie sits forward in her chair, leaning intently toward Gabe. "When would Sheila have gotten here?"

"I'm not sure." Gabe focuses on the burning ash of his cigarette.

"You said she called," Allie continues. "When did she call?"

"While we were at the brewery. I was going to listen to the message later, but then when we got here my phone didn't get any service."

Gabe's ash is bordering on Shelly Duvall in *The Shining* long. For as swaying on his feet drunk as he is, he must have every muscle flexed to hold that still.

Allie nods. "So, she must not have been here yet when she called you. She must have gotten here right before us."

Allie's right. Sheila couldn't have called from the campsite; there's no service and no phone.

Lauren stands with a dramatic slap to both her thighs. She heads to the tent, coming back with another bottle of wine. "Look, if we have to stay out here for another day, possibly two, we have to stop talking about this. Okay? We all need to sleep tonight, and if we keep acting like there's some crazed serial killer out here, we never will."

Ben laughs, a harsh humorless laugh. "Lauren, there really might be a crazed serial killer out here."

"I realize that, Benjamin. And we're doing all the things we can to stay safe. But us obsessing about it is not going to help. Let's talk about something else. Just for a little while."

I can't handle idle chit chat right now, and no one else is jumping to add anything to the conversation either. What Lauren is failing to realize is all the wine in the world won't change how utterly fucked we are.

Each and every one of us.

Allie

As if the situation couldn't get any worse, "Crash into Me" comes on the stereo, and I wish someone would just kill me and get it over with.

Oof, poor choice of words.

I walk over to the picnic table and flip through the CD booklet. Dana, Lauren, and Jennifer are all trying to figure out where else Jennifer can have the wedding after we get out of here. How can they think about the wedding at a time like this?

I mean, I know they've all been planning it together for a long time, but it seems insensitive under the circumstances.

Joe's staring into fire, a faraway look on his face. That guy gives me a weird feeling. I can't put my finger on why exactly. Maybe it's run-of-the-mill stranger danger or his super deep voice.

I scan through the CDs; it's one of those extra-large books with four discs to a page. They're alphabetized, which is surprising to me. Who alphabetizes their music? If you get something new, you have to go through and move the whole collection. I scroll to the middle, hoping there's some Modest Mouse besides their new album *Good News for People Who*

Love Bad News. No luck there. I flip instead to the back, hoping for some old Weezer or maybe even some Ween.

Instead, I find a burned CD that says *Wonderful Wendy's Ultimate Playlist*. I put it in the disc changer, and the Gin Blossoms blast out of the stereo. I skip the song and "Lovefool" comes on. Dana joins me from where she had been talking with Lauren, an actual smile on her face.

"Oh crazy. This is Nick's mix from high school! We listened to this thing over and over again so he could get it just right. Do you remember that, Ben?"

"Who was it for?" I ask.

Dana's smile fades. "It was for Wendy Robinson."

That name is so familiar. But I didn't go to high school with them. Dana never lets us forget it. They are the oldest and dearest friends of the group.

Ben's nodding. "We sat at his dad's clunky desktop for hours."

"Why didn't he give her the CD?"

Ben's brow furrows, deep frown lines etching along the sides of his mouth. "Huh?"

How am I the only one that sees it doesn't make sense? "He spent all this time making the perfect mixed CD, why didn't he give it to Wendy?"

"I thought he did," Dana says. "Maybe he kept a copy for himself."

She goes back to Lauren's side. I join them and scoot my chair a little closer to the warmth of the fire. "Dana, did you know Nick's girlfriend in high school?"

Dana laughs then stops abruptly, her eyes look horror-struck at her own moment of lightness. Twice in the matter of minutes. Once she's regained her composure, she says, "What girlfriend? No offense, Ben, but Nick was a loser in high school."

Ben chuckles. "None taken."

"I could never figure out why you hung out with him." Dana pulls her sweater closed. "Until college. He was totally different once we got to college, actually kind of hot."

"So, you didn't know Wendy Robinson?" I say.

There is a swift beat of silence, like even the fire sucks in a breath.

Joe speaks first, sitting forward in his chair. "Wendy Robinson, as in Wyatt James's second victim?"

Then with a sickening clang, it clicks. That's where I recognize the name. Her face suddenly fills my head from all the news reports. Wendy Robinson is usually the last photo they show whenever they report on Wyatt James. The youngest victim.

"Nick knew her?"

Ben motions to Dana. "We all did. We went to the same small high school. She was a sophomore when we were all juniors. Weren't you on the cheerleading team with her, Dana?"

Dana nods.

Jennifer stares at Ben like he sprouted another head. "You all knew her? Why didn't any of you say something about it before?"

Ben shrugs. "Haven't I?"

Jennifer says, "No, you haven't."

Ben throws his hands up in the air. "It's not like we talk about Wyatt James all that much. In fact, I've talked more about him in the past two days than I have ever, in my entire life."

Dana jumps in. "It's not really a pleasant time to revisit. It was super scary."

Joe sits back, but his face still holds something to it I haven't seen before from him. Like for once he's actually invested in the conversation. "Wyatt always claimed he was innocent. Did you ever think it could be someone else? Someone from your school?"

Dana takes in a shuddering breath. "No. It had to be him. Wyatt used to hang out at our practices sometimes. He was just so odd. As soon as Wendy went missing, I knew he had something to do with it. The whole school was terrified. I for one couldn't wait to graduate and get the hell out of there."

Jennifer mutters something I can't hear.

A chill creeps up my spine as the song changes to Lisa Loeb's "Stay." I jump back over to the stereo and switch it off.

Gabe joins me. "Not a fan?"

"It's just creepy. Did you know Wendy Robinson too?"

A shadow passes in front of his face. "I had already graduated when she went missing."

"You mean, was found murdered. It's pretty extraordinary, don't you think? That you four already have a connection to Wyatt James. That Nick dated, or I guess wanted to date, one of the victims."

Gabe's face doesn't move a muscle. "It is."

I lower my voice, not wanting the group by the fire to hear me. "How well do we all know Nick?"

Gabe sips his water, his eyes on the group by the fire. I press on.

"He's the only one that's been here before, right? He suggested this place. He's gone without a trace and now someone's dead. Where did he go?"

"I don't know."

A twig snaps. I turn, fully expecting to see Nick glowering at me, but it's Eric. He puts both hands in the air as if in surrender. "I didn't mean to startle you. I'm beat. Are you about ready to head to the tent?"

Nodding, still lost in thought, I walk over to the fire and grab what's left of my beer. "We're going to bed."

Ben looks at me with such an intense gaze, his blue eyes lit by the firelight. "Don't go anywhere alone. If you have to use the bathroom, you have to go together."

"Okay." Eric turns on his flashlight, and I follow him. We walk silently to our site, my mind spinning.

Did Nick kill that girl and run?

Gabe

Despite chugging water, my head's still swimming. I shouldn't have drunk all that whiskey.

Allie and Eric leave. Splitting up into our respective pairs suddenly seems like a really dumb idea.

The flames lick the wood while my thoughts whirl. Did Ben ever tell me that they were friends with Wendy Robinson?

I can't sit still; my thoughts are too fast, too loud. Walking to the edge of the path, I sit down on the step and look out at the lake. The moon's a sliver, a Cheshire Cat moon. It reflects off the inky water. I can't help picturing Sheila's face.

Lauren comes over and sits too close to me. "What are you thinking about?"

Clenching my jaw, I bite back a sarcastic remark. "Just...the situation."

She puts an ice-cold hand on my arm. "I'm so sorry about your girlfriend."

I shrug her hand off. The water laps at the shore, filling the silence.

Joe yells, slurring from across the fire. "I'm fine. You'll be around people, and I'll be fine." He stands and stumbles a bit.

Lauren and I rejoin the group. How much has he been drinking?

Dana stands too. "Let's go to bed."

Joe pushes her away, not forcefully. But it sobers me more.

He slurs as he says, "What's the point of sticking together? We're all going to die. You were with Wendy the day she died, and she was still cut up. Murdered. No one could save her. Just like no one can save you."

He strides toward the bathrooms, veering this way and that. I didn't think he'd been drinking that much. Maybe I wasn't paying attention.

Lauren asks, "Are you okay?"

"Of course," Dana says. "He's just had too much to drink. It's the stress. We'll use the bathroom and go to bed. See you all in the morning."

We all say goodnight as she runs after Joe.

Lauren makes a loud yawn, stretching her hands up over her head. "I'm pretty tired too. Do you mind if we turn in?"

I look at her, maybe for the first time since we got here. She's wearing a bulky cardigan over a sheer white cover up and white bikini.

She asks, "Should we go to my camp or yours?"

"Whatever you want."

"Yours is good."

I nod and take one of the flashlights off the picnic table. It's so dark, even with the light it's hard to make out the path. I hear Lauren stumble behind me. Reflexively, I catch her by the arm. "You okay?"

"Just tripped on a rock." She doesn't let go of my arm this time.

We make it to my tent, and I say, "You can take the bed. I'll sleep in the hammock."

"Don't be silly. We're both adults and the bed is huge. We can share it."

My gut tells me it isn't a good idea, but my head is nodding, and my stupid mouth says, "Sure."

Lauren turns on the small lantern on her side table. It puts out a faint orange glow.

I kick off my shoes and peel off my socks, but that's the only clothing I remove. Lauren, on the other hand, takes off her sweater and cover up, sliding under the covers in just a white bikini.

The only sounds are a distant owl and the light rustle of leaves in the wind. Then silence.

The leaves tremble again, and Lauren scoots closer to me. "Did you hear that?"

I try moving over more to my side of the bed, but there's nowhere to go. "It's just the wind."

"I didn't notice any wind before."

"Weather must be shifting."

Lauren scoots again and presses her body against my side. She snakes an arm around my waist, tucking herself into me.

Her skin is so cold, and I flash once again to Sheila's face. I jump off the bed. "We shouldn't do this."

Lauren sits up. "I wasn't doing anything. Oh my god. Did you think I was coming on to you?" She stands, grabbing her cardigan and wrapping it around herself tightly. "I'm seeing someone, asshole. I wasn't trying to fuck you."

I hold up a hand.

Shit.

Did I misconstrue the situation? It's possible. I'm still a little drunk. I replay it in my head, her arm draping slowly across my body. No. She was coming on to me.

A large crack echoes outside, and all the blood in my body

shoots to my toes in one frenzied pulse. I duck my head out the tent door.

The noise is gone. The wind must've snapped a branch.

I grab a blanket off a chair in the corner.

"Where are you going?"

"I'm going to sleep in the hammock."

Lauren slips into her Ugg's with a huff, her eyes flashing in the light of the lantern. "Don't pretend you're broken up about your"—she makes air quotes—"'girlfriend.'"

"What do you mean?" My head is swimming, trying to comprehend.

"Oh please. You were cheating on her."

My jaw clenches, uncomfortably tight. What does she know? Does she know about Jennifer? "Cheating?"

Lauren shakes her head. "No one checks their phone that much unless they're hoping for a sexy text."

"I was just waiting to hear from Sheila." That's not true.

"If you were so concerned, checking your phone every five seconds, then why didn't you pick up when she called? Or check the message she left when you had the chance?" Without waiting for my reply, she heads out of the tent. "I'm going to go bunk with Dana and Joe."

"You don't have to—"

She's already past the tree.

"Let me walk you."

She says over her shoulder, "I don't need anything from you."

Going back in the tent, I throw myself on the bed.

I should go after her.

But I don't.

Allie

Eric's snores fill the night air.

As I lie here, listening to his heavy breaths, my neck is taught, brimming with annoyance. How can he fall asleep so fast? Isn't he scared? Isn't he worried?

An owl hoots somewhere off in the distance. I turn on my side for the millionth time. I should've drunk another beer, then I'd be asleep now. I sit up in bed. That's a brilliant idea. I put on my sweater and shoes. I'll just walk next door for a shot of whiskey, and it'll put me right to sleep.

But should I really walk around by myself at night? With a killer out there? I hesitate at the door to the tent. Why didn't Jennifer put a bar cart in my tent?

Fuck it. I'll be quick. I'll be careful.

I grab the flashlight and wish again I knew where the knife I bought from the antique store went. It's possible I stashed it somewhere the first night. Where would drunky drunk Allie put her brand new dagger? I'd feel better with it in my back pocket. Safer.

The flashlight blazes a tiny circular spot on the trail. I focus on the light and not on the murky trees surrounding me. Eric's snores get quieter as the sound of the night gets louder. Crickets and the rustle of leaves in the wind. The crescent moon shines on the lake, and I can see the appeal. On a different day, in a different situation, this might feel peaceful.

When I get to the tent, I pour myself a large portion of whiskey into one of the crystal tumblers. I don't even have glasses this nice at my house. Who takes crystal to the woods? Not that I'd know. Camping was never my grandma's thing. I only went once as a kid with a friend's family. It was fine until I had to use the rickety old outhouse in the middle of the night with only a dim glow stick to light my way. I cried the whole time I was peeing. The next night when I had to pee, I tried to hold it. I didn't want to go to that dark hut all by myself. I had an accident in the borrowed sleeping bag. Too embarrassed to tell my friend or her family, I put the sleeping bag in the lake to clean it myself. When her mother yelled at me, I told her I was just seeing if it would float. I was not invited on another trip, which was fine by me.

This whole camping wedding is a ridiculous idea, and now we're stuck because of a landslide.

I sip my whiskey as that thought rattles around in my brain. A landslide. What are the odds? Gabe goes for help and instead finds a landslide and says we can't leave, that we're trapped. Then we find Gabe's girlfriend murdered.

A loud crack shoots adrenaline to my fingertips, jolting me out of my thoughts and making me drop my whiskey. I crouch behind the bar cart for a long time, waiting, listening, hiding. What is that? Is someone out there? I listen to footsteps approaching, my breath fast and loud in my ears. Will they find me down here? I look around for a weapon. The bottles. If someone's coming for me, I'll hit them with the whiskey bottle.

The tent flap rustles, and my pulse ratchets up a notch. I

lean a bit to sneak a look around the cart just as Lauren peers over it.

"What are you doing?" she asks as she snatches an open bottle of red by the neck and pours herself a glass.

My heart rate returns to normal slowly. I stand brushing off my legs. "I dropped my drink."

She holds up the bottle of wine. "Want some?"

"Yes."

She pours some in a glass and hands it to me then turns on the camping lantern and sits on the couch, curling her long bare legs under her. "What are you doing up?"

I take the chair facing her, my relief at seeing her here replaced with confusion. What is she doing wandering around at night by herself? "Couldn't sleep. What about you? Where's Gabe?"

"He's over there being an egomaniacal dick. He actually implied I was coming on to him?" She scrunches her nose as if smelling something rank. "What about Eric? So much for staying in pairs."

"Eric's sleeping so peacefully it was making me restless."

Lauren nods and sips her wine.

"Do you know Gabe very well?"

"Not really." Lauren purses her lips to the side, a gesture that looks a lot like Jennifer and I wonder which one of them started doing it first. "I've met him a handful of times. But I wouldn't say we were close at all."

"Do you really think there was a landslide?"

The tendons in Lauren's neck stiffen. "Oh my god. Do you think he's lying? Why would he lie about that?"

To keep us here and murder us all one by one, I think but don't say. Instead, I shrug. "I'm probably just being paranoid."

Lauren sighs and stretches out on the couch, covering herself with a fur throw blanket. "I'm going to sleep here."

The hairs on my neck stand on end. "By yourself?"

"Yeah. I'll be fine. I don't want to bother Joe and Dana. Honestly, Joe kind of gives me the creeps, but don't tell Dana I told you that."

"Oh right, because me and Dana are constantly having heart-to-hearts."

Lauren smiles. "Yeah. I know you haven't been close for a while."

"Or ever."

I set down my wine, grab the blanket off the back of the chair I'm sitting on, and cover myself snuggling deeper down, throwing my legs over the side. Eric will be fine on his own.

"Have you started snoring in your old age?"

"Bitch, I'm twenty-six." Lauren laughs. "And I do not snore."

"I'll stay here too then."

The chair is surprisingly comfortable, and Lauren's breathing is slow and even.

Dana
Friday, July 21, 2004

I'm not thinking clearly.

It's all the stress. I'm not thinking clearly. I shouldn't be out here. It's pitch black. At the very least, I should've brought the flashlight before I ran off. But I had to leave. There was no other choice and absolutely no time to grab anything.

My flip-flops slap painfully against the soles of my feet as I run down the trail. It grounds me—the sensation and the sound.

Slap, slap, slap.

My heart pounds in my ears. It mixes with the echo of my shoes and hammers out a song in my head with just one lyric.

Joe. Joe. Joe.

I thought I knew him. But it's clear now, I know nothing. I've spent my whole adult life doing the right thing. Getting good grades. Buying the right clothes. Styling my hair and makeup just so, even at the gym. And look where it's gotten me. What a fucking waste. I should've just been doing whatever the hell I wanted, like Allie.

But I was trying to make up for the terrible thing I did in high school.

I glance behind me, but it's so dark I can't tell if he's following me.

The moon provides only the smallest amount of light as I run, not knowing where I should go.

The car. Of course. It's so obvious I can't believe I didn't think of it earlier. I can take the car and leave. There has to be a way in. The landslide can't be all that bad, if there even is one. Who knows anymore? I can't trust any of them. Not even my best friends.

Tears roll down my cheeks, and I swipe them away.

Apparently, this is who I am now. A woman who cries.

When I'm far enough away from our tent, I slow down to a walk and zip up my hoodie. Maybe this is all karma. It's what we deserve, what I deserve.

I should've never put that picture on Wendy's locker.

It was such a bitchy thing to do. And it's why she left practice early that day. By herself. Instead of walking with the group she normally did.

That day set my whole life on a different trajectory.

What if I hadn't made that picture? I'd probably be happily married, with a baby on the way, a little girl. One I could protect from the horrors of the world. Teach her to be strong and stand up for herself but also be kind. Teach her to go after what she wants but not the way I have.

The site comes into view. But there's already someone there. Please don't let it be Lauren.

Wait, are there two people? It's hard to tell what shadow is what. What is a tree and what might be a person. A light shines into my face. I can't see anything at all, just streaks of lights and neon stars.

Allie

I wake up with a start and sit straight up, forgetting I'm on a small inflatable chair, and fall to the ground with a thud. The lantern's been switched off, and the tent is dark. I hold my breath and listen. Something woke me up, but now the night is silent.

"Lauren," I whisper.

There's no answer.

I crawl over to the couch, but it's empty. Where's Lauren?

Maybe she went to use the bathroom and that's what woke me up.

But there it is again, far off in the distance.

It's undeniably a scream.

Not bothering to put on my Van's, I run to the trail, flashlight in hand. I don't even remember getting it. When I get to the path, it's empty and silent again. I shine the light this way and that. A raccoon scurries out of the beam. An animal. It could've been an animal that made that noise. Or was it, Lauren? Where is Lauren?

I walk a little ways on the trail and hear another noise coming from the left. What am I doing? What if there is a psycho killer up here? What am I going to do with just a flash-light and bare feet?

But I have to go. If someone needs help, I'm not going to leave them high and dry. The next campsite over is empty. I lift the flap and point my light into the tent. I have no idea who's tent it is. "Hello?"

Eric's crouched by the bed fully clothed. He puts his hand in front of his face as the flashlight shines in his eyes. I point it away and turn on the lantern.

"What are you doing on the floor?"

Eric stands and runs a hand on the back of his neck, some of his tattooed diamonds stretching as he does. "I heard something, and I just didn't know what to do."

"I heard it too. But I couldn't tell where it came from."

"It could've been an animal."

I laugh—a hard, brittle sound that jars even me when it comes out of my mouth. Even though I had the same thought, out loud, it sounds crazy. I shake my head. "Uh-huh. We found a carved-up dead girl under a dock, but that scream was an animal. Sure."

Eric moves his hand to his face.

"Should we go check it out?" I ask. Eric looks frozen. "Never mind. You can stay here. I'll just go look around."

"No. I'll come."

I'm both relieved and a little annoyed that he wants to go. "Let me get my shoes. I left them next door."

He follows me next door in silence, almost like he's holding his breath. I slip on my shoes as the unmistakable sound of splashes comes from the lake, like someone or something is in the water. But it sounds far off, too. Maybe the other side of the lake. Eric catches my eye, and we're both so still it's like we're suspended. Listening, waiting, hiding.

Not anymore. I charge toward the sounds, Eric close behind

me, but the splashes stop before we reach the trail. The sky is a pearly gray with heavy looking clouds pushing in like a strong tide from the direction of the mountain.

"Which way did it come from?" Eric says.

I point in the direction of the lodge. "This way I think."

We walk farther down the trail to more serene nature, the lightening sky and the birds tweeting like they're mocking our fear. We walk past the lodge but still find nothing. I turn to Eric. "Do you want to keep going?"

He nods.

After about twenty minutes, I spot dark wet dots on the trail. Eric must see them at the same time because he stops dead in his tracks.

I kneel and run two fingers along the dirt. I examine the mud on my fingers, red and metallic.

Blood.

Following the trail of drops all the way to the water's edge, I brace myself for the worst. But I can't see anything in the lake.

My eyes go fuzzy, staring out at the dark expanse, trying to find something, but it's like looking at one of those magic pictures. Just like when I look at those, nothing appears. When I turn back, Eric's standing right where I left him, eyes wide.

"I don't see anything."

He points, and I follow the direction of his finger to a small broken boat on the shore.

Something could be under there.

Or someone.

Pushing my shoulders back, ignoring the nausea creeping up my throat, I make my way over to the boat. I slip off my shoes and wade into the water, the cold stinging my toes, my feet sinking into the slimy mud.

I take a hold of the side of the broken row boat and, with one great heave, I flip it over. It moves more easily than I bargained for, catching me off balance. I fall into the water on my ass with a splash. The cold steals my breath.

Eric yells—an odd squawk that sounds like it's lodged in his throat.

"I'm okay." I hold up a hand to prove I'm fine, but he keeps making the noise. Is he screaming?

I follow his gaze to the shallow water I just exposed by moving the boat. Lying there in a hot-pink bra and panties is the body of a woman face down in the water, long dark hair floating above her head like a demonic crown.

Gabe

In my dream, I'm running, my heart racing, sweat dripping down my back, the thud of each foot strike thundering in my ears. When I wake up with a jolt, the sound continues.

Nothing but crickets now. I run my hand on the side of the bed before remembering no one will be there. Who was I expecting? Lauren? Jennifer? Sheila?

A shiver racks my body. I shouldn't have let Lauren go off alone. But out of all the shitty things I've done recently, it's the least of my crimes.

I lie back and close my eyes, praying for sleep, but my brain is a slide carousel of images. Click. Sheila's gray flesh in that dark basement. Click. Jennifer's ass, bent over, her holding on to the tree. Click. Ben's cherub face.

Fucking Ben. He's like a golden retriever. Always such a good boy. Everyone loves him; our whole life it's been like that. I would say something snarky, and he would follow it up with a joke, lightening the mood, like we were doing a bit. Like we were in on it together. Everyone loved him best. Everyone. Each break from school, we visited our grandparents in Seattle. One summer, Ben couldn't go because he and Nick were working late that summer at camp. So instead of just having me visit, my grandparents canceled the trip. "We'll do it another time when you can both come," they said.

Ben never missed out. He always gets exactly what he wants.

I sit up again, a pit rolling around uncomfortably in my stomach. That doesn't mean he deserves to be fucked over by his own brother. I should've never invited Jennifer to my room that night. Should've never given her my number. Should've never—

A scream pierces through the night, breaking me out of my self-loathing spiral.

Jennifer.

It sounds like it came from the bathrooms, so I shove my feet into my shoes and run that way.

No one is here.

Heading back to the main trail, I walk toward the lodge. Where is everyone?

An awful sound fills the early morning air—somewhere between a yell and a wail.

I sprint toward it.

Eric's standing on the trail, shoulders hunched, head moving back and forth. Allie's in the water, arms tangled with other arms. No. Not just other arms.

A body. Sheila's body.

I join Eric.

"No. No. Why did you move her from the basement?"

Allie doesn't look at me. She inhales deeply like she's about to dive in the water but instead pulls the body a little more toward the shore and turns it over.

Bile immediately fills my throat.

It isn't Sheila.

It's Dana. In the middle of her chest is a bright-red wound, blood trickling into the water.

My limbs come out of their frozen state, and I run into the lake. "Is she breathing?"

Allie's staring open-mouthed. I shoulder her out of the way and put my hand in front of Dana's lips and nose. There's no warmth. No tickle of breath. Nothing.

Dana is dead.

"Gabe? Allie?" Jennifer calls from up the trail. She and Ben run toward us.

I turn to Eric and say, "She can't see this. Take them to camp."

Eric doesn't move a muscle.

"Go!" I snap at him.

Eric runs up the trail. I can't hear what they're saying, but they let Eric lead them away.

I turn my attention back to Dana. She's in her underwear, just like the last body. There are a few diamonds carved into her skin, but not nearly as many as Sheila had. Everything else on her looks the same, normal, except for the wound in her chest.

It's completely irrational, but I feel responsible. This is somehow my fault. My mouth forms the words before I comprehend what I'm saying, "I'm sorry, Dana. I'm so sorry."

Allie's looking at me with hard eyes.

"We should get her out."

She nods but doesn't speak.

Allie

Why did Gabe tell Dana he's sorry? Of all the things he could say right now, why apologize? Standing there in the water with him, I'm very aware of how alone we are. He sent away Eric, and Jennifer and Ben. How hard would it be for him to just hold me underwater?"

"Allie? Did you hear me? Can you help? We can't leave her here."

Tears stream down my face. Now is not the time to fall apart. I wipe them away, rolling my shoulders back, and picture my purple sparkly box again. I shove in all my feelings about Dana, add my helplessness and my guilt for never trying to work out whatever weirdness we held between us for years, and turn the key. I splash some water on my face and slide my hands under Dana's arms. Gabe gets her legs.

He looks me in the eye, and I ignore the chill creeping up my spine. "On three."

I tighten my core.

"One, two, three," Gabe says. We lift her; with both of us it isn't hard. "We should put her in the basement. To keep her protected."

I swallow hard. I don't want to go down into the basement with Gabe. But what choice do I have? He can't do anything to me right now. If he did, everyone would know it was him, since they all know we're together.

Just like Dana was supposed to be with Joe.

We carry her down the steep stairs and set her down.

I take one last look at Dana, the hanging light shining down on her like an interrogation. I pause. There's something in the waistband of her panties—something catching the dim light from the hanging bulb.

Once Gabe starts up the stairs, I quickly pull at it and hold it up to the light. It's a small piece of torn fingernail. The fingernail is white and short, cut clean at the top but jagged where it's torn.

I put it in the wet pocket of my cut off shorts before Gabe can turn around.

We head back to camp, Gabe leading the way. When we get there, the aroma of coffee is a welcome surprise. Jennifer pacing around the small fire is not. Ben's poking at the fire, and Eric's sitting in a camping chair, his head in his hands. I should've never brought him.

Lauren's making an obnoxious clinking, messing with enamel cups on the picnic table.

There's no sign of Joe.

Jennifer spots me and grabs my arms. "What happened?"

My heart quivers for a moment, but my voice stays strong. "Dana is dead. There's nothing we could do."

It's like someone presses pause. Or like that show where the girl touches her fingers together and freezes time. No one moves. No one reacts.

Gabe

I stare into the fire and half listen as Allie tells them Dana is dead. I snag my smokes from the cup holder of the camping chair. I'm too much of a chicken shit to tell Jennifer myself. Dana was her best friend, her maid of honor. I've done enough damage in her life. It's better she hears it from Allie.

I expected hysterics. Crying at least. But Jennifer just quietly sits down next to Lauren. It's the quietness that worries me. Lauren holds her hand and whispers something in her ear.

Allie comes over to the fire, dripping wet. Her jaw is set and her eyes are hard as she appraises the group. "Where's Joe? Has anyone seen him this morning?"

"Yeah," Lauren says. "I saw him go to the shower house on my way out."

Allie nods once then marches toward the bathrooms. My brain is having a hard time keeping up, but my gut knows this is a bad idea.

Throwing my cigarette into the fire, I follow her at a jog.

"Allie." I reach for her shoulder. She turns around, and I

flinch, thinking for a moment that she's going to slug me. I raise both hands in surrender. "What are you doing?"

"Joe was supposed to be with Dana. Someone stabbed Dana. You do the math."

She continues her determined stomp to the shower house and throws open the door to the men's side. This is idiotic.

"Joe!" Allie flings open the shower curtain where Joe is lathering up his hair.

"Allie. What the—"

If looks could kill, Joe would be dead on the spot. "What did you do?"

Joe backs up to the wall of the shower.

Allie follows him, pointing a finger into his chest. One jab for every word. "What the fuck did you do?"

"I can explain." Joe shakes his head. "It was nothing. Nothing."

"Nothing? You stab your girlfriend, and it's nothing to you?"

Joe's eyebrows rise in what looks to me to be genuine shock. "Stabbed? Wait. What are you talking about?"

I pull Allie out of the shower. "Go rinse off in the other bathroom. Warm up. Dry off. We can talk at camp."

Allie points and opens her mouth to speak, but I cut her off. "Allie, look at him. He didn't know."

Her fierce gaze moves from Joe to me and back again. "Fine."

She walks out the door, muttering.

I keep my eyes turned away from Joe as I say, "Get dressed and meet us at camp in ten."

Joe mumbles.

I leave the bathroom. Allie's right. Where has Joe been? He was supposed to stay with Dana. On the other hand, I was supposed to stay with Lauren and look how well that went.

A thought occurs to me. If Joe had something to do with

Dana's death, where would he do it? The most obvious place is their camp site. My feet are moving before I finish my thought. I half walk and half run to their set up, the last one in our little group.

When I get there, I'm not alone. Allie's opening the flap of their tent. She freezes when she spots me.

I take in the scene. Nothing looks out of place to me. No trail of blood on the dirt. The site's just like the rest of them. Two camping chairs, a hammock, a cooler, firewood, and a tent. Allie walks out, peering closely into the fire pit.

"Did you find anything in there?"

Allie's shoulders slump. "Nothing."

I nod.

"So maybe he didn't do it."

Allie scoffs. "That's a leap. Just because he didn't do it here doesn't mean he didn't do it at all."

Goosebumps line Allie's arms, and she rubs a hand over them.

"You need to shower and put on dry clothes. We can talk about this after."

Allie huffs. "Fine. But I don't need you to take care of me."

The last thing I want is to take care of her. But I just say, "Fine."

She walks away, and after a few minutes, I lift the flap and go into the tent. A rumpled comforter and tangled sheets litter the floor around the unmade bed. Both pillows have deep impressions in them. It looks like two people slept here. What was I expecting to find? I knew I wouldn't find blood-stained sheets. I knew I wouldn't find anything.

Allie

I let the warm water wash over me, my goosebumps subsiding, my muscles unclenching ever so slightly. I was sure I'd find a crime scene when I went to Dana and Joe's campsite. But I didn't. It was empty. No blood anywhere.

Did Joe kill Dana? If it wasn't him, then who? Could it be Nick? And if it isn't, where is he? Or is Wyatt James really out here roaming around? I shiver despite the warm water.

When I searched the tent, I found a pocket knife on the bedside table. I flicked it open. The blade was a shiny silver, clean, not a speck on it. I closed it and put it in my pocket. I was about to search through their bags when Gabe showed up.

Gabe's always showing up.

I dry off and dress with an inky black pit in my stomach. Jennifer's sitting exactly where she was when I left earlier, staring into the fire with an untouched glass of whiskey in her hand. Ben's sitting next to her. He turns to watch me. His face looks ten years older than when we arrived.

Joe's sitting by the fire now too, a beer in his hands, legs spread like his dick is too impossibly large to take up any less space. I almost laugh out loud. I just saw you naked, buddy, don't flatter yourself.

Lauren and Gabe are missing. I sit down in a chair off to the side, near Eric.

Jennifer looks up from her trance. "What happened?"

"Ask Joe." I lean forward, turning my body toward him. "What happened, Joe?"

Joe stands, and for a brief terrifying moment, I think he's going to attack me. But tears well up in his eyes instead. He turns and throws his empty can. The beer ricochets off, straight into a bush, as he grabs another one from the cooler. "I don't know what happened."

He comes back and sits down, taking some deep breaths.

Lauren slinks into camp and sits down as Joe continues, "I couldn't sleep. I was anxious. I went for a walk."

"Oh, okay. You went for a little stroll in the woods at night? When we were supposed to be sticking together." It doesn't make sense. He's lying. I know it.

"What about you, Allie? Did you stay with Eric all night?" Joe asks.

I don't answer.

"When I got back from my walk, Dana was gone," Joe says. "I laid down for a bit but still couldn't sleep, so I took a shower. I didn't even know that—"

He chokes on his last words, a sob catching in his throat.

Gabe comes in and sits down.

Jennifer takes a shaky breath. "Are you sure Dana is really dead?"

When I nod, a sharp animal cry escapes Jennifer. She holds her stomach and curls in on herself. Ben wraps his arms around her.

Joe lets out a shaky breath and opens his can. "I didn't do anything."

I stare into the fire, something niggling me about that statement.

Gabe clears his throat. "I think we have to accept the very real possibility that someone else is hiding out here."

"Where?" Lauren says. "What do we do? Should we try to find them? Is there any way we could all leave?"

Gabe shrugs and looks at Ben. "If you go further up the road, where does it lead?"

Ben's rubbing circles on Jennifer's back. "It's one way in, one way out. Further down just leads to a dead end."

Gabe sighs. "The road's totally blocked by the landslide."

I turn to Gabe. "The landslide, right. The landslide that only you saw."

Gabe's eyes shoot to mine, his pupils dilating a flicker. "You think I made it up? Why would I do that?"

"To keep us all here."

Gabe lets out a small laugh. "You think everyone did it, huh, Columbo? You are more than welcome to take the bike and see for yourself."

Lauren stands. "No. No. No. We're not splitting up this time. We're not pairing off. We're all sticking together. Witnesses. You can't be killed if you're surrounded by witnesses."

"So, we stick together and, what?" Joe says. "Just wait?"

Ben says, "Melanie should be arriving early tomorrow to set everything up for the wedding. She'll see the landslide and get help. We just have to make it through today and tonight and then we should be getting out of here."

I look around our little group. Everyone's faces are drawn, deep frown lines, furrowed brows. Is someone really hiding in the woods waiting to murder us one by one? Or is one of these people sitting with me a killer?

After all of my accusations float away with the growing

wind, the group falls silent for a while. I pour myself a cup of coffee and take it to sit on the stairs leading to the trail.

Dark clouds have rolled in, obscuring the view of the mountain and reflecting ominously off the water. I sip my coffee, the hot bitter taste a welcome distraction.

When Eric made that Voorhees joke in the car, I never for once really thought I'd end up in a real-life enactment of *Friday the 13th.*

One idea keeps circling me—Nick. Nick knows Lost Lake better than any of us. And Nick is nowhere to be found. He has to have something to do with all this. He has to.

Another thing that keeps bothering me is when was Sheila killed? If it was Nick, he would've had to do it right when we got to camp. I think back to when we first arrived. We all went our separate ways right when we got here. It's possible.

Eric sits next to me with a steaming mug in his hands. "Can I join you?"

I scoot a little to the side to make more room on the stairs. "Knock yourself out."

Eric gazes out at the lake. "Looks like rain."

"That's all we need."

Eric shrugs, his coffee sloshing over the side of his mug, mixing in with the dirt, reminding me of the spots on the trail. "It can't get any worse."

In my gut, I know he's dead wrong.

Eric

Gabe walks between us, down the stairs, coffee in hand, his face a wall of determination. For a second I think he's going to sit, but thankfully he keeps walking.

"Where are you going?" Allie asks.

Gabe doesn't slow down. "To the map."

Allie sets her coffee down. "Wait, we need to stick together."

I really don't want to go. I don't trust Gabe, and I know he doesn't trust me. I'm done tiptoeing around his moods.

Gabe walks faster and says, more to the trail than Allie, "You're welcome to come too."

She follows him. Why?

"Babe," I say. Which makes Allie pause for a microsecond, but then she keeps going.

Fuck. I take one more sip of coffee and walk at a more leisurely pace behind them both. When we leave this place, I'm going to write a book about an egomaniacal smoker who lights up one day and turns into a serial killer. Not that I really think

Gabe did it. I know it wasn't him. But it might make for a good story.

When I arrive at the lodge, Gabe and Allie are already in the office. Allie's finger lightly traces the drawn on trails.

I ask, "Is there anything new?"

Allie points, and I get an almost overwhelming jolt of déjà vu.

I follow her finger to a new diamond drawn on the map, a second diamond, right where the boat was in the lake, right where we found Dana. She moves her finger again to a third diamond right where we're standing. It's drawn over the clubhouse like a *you are here* symbol.

Now I know what they mean when they say, *my heart races.* My heart literally feels like it's galloping in my chest. "Shit."

Gabe's pacing behind us, back and forth in front of the office desk. "I don't understand. What does it mean?"

I don't answer, there's no point. Allie stares at the map as if hypnotized. Gabe's footsteps are the only sound for a few long minutes, then he answers his own question.

"It might not mean anything." He keeps pacing and rambling—the guy loves the sound of his own voice. "Maybe there's a leak and it's dropping stuff onto the map and it just kind of looks like diamonds."

Allie finally comes out of her trance. "That is a very optimistic thought and completely ridiculous."

She turned back to the map, still staring at something, but I can't tell what. We need to leave before this all gets so much worse.

Gabe

I t's like Allie sees something on the map that we don't. Maybe she's just looking at the ominous third diamond. But maybe she's trying to decipher another part of the map. Like where the car is in the bushes. We could've missed something there.

"I'm going to take a look around and then head back to camp," I say. "Are you two going to be okay?"

Allie nods, her eyes never leaving the map, and I walked out the door. I take a quick walk through the little convenience store, but everything's the same as before.

I go down the hall to the back room. It's all forest green and dark woods. A deer with massive antlers hangs on the wall. His glass eyes seem to watch me as I move through the space. I grab one of the foosball handles and send it spinning with a flick of my wrist. This would've been a really fun wedding, if I wasn't sleeping with the bride-to-be and if people weren't turning up dead.

I'm not sure what I'm looking for, but it's not here.

I leave out the back door, not wanting Allie and Eric to see me go the opposite way from camp. I walk at a steady pace down the trail toward the car. We must have missed something.

The sky is a blanket of clouds, but not the cozy kind. More the suffocating kind that you find yourself tangled in on a hot summer night. Sweat trickles down my back. I'm almost to the car when a twig snaps up ahead. I duck behind a tree.

Not sure who might be out here, but I don't want them to see me. Crouching low, I listen. Birdsong fills the air, but no other sounds of twigs breaking or footsteps. I peek around the tree and the trail is empty, so I press on.

The camp looks the same as before. I try all the doors on the car. Locked. I try to open the trunk. No luck. But when I pull my hand away, there's something on my fingers, brown and sticky. Is it blood?

I have to get into the car.

There are rocks around the fire pit.

I grab one and hurl it at the back passenger window. It sails right into it with a satisfying crack. Little bits of glass fly everywhere.

With a stick, I move the rest of the glass, then I put my arm through and open the car.

On the backset, now covered in glass, is a black suitcase. I want to look inside, but first I need to see what's in the trunk. I climb over the seat and reach to unlock the driver's side. I walk around and open the door, searching for the trunk lever. All the switches are plain black. I try each one. The door to the gas opens, but nothing else happens. I push them again and again. Still nothing.

Under the seat, there's a bunch of papers. I pull them out. It's printed out MapQuest directions to Lost Lake, and in Sheila's unmistakable neat cursive it says 11:30. 11:30? Is that when she thought she'd get here? Or was she supposed to meet someone?

Throwing the paper on the seat, I move on to the suitcase. Colorful sundresses, khaki shorts, bikinis, and elegant lingerie. I hold up a black lace teddy, trying to puzzle out what strap goes where.

This one is new.

Was it for me? Or was she planning to wear it for whoever she was meeting. Maybe she was meeting them at 11:30 and then coming here after?

I throw the teddy back in the suitcase. There's a metallic purple cosmetic bag, and I unzip it. Night cream, day cream, eye cream, sunscreen, you name it, Sheila has it.

Had.

The bag rattles when I move it, so I dig my hand to the bottom to find the source. A small amber pill bottle, the white printed label reading alprazolam, *take one pill thirty minutes before flight*.

I put the pill bottle in my pocket and put the bag back in the suitcase.

What were you doing out here, Sheila?

She was afraid of flying, I know that. I thought it would be better if we flew together, but she couldn't get the time off. Only it turned out that she could because she's here.

The last place to look is the front zippered pocket of the suitcase. At the very bottom of the pocket is one of those flash drives, the small ones that plugs into the side of the computer. I put that in my other pocket and do one more once-over of her suitcase, but I don't find anything else. No phone. No wallet. No purse.

She never went anywhere without that pink snakeskin Prada purse. It was a real Prada, or so she liked to tell me all the time if I threw it on the floor from the couch.

So where is it?

Allie

Eric's rifling through papers on the desk. The sound of the crinkling paper is setting my teeth on edge. What's he even looking for?

I say, more to myself than him, "The old guy that runs this place must live somewhere on the grounds, right?"

Eric stops the infernal rustling of paper. "You're right. He must. Is he here now? Do you think he killed the girls?"

I point to a small house that sits behind the clubhouse on the map. "I think he probably lives there."

No time like the present, I bolt out the door, Eric following close on my heels. There's a trail that leads from the back porch, through the field behind it. The open patch of grass gives way to a wall of trees. The trail narrows. What I would give for a sidewalk right about now. Stupid dirt. Nothing good ever happens in the woods.

I slow down to a walk, apprehensive about going to an unknown house in the middle of nowhere. What if the old man's in there? What if he's a psycho killer? What if that's where Wyatt James is hiding? Or Nick? "It looked closer on the map."

Eric says, "It really did."

After walking for a few more minutes, Eric says, "Do you think it's still here?"

"Yeah, the guy has to live somewhere, right?"

Finally, the trail opens up and turns into a wider gravel path. It winds through the trees. A small house sits tucked away at the end. It's an old barn red, with white trimmed windows. With the amount of moss growing on the roof, it appears thatched. There's a small glass greenhouse to one side, like a clear shed. It looks like a freaking Thomas Kincaid painting. It seems utterly absurd that this picturesque house is sitting here while people are getting murdered left and right.

Eric lets out a long breath. "Should we knock?"

I nod, roll my shoulders back, and walk up the small steps, hesitating only slightly before rapping on the white front door. No answer. I knock again, and again no one comes to the door. Eric's saying something, but the idea in my head is too loud to hear him. I go around the side of the house to the back.

The backyard isn't a lawn really. Just a small porch with a hammock hung on a metal frame and a few folding chairs. Twinkle lights swing above them in the wind. Beyond the porch is more gravel and what looks like an empty parking spot.

Eric joins me. I turn to the house, looking at the windows. Are any unlocked?

"No one is home," Eric says, stating the irritatingly obvious.

I continue scanning for a way in. We can break one of the windows. Maybe one of the small ones in the front.

"Should we head back to camp?" Eric asks.

I shake my head, and he follows me back around to the front of the house. "We need to get in. There might be a phone, or a radio, or something."

That's when I spot it. A perfect rock at the foot of the stairs. Not a hint of moss or dirt on it. The bottom of the rock is perched on the soil, too flat for a real rock. There's an impression in the dirt next to it, like it's been moved slightly. Picking it up, I smile at how light it is. I turn it over, and bingo, a plastic sliding door. It's a hide-a-key.

Eric stands mouth agape. "Whoa, dude. How did you know that was there?"

"I didn't." I pluck the key out and climb the steps again. The key slides easily into the lock. I hesitate for a half a second—then turn the key. The house has a slightly stale smell, like a parked car that's been sitting in the sun for a while.

"Hello," I call out. Relief washes over me when no answer comes back.

There's a compact mudroom at the front of the house. A simple wood bench with boots lined up underneath, winter boots and rain boots, both male, both the same size. Further down the hall, there's a sitting room to the right and a closed swinging door to the left. I go into the sitting room. There's a tattered plaid couch and a leather wingback chair by a brick fireplace. A small television on a rolling cart in the corner looks like it's original to the house. There's a cabinet against the wall with various liquors on top. Two end tables sit by the couch and the chair, a brass lamp on one, a remote on the other. No phone.

My heart jumps into my throat as footsteps come from upstairs. I run to the doorway, right into Eric. "You scared me."

He backs up, his fingers grazing my hips as he does.

"Sorry. Didn't mean to." Eric walks past me and turns the channel knob on the television. "This place reminds me of my grandparents' house."

The sitting room is homey, cozy. Nothing like the stark white couches of my grandmother's house. What kind of grandma has white couches? The kind that doesn't want little berry-stained fingers to sit with them, that's who.

I cross the hall, through the swinging door into the kitchen and freeze. Scratchy gramophone music plays softly. There are white cabinets, wood butcher block counters, and a large farmhouse style sink. In the corner is a built-in breakfast nook with a silver radio sitting on the table playing the music. A half-empty cup of coffee sits on the table next to a folded newspaper and a pencil. I pick up the mug; it's cold to the touch. The radio switches over to the host of the program, but the static makes it hard to make out what he's saying as I take a seat on the bench.

"That...'Midnight, the Stars and You.' We have breaking news. Convicted...killer Wyatt James..."

I quickly turn up the radio, but I'm met with only loud static. I try the tuner this way and that and finally, the radio host comes back on.

"Now for one of my all-time favorites 'It's All Forgotten Now.'"

The scratchy music returns as a shiver racks my body. I click off the radio.

What was he saying about Wyatt James?

Taking a deep breath, I look up, my eyes going straight to the olive green phone hanging on the wall like a beacon of hope. It's one of the prettiest sights I've ever seen.

The olive green plastic is smooth but heavy in my hand as I bring it to my ear.

Tears well up behind my eyes and my legs wobble. I nearly hum along to the sweet, sweet sounds of a dial tone.

Immediately, I call 9-1-1.

The phone rings once, twice then picks up. I start talking before I hear anyone on the line.

"We need help—"

"Your call is very important to us. Please stay on the line and an operator will be with you..."

Fuck.

I twirl the spiral cord around my finger as I wait for an operator.

The lights flicker, and the phone turns to static. This isn't going to work. I can't just sit here on hold all night.

But who else could I call?

There's only one number I know by heart. Without over-thinking it, I hang up the phone and dial again.

"Hello?"

Just the high pitched, smooth voice makes me want to hang up. But we need help.

"Hey, grandma."

"Oh my word. Allison, is that you?"

"Allie." She knows I hate the name Allison.

"Allie is a stray cat. An Allie is a seedy meeting place. Allison was your great aunt's name."

Inhaling deeply, I let it go. I can't be pulled into this right now. We need help.

"Grandma, I need—"

A massive sigh, so large I can almost smell the alcohol on her breath through the line. "How much this time?"

"What?"

"Money? How much do you need?"

I pull the phone away from my ear. This was a mistake. Should I just try 9-1-1 again? Another flicker of the lights. I take a large inhale, like I'm about to jump in a pool.

"I don't need money. Me and my friends are out at Lost Lake Campground, and Wyatt James is out here killing people. We just found my friend in the lake. We need help. I couldn't get through to the police."

"Are you high?"

"What?"

I can hear some rustling across the line. "This isn't funny, Allison."

"It's not a joke."

Grandma laughs. Actually laughs. "Isn't everything with you? They caught Wyatt James just about an hour ago. It's all over the news. How silly of me to think you called to catch up. Check on me. When you're ready to really talk, you know my number."

The dial tone is back. She hung up.

An hour ago. Is it possible for Wyatt James to have been here at Lost Lake, killed two people, and then left? He would've had enough time. But not with the landslide, if there really is a landslide. Dana was alive when Jennifer and Gabe came back telling us about the blocked road.

I call 9-1-1 again, but the phone cuts out as I'm pressing the last number.

Frantically, I push down on the button in the cradle of the phone. But nothing. No dial tone.

I hang the phone back up. "Shit."

Eric comes through the swinging door. "What?"

Should I tell him what Grandma told me about Wyatt James? The thing is, if it wasn't him, then it has to be someone here. Either someone is hiding, or it's one of us. I shake my head and decide not to tell Eric more than I have to. "Phone doesn't work."

Eric frowns. "I thought I heard you talking to someone?"

I let out a long sigh and shake my head as I open the fridge. Plucking one of the three beers off the top shelf, I twist the metal cap and take a seat. We're never getting out of here, might as well drink up. I sit down at the kitchen table. "Nope. You can check the phone if you want. It's dead."

Eric grabs a beer and joins me. "What should we do?"

I shrug. "Nothing. I don't think there's anything we can do but wait for help."

It feels more like waiting to get murdered.

"We could just stay here. Lock the doors. Start a fire." Eric smiles, his most charming smile. "Watch some television. Snuggle on the couch."

He sips his beer, the skin on his neck stretching as he tips it back, the diamond tattoos distorting. The kitchen knives gleam on the wall behind him, and suddenly the room is impossibly small. Like there isn't enough air for us both to sit here. Why *is* he covered in so many diamonds? Is it really just illustrations from a children's book?

I stand, knocking into the table and spilling the mug of coffee onto the half-finished crossword puzzle. "We should go."

Eric moves out of the booth calmly. "Okay, not a fan of TV. I get it."

I hurry out the front door, feeling better in the open space, the fresh air, for once. I inhale deeply the smell of dirt and trees and that sweet, pungent smell of ozone as my eyes snag on the thick menacing clouds above.

Eric joins me.

"Let's head back to camp."

"Whatever you want."

None of this is what I want. I want a mug of whiskey, fuzzy socks, and an episode of *Columbo*, maybe the one with Johnny Cash. I don't want to be trapped out here with a killer.

Murder? What murder? Episode 189 July 20, 2024

"Who was driving the truck?"

"Wyatt Motherfucking James."

"What? NO! Did he kill the girls at Lost Lake?"

"Well, that's the thing. So, Wyatt James was arrested at a small bar in Dee. The bartender had been watching the news reports about the escape non-stop, so when Wyatt walked in with a bloody head and covered in dirt, he recognized him right away. He got Wyatt a Pabst then went in the back and called the cops. The cops showed up in record time."

"Ha. No doubt."

"They arrested him and took him back to prison. The light-green truck that he stole and ran into the tree was probably around four or five hours away on foot. So, it's completely possible that Wyatt James could've killed Sheila, the first girl they found. But there's no way he could've killed Dana—"

"Wait, why couldn't Wyatt James have killed them?"

"They found Dana after the landslide. Wyatt James caused the landslide and was stuck on the other side. He couldn't have gotten to them."

"Oooh, what does that mean?"

"What it means, Jules, is that whoever the killer was, they were out at Lost Lake with our hot bridal party, also trapped, and most likely one of them."

"Oh shit."

"Yep. Their cell phones didn't work. The landline's main cord, the one that runs underground or to telephone poles, was cut. There was no phone service out there at all."

"Oh boy. So, they're stuck out in the woods with no phone and two dead bodies."

"Wow, you really don't know *anything* about the case. It's going to be more than two."

"What the actual fuck? Who else dies?"

"Ooh, I'm not sure we're ready for spoilers yet. But... I have a surprise for you."

Allie

We walk back silently, sipping our beers. Back at camp, Jennifer hasn't moved from her chair but now has a blanket over her lap. Ben's pouring a drink in the tent. Near the grill, Lauren and Joe are huddled together in a hushed conversation.

Ben brings his glass and sits next to Jennifer. "Where did you go?"

Eric speaks first. "To this little—"

I cut him off. I'm not sure why exactly, but I don't want him to tell the others about the caretaker's house. "Back to the clubhouse. Hoping we missed a phone or a radio."

Eric gives me an odd expression then closes his mouth.

Joe and Lauren walk back over and take seats next to each other by the fire. Ben leans forward in his chair. "Find anything?"

I catch a whiff of sandalwood. Ben still smells like him, even after all this tragedy. For some reason, this doesn't feel right. His face, on the other hand, doesn't look normal. Usually he looks relaxed, his jaw slack, his strong brow and deep dimples doing the bulk of the work to make him appear handsome-ish, but today the muscles in his neck are taught. His lips a tight frown. "Nope. No luck."

Gabe trudges into camp, his jaw set so tight he's going to break his teeth. He walks straight to the bar and pours himself a tumbler of whiskey.

Where has he been? I thought he was headed back here when he left the lodge.

"What about you, Gabe?" Ben says. "Did you go to the lodge too?"

Gabe takes a large gulp of whiskey. "At first. But then I went back to—" He stops himself. "For a walk. I can't believe all of this is really happening."

Nods ripple all around the group.

Out of everyone, Lauren seems oddly unaffected. She looks like any normal girl out camping with friends. Her hair is pulled back into a high ponytail, and her cut off shorts and tank top are spotless, perfectly in place. It's true she didn't know Sheila, none of us but Gabe did, really. But Dana was one of her closest friends. How is she so perky looking?

Gabe sits down. "We all need to stick together. We said that before, but none of us did and now another person is dead." He holds up his hands. "I'm not pointing fingers. I broke off from the group. Hell, I just did. We all have at some point." Lauren and Joe mutter agreements. "I'm not saying anyone here is responsible for the deaths of the others."

Is it my imagination, or does he look right at Eric when he says that?

Gabe continues, "All I'm saying is for safety reasons, we all need to stay together, for real this time."

"What about when we pee?" Lauren asks. "Are all seven of us going to go to the bath house?"

Gabe runs a hand over his chin. "We can go to the bathroom in pairs. Is everyone agreed?"

There are nods and a few mutters of yeses.

Joe stands, slapping his palms on his thighs. "I'm going to make some food before it starts to rain."

Jennifer gets up too. "I have to pee." She makes eye contact with me. It's the look we used to give each other at the club when we're done talking to a guy that just bought us a drink and need an exit. "Allie, will you come with me?"

There's a hard pit of fear in my stomach, but I stand anyway. "Yep."

Jennifer walks to the bathroom, her shiny golden hair swinging back and forth. As she flings open the door to the bath house, I swallow hard and hesitate a moment before pushing my way through too.

Jennifer's leaning, half sitting on the sink, her arms crossed in front of her.

"Are you going to…" I motion to the stalls.

Jennifer bites her lip, crossing her arms tightly in front of her chest. "I just needed to get away for a minute. What do you think of Gabe? Barking orders like that. Like he's suddenly in charge. I told everyone to stick together last night. Everyone should've listened…" Her last word dissolves into a sob. Her shoulders shaking.

I cross the tiny space and rub my hand on her back.

Once she's calmed down a bit, she says, "We really should stay together, so nothing else happens." Then she sighs. "But I don't feel safe with Gabe. How do we know he doesn't have something to do with all this? Who else would want Sheila dead? No one else even knew her."

She's right. I don't trust Gabe either. But he's not the only one I don't trust.

Her jaw tenses then she says in a rush, "I don't even trust Ben anymore."

"Ben?" What in the hell is going on that she doesn't trust her Ben. They've been together for years. They're out here to get married. And if anyone shouldn't trust someone in the relationship it seems like Ben shouldn't trust her.

She shakes her head. "It's just. The past couple of months... I'm worried he's cheating on me... or something. Something's been off."

God, project much.

She shakes her hands out. "Do you think this is all a sign? That we shouldn't be together?"

As much as I love Jennifer, she is a certified narcissist if she's taking two girls being murdered as a sign from the Universe for her. But maybe the stress is just getting to her. It's definitely getting to me.

"Let's get back to the group," I say. "We just have to make it through the night, and then help will come."

Jennifer runs her hands over her still impeccable face, then stalks off toward the stall. "That might be easier said than done."

I turn on the faucet and stare into the cloudy mirror. Big bags hang under my eyes. I splash cold water on my face. It shouldn't matter what I look like, especially not under the circumstances, but it bothers me. Jennifer still looks smooth and put together. Why do I look like something the cat dragged in? Maybe because I'm the one running around trying to figure out what the fuck was going on here?

I'd feel better with a weapon. I wish I hadn't lost my knife. It might be tucked away in my bag.

Jennifer comes out of the stall and washes her hands. While she's drying them, I ask, "Will you come to my site with me? I just want to try to find something."

"Sure."

We start to walk in the direction of my tent. A flash of memory from the first night comes to me. Lauren was whispering with someone late at night near the bathroom.

I shake my head. I'm not sure it was Lauren that night. It could've been Dana or Jennifer. Truth be told, I'm not even sure the memory is real.

We get to my site, and I go into the tent, Jennifer follows close behind me. "What are you looking for?"

I throw my duffle bag onto the bed. "That knife I bought. It's been missing since our first night here."

Jennifer covers her hand with her mouth. "Really? Why haven't you mentioned that?"

I rifle through my clothes, getting nowhere quick. So, I turn the whole thing upside down, dumping it all out on the bed. No knife. I pick up my camera and try switching it on with no luck. The battery's dead.

Jennifer's pacing at the foot of the bed. "I don't understand why you even bought that ugly naked lady knife."

"I didn't know we'd be stuck out here with a psycho killer." I wish I could've come look for it alone. I don't need Jennifer's judgment right now on top of everything else.

I look on the nightstand for the billionth time. I know that's where I left it. At least I thought that's where I left it. Then I spot Eric's bag.

I hesitate for half a second. It's a violation to go through his stuff, and what if we don't find anything? But these are desperate times. I pile my shit back into my duffel bag. Then I grab Eric's backpack and dump it unceremoniously onto the bed. There are some socks, underwear, and a tarnished Zippo lighter.

Jennifer wrinkles her nose as she picks up a stick of deodorant. "I didn't even know they still made Old Spice."

"I guess they do." I actually love the way Eric smells—clean and with a little bite to it.

Picking up Eric's tattered copy of *On the Road*, I roll my eyes. Of course, he's a Kerouac fan. There's a weird bookmark, though. I pull it out and unwrap the tightly wound paper towels and gasp. It's unmistakably my knife, with the golden naked lady handle.

Gabe

The girls have been gone too long. Pacing by the picnic table, I keep my eye on the stairs toward the bathrooms.

"I'm sure they're fine," Joe says from the grill where he's throwing some burgers on. The sizzle sets my teeth on edge.

I want to snap at him. Say, *Oh because Dana was just fine, right? Sheila was just fine?* But I clench my teeth harder and try to will Allie and Lauren to come back.

Three more minutes pass.

"I'm going to go check on them."

Ben throws his arms out wide. "We're splitting up again? We just all decided we were going to stick together."

Is he being serious? We can't just sit and wait. "What if something happened to them?"

Lauren speaks for the first time in what seems like hours. "I'll go."

She's definitely still pissed at me for last night.

Not waiting for anyone's permission, she traipses off to the trail, hips swinging. Ben's face is a mix of emotions as his eyes follow her. I put a hand on his shoulder. "I'll go after her."

I nearly run into her waiting at the top of the stairs. Allie comes storming down the trail. Jennifer, running after her, yells, "Wait. Let's make a plan. We can't storm in there half-cocked."

Allie laughs. "Watch me."

She doesn't even look our way as she passes us with a knife in her hand.

Lauren's eyes are wide as she asks Jennifer. "Did she have a knife?"

Lauren takes off down following Allie, not waiting for an answer.

Jennifer looks at me, her light-blue eyes brimming with tears, and whispers, "I think Ben knows."

Before my brain can process what she's saying, she's running down the stairs.

Allie, still with the knife in her hand, walks right up to Eric sitting at the picnic table. The world slows as she holds the knife up.

She raises it up to the sky. She's going to bring it down on his chest. I reach out to stop her, but she's too fast.

Plunging the knife into the wooden table with a sickening thud, she says, "What the fuck is my knife doing in your shit?"

Eric

It's becoming more and more clear to me that I've misjudged and underestimated Allie. This isn't the first time I've fallen for the wrong girl.

One, I never thought she'd really go through my stuff. And two, if she did, I never thought she'd look in a Kerouac book. She doesn't strike me as a fan of the Beat poets.

For a brief shining moment, I thought Allie was going to stab me, but she didn't. I scramble backward, untangling my legs from the picnic table, and try to put some distance between us. "Whoa."

Allie advances again, poking me in the chest. "Why did you have my knife?"

"I didn't want you to hurt yourself. That first night you were so wasted. I was going to give it back after the trip. I've seen you slice limes enough times to know you can handle a knife, just not so drunk."

"Enough times? What does that mean?" Allie's eyes are narrowed.

Shit. I fucked up, again.

"You just started at the bar," she says.

My pause fills the space between us. Everyone is watching us now.

Fat rain drops splatter around me, hitting the table, the dirt, the tip of my eyelashes.

Allie's face falls. "Have you been watching me?"

"Watching..." I put my arms out palms up, a plain and simple sign I'm trustworthy. "It's such a strong word. I've just been in the bar a few times."

"Earlier, you said coming here was your idea."

Shit. "I thought it would be fun for us to get to know each other a little better. I just suggested it."

"But that morning...you said I invited you." Allie's eyes look almost wounded.

"I never said that, I just asked when we were leaving. I thought you remembered..." That's not true. I was pretty sure when she passed out the night would be fuzzy at best. But what is it that Ginsberg says, "there is no truth...only points of view."

Something like that.

Joe grabs the plate of burgers as the rain falls in sheets. "We should move into the tent."

How can he even consider food after what happened to his girlfriend? The longer I live, the more I realize I'll never understand people. Allie's still looking at me like I hit her cat with my car.

Gabe puts a hand on her shoulder. She turns on him, her chest rising and falling rapidly.

His hand flies up as he asks, in a voice barely a whisper yet loud enough for me to hear, "Was there blood on the knife?"

I get it, I really do. I'm the outsider. Story of my life. They don't know me, so they suspect me. Makes perfect sense. But do they really think I'm dumb? That I'd come out here, murder a bunch of people with a stolen knife, then not only keep it, but keep it with all the evidence on it.

She shakes her head. The rain picks up speed.

"I really was going to give it back," I say.

We're all getting wet at this point, the rain picking up in speed and intensity.

Gabe blows a breath, holding it in his cheeks, then says, "Let's talk about it somewhere dry."

Everyone heads for the tent, except Allie and Gabe. They stay for a few minutes talking with their heads bent close together. Since when have they gotten so close?

When they finally come into the tent, Gabe goes straight to the bar cart and pours himself a generous whiskey. Seems like a bad move. All this shit going down and he's going to get wasted. Now *that's* dumb.

The group is huddled into various corners of the small space. Jennifer and Ben are sitting next to each other on the couch. Lauren's sitting in a chair, her face pale, her fingers fiddling with the tassel of a throw blanket. I'm standing with my arms crossed near an end table in the corner, trying to make myself invisible again.

Joe sits in the other chair, a burger in hand, legs spread. "I think we're doing this all wrong."

He pauses to take a giant bite. I want to smack the whole thing out of his hand, but instead I move farther into the corner.

"What do you mean?" Lauren asks.

Joe holds up an obnoxious finger as he finishes chewing and swallows. "We should be working together."

"Joe's right," Gabe says. "It feels like some people think Wyatt James is hiding in the woods somewhere and some people think one of us is responsible for the deaths of those two girls."

Allie scoffs and stalks over, bottle of water in hand. "Dana and Sheila. You can say their names. You were sleeping with one of them."

Gabe sighs. "I was being delicate. Dana and Sheila. We're all suspicious of each other when what we should be worried about is who's out there." He points to the tent door.

Who's out there? At this point, we all must know the real threat is in here.

Ben nods. "It can't just be a crazy coincidence that Wyatt James escaped at the same time we found a dead body."

Allie runs a hand through her hair. "Wyatt James is not the killer. He was arrested."

We all look at her.

Wyatt James was arrested. When?

Jennifer shakes her head. "What? How do you know that?"

Allie looks like a trapped animal while everyone waits for her answer. How does she know that? And why didn't she tell me?

"I heard it on the radio, in the lodge."

The lodge? No. She could've heard it on that little radio in the house, maybe.

Gabe rubs a hand over his stubbled chin, making a scratchy sound that grates on my nerves. "I don't remember a radio there. Where was it?"

"In the back, with the pool table and stuff." Allie isn't making eye contact with anyone, suddenly she seems mesmerized by the pattern of the carpet.

"What did it say?" Lauren asks. "About Wyatt James? Did it say anything about the landslide?"

She shakes her head, her brown hair catching the light of the lantern as she does. "It said he was arrested."

Ben asks, "When?"

"Earlier today."

Gabe nods. "So, he could've been responsible for their deaths."

Allie lets out a long breath. "It's like you're not listening. I don't see how."

"Well, if he was arrested today, he could've been here, killed the gir—Dana and Sheila, then left and got arrested."

"What about the landslide? Dana...We found her after." Jennifer clamps her mouth shut, tears streaming down her face.

Gabe sits on the other side of Jennifer on the couch with a heavy sigh. "Right."

Ben's brow is furrowed. "Maybe there is a way around?"

I should've gone with Gabe. I could've seen the mess for myself and known for sure what we're really up against.

Lauren's face lights up. "So, we're safe."

She walks over to the bar cart and grabs a bottle of champagne sitting there and with one swift motion, thumbs out the cork. The loud pop makes me jump despite knowing it's coming. Foam spills out of the bottle, and Lauren sips it then pours a glass. "Who wants champagne?"

Lauren is not in touch with reality. It's like she hasn't processed the fact that people are dead, as in never coming back.

Gabe shakes his head. "It's a little early to celebrate. There's no way around that landslide. If he was here, he would've had to leave before it happened."

Lauren shrugs. "Maybe there was a way you didn't see, or they could've cleared it away, cleaned it all up by now."

Gabe sighs. "It's possible. I guess."

"I'll take a glass," Joe says to Lauren with a look that makes my stomach lurch. Something about Joe bothers me. They all bother me, except Allie.

Gabe's still talking. "I don't think the plan should change, though. We should all stick together."

The group mutters their agreements.

Allie

The afternoon passes at a crawl.

Jennifer curls up on the sofa and takes a nap. Ben finds a book lying around and reads it. Gabe paces, a lot. Lauren and Joe find a deck of cards and play Gin Rummy. Eric falls asleep in one of the chairs. I sit in the other chair watching them all while hoping they don't notice.

For some reason, I keep thinking about the movie *Clue*. Maybe because it was always a rainy day favorite of mine, but also our situations seem similar at the moment. There's one line from the movie rattling around in my head on repeat, "Whoever's got the gun shot the girl."

My knife is clean. But what if someone is hiding another weapon? Or bloody clothes. Or some evidence of something. Sighing, I look at each face. Could one of them really be a killer? My eyes land on Jennifer, and some of the tension in my mouth eases. Definitely not her. She would never hurt someone, physically.

Ben's face catches my attention. I don't think he could've done this either. When I first met him, I got a bad vibe. I think I was making myself feel that way just because he's so boring.

But no one knows Joe. I just need to go look. I've already been in Joe's tent, but not in his bag. I'd like to check out Gabe's stuff too. Something definitely isn't right about him. But how can I search their stuff without them noticing? With us all sticking together?

I rise and gaze out the tent window. The rain has subsided, but the sky is a mass of dark clouds. The break in the weather won't last long. I have to move quick. I glance around at the group again.

"Lauren, can you go to the bathroom with me?" I clutch my stomach. This has to take longer than a usual pee break. "I'm not feeling too well."

Lauren looks up with concern. "Oh no." She throws down her cards. "Sure, let's go."

"Straight to the bathroom and back," Gabe barks out.

I resist the urge to flip him off.

As soon as we're up the stairs, I grab Lauren's arm and lead her the opposite way from the bathrooms.

She tugs back. "Where are we going?" Her words come out slightly slurred. How much of that champagne has she drunk?

I whisper, "We have to look through Gabe's stuff. Maybe Joe's too."

"But Wyatt James did it. And now he's caught."

I frown. "Trust me. This is important. If we don't find anything, then we don't find anything, right? Please. I need to see."

She lets out a large huff but says, "Okay." I lead the way to the site I think is Gabe's. But once we go inside the tent, it's obvious from the propped open pink suitcase that it's Ben and Jennifer's.

"Wrong site," Lauren says and turns to go.

I hold out a hand. They may not be responsible, but what if

they have something that might help? "Wait. We're here. We might as well take a quick look."

Lauren frowns. She clearly wants to leave, but I don't wait for her to protest. I search through the nearest thing to me, the pastel-pink suitcase. Jennifer packed cute sundresses, cut off shorts, bikinis, typical camping stuff. I get to her toiletry bag. It's a brown and gold Louis Vuitton zip up cosmetic bag. It seems so dumb to spend this kind of money on a kit for her face wash.

I unzip the bag and dig through the mascara and various foundations. My hand hits a cold plastic stick. I know the shape from clutching my own, praying the outcome would go my way on a dark Thursday last winter. I pull out a pregnancy test. In the little window are two pink lines.

It's positive.

My fingers shake slightly as I hold the smooth plastic stick. Lauren frowns. "What's the big deal? She's always said she wanted kids. Her and Ben just got started a little early."

I nod still staring at the test, but seeing Jennifer and Gabe huddled together at the general store. What aisle were they in? Did Jennifer buy the pregnancy test there? And if she did, why would she be talking to Gabe about it?

Lauren's already moved on to looking around the rest of the tent. I want to keep the test as proof of something, but that's weird. Proof of what? Who would I show it to? I put it back into the toiletry bag.

"Where's Ben's bag?" Lauren says.

I glance around, but there is no other bag. That's odd. "I don't know."

Lauren lifts the blanket. "Maybe he left it outside. If he did, it's probably soaked now. I'm going to go see if it is and bring it in."

"Okay." I turn my attention back to Jennifer's suitcase. I

don't know what I'm looking for, but I know I'm missing something. I look through her clothes but don't find anything. Shifting things, I try to make the suitcase look exactly as it did when I found it. Before leaving the tent, I take one last look around.

The sky's getting dark, the kind of dark that makes trees appear more looming than stately. The tree sitting in the middle of the campsite is making me nervous, its gnarled limbs blowing in the wind.

My grandmother's words come back to me. "Never tip your hand. Just keep walking by, cool as a cucumber."

Just like Joe. Joe is always so calm, so collected. Cool as a cucumber. I call out, "Lauren, I'm going to look next door."

In Joe's tent, the bed's rumpled and there's a bag on each suitcase stand. Ugg boots shoved in the corner along with a dingy pair of men's hiking boots. My stomach lurches. Dana's stuff, of course she brought stuff that we'll have to take with us. We'll have to get it to her family. We'll have to call her mom. Bile rises in my throat.

Turning away from Dana's things, my eyes snag on Joe's sensible black carry-on size suitcase.

I unzip the case with trembling fingers. Inside, there are jeans, shirts, boxers, an extra pair of shoes. I move on to the pocket on the side. There's a wallet. When I open it, a picture of Joe stares back at me.

But the ID doesn't say Joe.

The first name on the ID is Matthew, his middle name is Joseph.

Why does he go by his middle name?

Then I read the last name and the wallet slips through my fingers, hitting the floor of the tent with a dull thud.

My feet start running before I've fully processed what is

going on. But I need to talk to Lauren. She would know Joe's last name—or Matthew, or whoever he is. I head back into the site.

"Lauren?" I try to yell, but it comes out as a whisper.

Murder? What murder? Episode 189 July 20, 2024

"Ooh, I love surprises. Hit me. What is it?"

"We have a survivor from Lost Lake here on the show today!"

"What? Thank god *someone* survives."

"We'll talk to them a little bit later. So, they were trapped out at the lake, they found two dead bodies, someone is missing, and there was a landslide. And nature wasn't done with them yet. Do you remember how I mentioned it had been a record-breaking year for rainfall?"

"Yeah."

"A gigantic thunderstorm rolled in while they were waiting for help to arrive."

"Thunderbolts and lightning, very, very frightening. Tent poles and lightning do not mix."

"No they do not. A little like secrets and friendship. Do you keep secrets from your friends, Jules?"

"Who have you been talking to? Just kidding. I'm terrible with secrets, but I definitely don't tell everyone everything…"

"Right, but where's the line? When does keeping some

things private turn into harmful secrets? Almost every single person at Lost Lake had a secret, and one of them was motive for murder."

Gabe

I walk back and forth, back and forth in front of the bar cart in the tent. Like I have to keep moving. Like if I stop, I'll die. Like a shark. But I'm not a shark. I'm not the predator here. I'm the prey. We all are. All of us except one.

Jennifer's sleeping on the couch. She looks so beautiful when she sleeps, blonde hair spilling over her shoulders, pink full lips parted. I tear my eyes away and keep walking. Lauren and Allie left a while ago for the bathroom. Too long.

"I'm going to go check on them."

Joe shakes his head. "Just give them a minute. Allie didn't look too good. She probably wants to yak in peace."

I sigh.

"Sit." Joe motions to the empty chair. "We can play." He holds up the cards. "What's your game?"

How is Joe so relaxed? The girl he was dating was stabbed and found dead in a lake, and he's sitting here drinking, playing cards, relaxing. "How long were you and Dana dating?"

Joe shuffles the cards, but I see the tendon in his neck pulse. "Not long."

I sit across from him. "Five card draw."

Joe smiles. "Figures."

"Is that why you're not more broken up? About her death?"

Joe frowns. "This isn't the first time someone close to me has died."

What does that mean?

He deals. I pick up my hand. It's absolute shit. A nine, a queen, a three, a four, and a jack. All various suits. I lay the whole hand down. "I'll take five."

Joe's eyebrows go up. "All five?"

I give him a nod. "Sometimes it's better to start fresh."

Joe purses his lips and deals me five new cards.

I rearrange my hand as Joe grabs two new cards. Ben chuckles in the corner.

Joe looks over. "What? Is he cheating?"

Ben comes closer. "No. At least I don't think so. Not Gabe." He gives me a look I can't read. "It's just Gabe's been pulling that move since we were kids and would play with my granddad for spare change. He never wanted to work with the cards in his hand. Always wanted to start over."

My pulse ratchets up. "What would you know about starting over? You were always dealt a full house or a royal flush."

He always gets the good cards. Always made friends easily. Always the golden boy. All I have in my new hand is a pair of eights. I throw my cards down. "They've been gone too long. I'm going to go check on them."

Eric sits up, rubbing his eyes. "I'll go with you."

I'd rather go alone, honestly, but we should at least stick in pairs. The light's dwindling outside. Night is coming, and a light drizzle has started from the dark clouds above. Even darker than before. We check both sides of the bathrooms. No one is there.

I let out a frustrated sigh. "Where did they go?"

"Maybe they needed something from their stuff?"

It's not a bad thought. "Come on, let's go. Which way is your and Allie's tent?"

Eric motions his head to the left, and I tell him to lead the way. When we get there, the tent is a mess. All Eric's stuff is dumped out on the bed.

He breathes hard through his nose and quietly puts his stuff back in his backpack. "Guess she doesn't trust me."

I smile. "It's not like they didn't find anything. You did have her knife."

"Yeah. Well." He shrugs. "She was so drunk that first night I didn't want her to accidentally slice a finger off. Hers or mine."

"Fair enough. Have you seen her that wasted before?"

He rubs a hand on the back of his neck. "No, but we haven't known each other that long. Let's keep going this storm is going to get a lot worse before it gets any better."

He's right.

Rain falls in fat chunks on our shoulders as the sun makes its last beams of light before dipping below the mountain. "Should've brought flashlights."

We walk on the upper trail past the bathrooms again. Someone's running down the dirt path frantically.

Allie

A mix of relief and dread swirls in my stomach as I run toward Eric and Gabe. I reach them and bend to catch my breath. "I can't find Lauren."

They're frozen, staring at me.

"We have to find her," I practically scream.

Not Lauren too. Please let her be all right.

Gabe looks in the direction I came from. "Where were you?"

I flail my arms around and move past them toward the bathrooms. "Looking for her."

Gabe says, "No, I mean where did you last see her?"

I hesitate. Should I tell them about Joe? I don't want to tell them about our search. I'll keep it to myself for now.

"I was using the bathroom. She heard a noise outside and went to look, when I came out, she was gone." The lie tumbles out of me. It actually calms me down, the lying. "She probably just went back to the bathroom. I'll go check."

I walk slowly, deliberately down the hall.

"Lauren." My voice echoes off the tiles, but there's no other sound. Where the fuck would she go? I should never have left like that. I should've brought her with me.

A loud knock on the aluminum door makes me jump out of my skin.

"Allie," Eric says. He opens the door a crack. "Is she in here?"

I open the door wider and come out of the bathroom. Gabe and Eric both stare at me expectantly. "No."

A flash lights up the rapidly darkening sky.

"Shit," Gabe mutters.

Eric's counting under his breath. About ten seconds later, a small vibration rumbles in my chest. It slowly gets larger as a dull menacing peal of thunder rips through camp.

"We have to find her," I say.

Gabe

This isn't happening. Now Lauren's missing. I knew I should've gone after them sooner. "She might've headed back to camp."

Allie's eyes look skeptical, but she follows me as I lead the way back. When we duck into the dry tent, I notice for the first time how soaked I got outside. My wet jeans cling to me uncomfortably, bringing me back to when I stupidly threw myself in the lake.

Jennifer's still sleeping on the couch.

Joe and Ben are gone.

Shit.

I nudge Jennifer lightly by the shoulder.

She rubs a hand on her eyes. "What? What is it?" Her voice is still thick with sleep.

"Where's Ben?"

She sits bolt upright, the pulse on her neck beating wildly. "What?"

"Did Ben tell you where he was going?"

She shakes her head.

I kick the coffee table, and the playing cards go flying

through the air and scatter onto the floor, glasses knock over and spill. "Why do people keep leaving?"

The tent flap opens. Ben and Joe come in. "What's going on? We had to take a piss. Or Joe did anyway."

A small flood of relief washes over me at the sight of them, however, it's short lived. "We were just at the bathrooms. We didn't see you. Either of you."

Ben shrugs. His eyes narrow, and I can tell he's counting heads, always the Boy Scout. "Where's Lauren?"

Allie lets out a small noise somewhere between a gasp and a pained shriek. "We can't find her."

"What?" Jennifer's standing now, her thin arms wrapped around herself, and it stirs something in me. I want to put my arm around her shoulders. I want to tell her it's all going to be all right. But I have a sick feeling it's not.

Another huge clap of thunder shoots adrenaline straight to the tips of my fingers. I'm suddenly very aware of all the metal poles it takes to keep these fancy white tents upright.

"We have to go," I say. "Split up. Find Lauren. Then get to the lodge. It's not safe here."

"He's right," Ben says. "I'll go with Jennifer. Gabe, you go with Joe. Allie and Eric, you go together. Look where you can, but don't stay out too long. The storm is getting closer."

Allie says softly, "It's already here."

Ben continues as if she didn't say anything. "We'll all meet at the lodge in about fifteen minutes. Got it?"

Ben takes Jennifer's hand. They're the first two out of the tent.

Allie's brows draw close together. "I really don't know where else to look."

Joe picks up the table, putting it back in place. "I say we look in the lodge itself."

That isn't a bad idea. It also feels a little like giving up, though.

"Allie, you and Eric go straight to the lodge and search. Joe, let's look in her tent. She might've just needed to grab something."

Allie rolls her eyes. "I looked there."

I rub the scruff on my chin. It'll be a full-on beard soon. I really should've shaved before coming. Strike that, I really shouldn't have come at all. I'm starting to lose what little patience I have left. "We'll check it again. Did you hear anything when she went missing?"

Allie shifts her eyes to the right ever so slightly. "No."

Is she lying? I read a study called "Deciphering Deception," and it said when someone is lying their eyes look to the side. But I can't remember which side.

"You're sure?"

She nods. "I didn't hear anything."

We part ways. Joe and I head out into the rain, with Joe leading the way. Joe walks right to Lauren's site with no hesitation. I'm still getting all the sites mixed up. How does he know exactly where to go?

"Lauren," Joe calls out with his gravelly voice. He goes into the tent, and I look around. The rain is starting to turn the dirt into mud. The fire pit has formed a puddle. No trace of Lauren.

I yell at Joe, "I'm going to look at the site next door real quick."

Going as fast as I can without falling on my ass in the mud, I run to the site next door. It's Ben and Jennifer's. I quickly look around their tent, but Lauren isn't here. A huge clap of thunder spurs me on.

I go back to Lauren's tent, lift the flap, and enter. Joe's putting something in his pocket. He brushes his jeans off. "She's not here."

I'm about to ask what he put in his pocket when another flash lights up the dim tent, followed shortly by a rumble of thunder. All the hairs on my arms stand at attention.

Joe looks outside.

When I find my voice I say, "We need to be indoors."

"What about Lauren?"

Then I remember the third diamond on the map, the one drawn right over the lodge. "I think she's already there."

Allie

Eric and I make our way to the clubhouse like the sky is falling. It feels like it is. We quickly search through the rooms, not finding anything. We go into the dark game room last. I flip a switch, and two brass candlestick lamps with dark-green glass shades turn on. One by the couch and one near one of the leather wingback chairs. The soft amber glow confirms that the room is empty. Not a soul in sight.

Eric shakes his head. "She's not here."

An idea comes to me. "What about the caretaker's house? She could be there." A shiver passes over me like a convulsion.

Eric puts a hand on my arm. "You're ice cold."

"I'm fine. Let's go look at the house." But I can't help my teeth chattering as I say it.

Eric leads me to the couch. "Stay here." He points to a throw blanket. "Warm up. I'll go check the house and come back."

We're supposed to stay in pairs. But the idea of going back into the bombarding rain and thunder—no, I can't do it.

"Okay," I say, not even recognizing my own meek voice.

Eric goes out the back, and I sit on the couch, curling into the blanket.

This is all my fault. I should've brought her with me. Or better yet, I should've never insisted we go searching the campsites like we were detectives.

Burying my head in my hands, I try to slow the swirl of thoughts.

I knew I shouldn't have come to this stupid wedding. When will I learn to trust the tiny voice in the back of my head?

I'm so lost in my own thoughts, it could've been five minutes or fifty when Eric comes back into the room through the hallway. He rubs his wet hair. "It's really coming down now."

"Did you find her?" Of course he didn't. Would he really be talking about the weather if he had?

He shakes his head, small water droplets flying with the motion. "No sign of her. Why do you think she took off?"

I swallow back tears. Crying won't help; crying never helps. "I have no idea."

"Do you think she tried to leave?"

"Like leave Lost Lake?"

"Yeah," Eric says. "I just wonder if maybe she tried to get around the landslide. I'd be lying if I said I hadn't thought of doing the same."

Eric goes to the fireplace and starts breaking kindling. Each snap of the wood sends a little jolt of shock all the way down to my toes. I mull over what he said. Lauren might've taken the bike. She doesn't trust Gabe, maybe she really doesn't believe him about the landslide. But why wouldn't she have told me what her plan was?

The fire burns bright, and some of the ice in my bones begins to thaw. After a while, Gabe comes in and then leaves again.

Time's moving in spurts and stutters, like a car that just can't quite get into the next gear.

Until a scream claws through the air.

It's a primal scream, not even human. I'm on my feet and out the door before I even fully register what it is, Eric following close behind me.

Ben's running down the trail, his hair and clothes soaked.

He's alone.

He half yells, half sobs, "I can't find Jennifer."

I look toward the lake. Gabe is already in the water but the picture doesn't make sense. There's too many limbs. A bare skinned leg peeks out from under the dock like a dancer lifting up her skirt. My insides melt into pure acid.

Gabe gently pulls her out and turns her over, blonde hair floating like tendrils. Floating in her shorts and tank top, a red gash over her heart is Jennifer.

It can't be. This is all wrong. What is going on?

I cover my mouth and turn away, shivering. Eric puts a hand on my back.

He leads me inside. My limbs somehow move, but I can't feel any of it. He sits me by the fire. Joe's drinking a beer in one of the wingback chairs.

The flames dance in the hearth and I can't tear my eyes away. The rest of the group trickles in one by one.

Ben sits in the other wingback chair, shaking his head.

Gabe's pacing by the pool table throwing a ball up in the air and catching it, over and over. Eric keeps touching my arm or my leg. I move over on the couch.

There's still no sign of Lauren.

My voice is a whisper as I ask Ben, "Why weren't you with her?"

Ben looks as if I slapped him. "We heard a noise and thought it was Lauren. We both ran toward the sound but after a while it stopped. Then when I looked behind me Jennifer was gone. I thought she was with me the whole time. We run together every Sunday. She always keeps up."

Ben hangs his head in his hands. His body heaves with great sobs. It's almost exaggerated in how much his body moves with every fresh wave of tears.

For the life of me I can't tell if it's real, or if he's putting on a show. Jennifer's words in the bathroom come back to me. "Sometimes I look at him and it's like I'm looking at a stranger. I don't know him at all."

I look around the room again. Chiseled jaws, stubble, prominent forearms. It even smells masculine—fire and musk.

I'm the only woman left.

As the reality of that sinks in, it feels like I'm physically sinking into the couch. Like I can disappear. I look at the faces around me. One of these men is a killer. They have to be. It can't be some stranger lurking in the dark. No.

It has to be one of us.

My attention lands on Joe. Or should I say Matthew.

"What?" Joe says.

I shrug and point to the six-pack next to him. "Can I get one of those?"

He pries one out of the ring and makes a motion to throw it to me. "Can you catch?"

"It's not my strong suit."

Joe grins and walks the beer over to me. Our fingers brush as I take it from him, and I suppress a shudder. His fingers are rough and dry, but he smells clean. Like soap. I picture him backing up in the shower when I was yelling at him. Something about that interaction has been bothering me in the back of my mind, like the hum of static on a television in another room. It's what he said when I accused him. He didn't say *what are you talking about?* He didn't ask what was going on. He didn't even say *it wasn't me.*

What had he said again?

"You said, 'It was nothing.'"

Joe looks to Ben and then to Eric. "Huh?"

I sit up. "When I confronted you in the shower. You didn't deny it or ask what was going on like any normal, innocent person would have. You said, 'It was nothing.' What was nothing exactly?"

The whole room stops breathing. Even the dead deer on the wall is silently staring at Joe.

Gabe

Joe the stranger. Joe who was supposed to be with Dana when she turned up dead. Joe, who when accused of murder said, "It's nothing."

My blood boils despite my clothes being soaked from the frigid lake. My feet take me over to Joe's chair, unbidden. I pull him up by the sleeves of his shirt. "Did you kill Jennifer?"

I can't keep the crack out of my voice.

Joe's shaking his head back and forth so fast he's a blur. "No. No. I didn't kill anyone. That's not what I meant."

His eyes look so sincere. My heat drains away. I let him fall back into the chair.

Allie's sitting perched on the edge of the chair like an eagle watching a field mouse. "That's not what you meant? What did you mean?"

Joe sighs and snags a fresh beer. He opens it in slow motion, clearly stalling.

"Just tell us," I snap.

"Okay." Joe holds up a hand. "I'm not proud of this."

"Spit it out," Allie says. Ben's even sitting at attention now.

If I feel like my heart was ripped out of my chest and smashed on a lemon juicer, I can't imagine what Ben's going through.

"I fooled around a little with Lauren. It was nothing. Dana and I weren't serious, and it was just a little fling with Lauren. No one was supposed to get hurt."

No one was *supposed* to? Allie's quicker on the draw. She says, "Did Dana find out?"

Joe gulps his beer. "Yes. Okay. She found out and stormed off, not before she slapped me, though. I'm a dirtbag, I'll admit that, but at least I'm not violent. I could press assault charges."

"Could *have*," Allie bites out. "She's dead, asshole."

"Right." Joe sighs. "I keep thinking she's just off, pissed at me somewhere. It still doesn't feel real." He takes a huge gulp of beer, probably not helping with his grasp on reality. "That's why we weren't together when we were supposed to be."

Allie purses her lips. "Were you with Lauren when she disappeared?"

"No," Joe says. "You were."

Allie sits back a little. He's not wrong. Allie and Lauren were supposed to be together at the time she disappeared.

I clear my throat. "How long were you sleeping with Lauren?"

"Just since we got here. Like I said, it was nothing. Just a summer fling."

I know I have no room to judge, but I'm disgusted with him all the same. How can he come here with the girl he was seeing and sleep with one of her best friends? Part of me is also vindicated. Relieved that I'm not the only person in the room who was fucking the wrong woman.

Allie stands and paces behind the couch. "Did she know your other secret?"

Joe flinches. It's minuscule. If I had blinked I would've missed it. What other secret?

He shakes his head. "That was it. That's all I was hiding."

Allie bites her lip, her eyes moving back and forth over Joe's face. Then she explodes. "You're not going to admit it. I found your fucking wallet. Sleeping with your girlfriend's best friend and now you're going to try to gaslight me. I can't believe you. I cannot fucking believe you. Fucking men."

"Hey!" It's an instinct. A reaction. It came out without a second thought. I want to take the word and scoop it back in my mouth.

Allie turns on me. "Hey? Really? You of all people are going to defend your gender when you're boning your brother's fiancée?"

Fuck.

All the air is sucked out of the room.

I freeze.

How does she know? Did Jennifer tell her? How long has she known?

Ben's on his feet. "Gabe?" His voice is soft, like when we were kids. "Gabe. Tell her she's crazy. Tell her she's wrong."

I don't move. Can't speak.

Ben's face looks so small. Despite his manly jaw, I can still see the little boy he used to be. He had the same look on his face when he came to me and told me Bobby across the street said there was no Santa Claus. He's waiting for me to deny or confirm. To let him live in a world of magic or introduce him to life's harsh realities.

He's just waiting for me to speak.

On that day long ago, I made the decision that he needed to grow up. That at six years of age he was too old to keep believing in fairytales.

Can I let him buy this fairytale now? That he has a good brother? Jennifer's gone. He never has to know. There's no proof.

The longer my silence stretches, the more convincing I know I'll need to be. But I have nothing left in me. I have no energy to lie. I keep seeing golden hair floating in murky water and Ben's shattered face.

I put my hand over my mouth to muffle my sob.

Eric

Ben staggers his way back to the chair. And I thought my family had drama. This is so messed up. What did Allie mean when she said she found the wallet? An even better question is why did I follow a hot girl and her psycho friends into the woods?

Allie shouldn't have said anything about the affair. It's none of anyone's business. Gabe has yet to confirm or deny that he's been sleeping with Jennifer, but his sobs are a pretty strong confession.

Love can make people do such terrible things to one another.

"It can't be true," Ben says quietly, shaking his head. "When? How? It's not even possible. We don't even live in the same city." His voice gets louder. "Tell them, Gabe. Tell them it's not possible. Tell Allie she's wrong."

Gabe sniffs in a giant breath. "I can't."

Ben's face turns almost purple. He storms out the door.

He shouldn't leave. This has all gone too far. We need to all stay here. I say, "Wait —"

Allie puts a hand on my arm, sending a shot of electricity to my fingertips. "Let him go."

Gabe stares at the door Ben left out of. Allie catches his eye and shakes her head. "You're the *last* person that should go after him."

He nods once, curt, definite—just like Gabe, or what little I know of him. Like if you could get the whole vibe of a person in one body gesture, his would be a rude nod. Gabe walks over to where Joe's sitting.

Joe curls in the chair as far as he can, covering his face with his arm, but Gabe just plucks a beer from the plastic rings then stalks out the back door.

All the muscles in my neck are still tense, bracing for something to happen. Allie gives me a half smile, melting some of the tension. "Bet you're wishing you couldn't get out of working that shift at the bar."

I bark out a surprised laugh. And that's part of what makes Allie so special. She knows just what to say. "You have no idea."

"I think I have some."

"Fair enough." I run a hand through my hair, flexing my bicep a little as I do. "What are we going to do?"

She shrugs.

Joe sits forward. "Nothing we can do, right? Just wait for help."

I don't want to admit Joe's right. There has to be some way out of here. If not, I know in my bones someone else will die tonight.

"Why have you been lying about your name?" Allie asks, her attention solely fixed on Joe.

"I don't..."

"Stop lying," Allie says so loud my heart hammers in my chest. "I saw your fucking wallet. Matthew Joseph Robinson."

Robinson?

Joe sighs. "I've gone by my middle name since I graduated high school. And no one asked my last name. I wasn't lying."

Allie's eyes go wide. "Dana never asked your last name?"

"Okay, I lied to her. Wyatt always said he was innocent. Then those other girls turned up, and he couldn't have killed them. I went to his trial. I talked to him in prison. I believe Wyatt. So, it got me thinking if it wasn't him, then who was responsible? In high school, Nick was always following Wendy around. Leaving notes for her. Flowers on the doorstep, but not nice store bought ones. Ones clearly picked from our own garden. It was weird. Wendy didn't even like him. But she idolized Dana and all the other older cheerleaders. They were all such bitches. I thought Dana knew something she wasn't sharing."

It's like I'm watching a movie in a different language, my brain struggling to keep up. "Are you...Were you related to Wendy Robinson."

"I'm her brother."

An enormous rumble of thunder rattles my teeth and a flash blinds me. Allie screams, shrill in my ear, as both lamps go dark. The only light in the room is the amber glow from the fire.

Joe sits back again, legs spread, and takes a sip of beer. "Ooh spooky."

With the lamps off, I can see now how truly dark it is outside. It must be night. I'm not sure what time, though. There's no clock in the lodge.

Allie curls into a smaller ball on the edge of the couch, tucking her knees into her chest. "So, you met Dana on purpose?"

Joe nods. "I tracked her down. She was easier to get close to than Nick. I just wanted to see if she knew anything. If any of them did."

"Weren't you worried she'd recognize you?"

"Nah, I was a couple years behind and scrawny. Dana never gave me a second look back then."

Allie is shivering. I move to put my arm around her, but she scooches closer to the arm of the couch.

"Did you..." Allie trails off.

"Look, I know this is hard to believe, but I didn't kill anyone. When I got out here, I realized it was a mistake. They were all too self-involved to know anything about what happened to Wendy. So, I figured I'd cut my losses. Lauren was flirty and hot. I fucked up, okay? I should've never come here. But I didn't kill anyone."

Allie is staring into the fire. Not reacting.

"You don't believe me."

"I do." I offer, but it doesn't help.

Joe sits silently staring into the fire.

Joe is Wendy Robinson's brother. Joe has been lying about who he is. Joe was with Dana when she died. All signs point to Joe being the killer among us. Good. Good. We can handle Joe.

My fingers itch for something to do, so I put some more wood on the fire. "Help should be here tomorrow. We'll stay up tonight. Stay here together. There's plenty of wood. We'll keep the fire going."

I wish I had my book. I've read *On the Road* so many times I could probably recite it from memory—lines of it are ingrained in my soul. My favorite quote is literally tattooed on my arm. I raise it to the light of the fire and read it.

"My fault, my failure, is not in the passions I have, but in my lack of control of them."

I throw another log on to make a fire that will hopefully last hours. The flames, the warmth, it'll soothe me, it'll soothe all of us. "We'll be fine."

Murder? What murder? Episode 189 July 20th, 2024

"What in the actual fuckity fuck?"

"Jules, it's so bananas."

"Well, Gabe did it, obvs."

"Interesting, even with Joe's last name being Robinson? Explain."

"Okay, the Robinson thing I can't explain, so I could be totally wrong. And this is assuming there's not a random psycho killer lurking in the woods, and it's just an assumption because I honestly don't know what happened. But Gabe was sleeping with two of the victims and sex makes people do crazy things."

"So, true. It's a good theory."

"Hmm. But it could also be Nick. Where the hell is he? If he was killed too, then why hadn't they found the body?"

"Well, they'd been pretty busy. Aside from when they first noticed he was gone, I'm not sure they looked that hard."

"Or wait, even better, what if one of the victims wasn't really dead? What if it was Jennifer?"

"Jules. They found Jennifer in the lake. How could she do it?"

"Well, but they found her so quickly, right? And she was

still dressed and there were no diamonds. So maybe, just maybe, she Wargraved them."

"She what?"

"She Wargraved them. Justice Wargrave from *And Then There Were None* by Agatha Christie. Okay, listeners, spoilers coming. Justice Wargrave pretended to be dead but wasn't and killed everybody. No one suspected him because he was supposedly murdered."

"So, you're suggesting Jennifer faked her death."

"Yes."

"Oh, Jules. I love you and your twisted mind."

Allie

Too antsy to sit, I go to the sliding glass door, pressing my forehead against the cool glass. Rain falls in great sheets, dripping off of trees and making puddles on the back deck.

Are we just supposed to sit here with a killer?

Joe is Wendy Robinson's brother. He lied to Dana to get close to her. He has to be the one responsible for all of this. He has to be.

I shouldn't have confronted him like that. I should've lured him into the basement and locked him in.

Another flash. In the brief explosion of light, I just make out Gabe sitting on the little staircase at the end of the deck, his face tilted up to the sky. The night goes pitch black again. A loud rumble of thunder vibrates in my chest.

Will we really be okay here all night with Joe sitting there? Where is Lauren?

A few minutes later, there's more lightning and thunder, but this time Gabe is gone.

I cup my hands over the window to make sure I'm not missing him somewhere, but he isn't anywhere to be seen.

"He's gone."

"Who?" Eric comes over to the window. He's been fidgety since we found Jennifer, it's like he can't stop finding things to do.

"Gabe."

"He probably went after Ben. They'll be okay. I'm going to go grab some snacks."

"Snacks? How can you be hungry?"

"I just need to do something."

There's no way in hell I'm staying in a room alone with Joe. "I'll come."

He grabs my hand, his palm rough and calloused. "For safety reasons."

Despite myself, I smile. We make our way through the dark hall, feeling along the wall.

Eric's hand doesn't feel as good as when we got here. It's cold and clammy. If it had been any other situation, I'd just continue to hold his slimy hand, but here in this dark lodge, with my friends dying one after another, I can't do it. I pull away and itch my face, trying to cover it.

"We should look for a flashlight in the store too. We should've brought ours."

"Yeah, but the store probably has some," Eric says. "I really don't want to go back to those tents. Ever again."

We walk through the aisles and find two red Coleman personal size lanterns. I pick up the box. "You think there's batteries around here?"

"I saw some up front."

Eric takes the other box, and we get the batteries. After a few minutes of fumbling in the dark with packaging and tiny plastic doors, Eric's face is suddenly illuminated from below, his eyebrow ridges making long shadows like an old Vincent Price movie.

"Let's find some Pringles."

We load up with a variety of snacks, even though the thought of eating right now turns my stomach, and head back to the warm game room. The chair by the fireplace is empty.

Joe is gone.

Gabe

My first instinct was to go after Ben, until Allie stopped me. She's right, if he wants to be alone, I should grant him that at the very least. But I'm too antsy to sit. Leaving the deck and the lodge behind, I set off down the trail.

The rain feels good on my face. Cleansing. Now that Ben knows, I'm—relieved. A tremendous weight has been taken off my chest. I take a long sip of beer. There's nothing to hide anymore.

I let the rain wash away any remaining guilt. There's no going back. No changing history. I can't change anything. And even though it was wrong, I loved Jennifer. It wasn't some meaningless fling. Despite us being the wrong people for each other, it was love. It had to be.

If it wasn't, what does that make me?

I stop for a moment, tilting my face to the sky. There's a flash, bright even through my closed eyelids.Thunder vibrates all around me.

My eyes shoot open as a noise off in the distance snatches

the tiny sense of calm I had. It's a woman. It's Jennifer. But it can't be.

I follow the sound. There's a trail I hadn't noticed before that goes through the field and into the woods behind the club-house. It's so dark. The further I walk, the darker it gets.

It's like walking into space.

My foot hits something hard, and my mind flashes to Jennifer's body in the lake. My arms flail but can't save me. The mud squishes under my stomach as I slide to a stop, my face inches from the ground. A rock in the path tripped me. I push myself up and there's the noise again, but this time it's coming from the opposite direction.

Is someone fucking with me? The sound vibrates through the night, not quite a scream, more of a moan.

I follow the trail back the other way, heading in the direction of the wedding party's tents. *Wedding.* It was a lifetime ago that we got here to celebrate Ben and Jennifer.

The noises intensify with each step I take. It's definitely a woman. But it doesn't sound like she's in trouble.

It's moans of pleasure.

The white tent at the group campsite glows. I don't see a silhouette. No shadows of movement. There's a man's grunts mixed with the woman's. Who's in there? Ben and Lauren? There's no way. My brother would never do that, not so soon after Jennifer's death. I open the flap of the tent, fully expecting to find two lovers, but instead there's a handheld tape recorder sitting on the couch.

The moans are unmistakable now. The woman gasps and says, clear as a bell, "Gabe."

Fear prickles the back of my neck.

It's Jennifer's voice. I grab the device and fumble with it, the sounds of our love reverberating through my skull. Finally, I find the off switch and click it. The sounds continue in my head. I throw the recorder at the tent wall. It hits the shiny fabric with an unsatisfactory muffled thud. I want a crash. I want it smashed to smithereens.

How can she be gone? Rage creeps up my neck, hot and sticky.

Who put this here? And why? I open the tent door as if whoever put this here is just right outside. As my eyes adjust again to the dark, it's evident no one is here.

I pour myself a glass of whiskey from the bar cart. Who could've done this? Lauren? Ben? Hell, it could've been Allie, or Eric or Joe. I have no way of knowing if any of them stayed at the lodge after I left. It could've been anyone. How did they get the tape? When is it even from?

I walk back over and pick up the recorder. It's been a bit since I've seen or used a cassette player, and I've never had one of these micro ones, so it takes a little time to figure out how to rewind the tape. I press play.

There are sounds of fabric, muffled voices, but I can't tell what we're saying. I crank the volume up as loud as it will go. It doesn't help.

Whoever played the tape out here, they would've had to turn on the recording near the clubhouse and lead me to the campsite. I wouldn't have heard the tape from that far away.

I walk back into the night, spreading my arms wide, tape recorder still in one hand. "You wanted me here! Here I am! Come and get me!"

Allie

Despite the fire, I can't help shivering. "Where do you think Joe went?"

"I wouldn't worry about it." Eric plops down on the couch and opens a package of Ho-Ho's.

Wouldn't worry? "He killed everyone."

Eric frowns. "I don't think he did."

"He lied about who he is. He tricked Dana to bring him out here. He's Wendy Robinson's brother. In what world didn't he do it?"

Eric pats the couch next to him, but I don't move. "He seemed genuine when he explained it all. If he killed them all, why would he admit to being Wendy's brother? Robinson is a pretty common name. He could've said it was a coincidence. But he told the truth."

As I sit next to Eric, he offers me the open package. How can he eat?

Is he right? The thing is, if Joe didn't do it then who did?

I sit back and play with the fray on the end of my shorts. "Do you think help is really coming tomorrow?"

Eric nods slowly. "Yeah—eventually."

My heartbeat races at his tone when he says, *eventually.* "What do you mean?"

"Well, if the landslide is as bad as Gabe says it is, it'll take a while to clear away."

"Longer than a day?"

"Maybe."

I don't know what I expected him to say, but something more hopeful than maybe. I stare into the fire. With every rise and dip of the flames, I get more and more anxious. I grab the poker and stab at some of the logs, hoping an activity will make me feel better. But it doesn't work. There is no feeling better.

Where is Lauren? And where is Nick? Could he be responsible for all this? Joe said he was creepy back then. He never seemed like the serial killer type, but who knows? Maybe he was, and he just hid behind his easy smile and athletic ability. What if he killed Wendy Robinson in high school and just never stopped? Maybe he's out lurking in the shadows, hiding in the trees, waiting for us to break out of our group and pick us off one by one.

Being the only woman left, I'm probably top of the list.

A deep voice startles me out of my spiral. "Are you trying to put the fire out?"

Joe strides through the door.

"Where did you go?" I ask.

"Bathroom." He walks over and stands so close to me I can smell the beer on his breath. He grabs a log from just behind me and puts it on the fire. Then goes back to his leather chair.

I huddle closer to the flames.

What about Gabe? He is—no, not anymore—was sleeping with Jennifer, his own brother's fiancée. He's already on another level morally than most of us. I've done some questionable things in my life, sure, but I've never betrayed someone like that.

Plus, he was in a relationship with Sheila. Why would anyone else kill her? She's a stranger to everyone but Gabe.

As my brain circles around Sheila, something occurs to me. The rental car. There must be keys to the rental car. They must be somewhere. Where? If we can find the keys, we can drive away.

Joe and Eric are both staring into the fire. I don't trust either one of them.

I can drive away. I'll be safe alone. And I won't leave them stranded for long, I'll send back help. If I can get around the landslide. But if Gabe really is responsible for all this, then it's quite possible there's no landslide. I just need to find the keys.

Checking to see if Gabe's back, I walk over to the window again, cup my hands on the glass and peer into the night. My heart jumps in my throat. I throw my body back as Lauren's face appears.

She quickly presses her pointer finger against her lips. Her soaking wet hair plastered to her head.

I nod, showing her I understand.

"What is it?" Eric gets up from the couch as Lauren makes a half circle with her finger then disappears into the shadows again.

"Huh?" I say.

"You jumped like something scared you." Eric looks out the glass door.

"Raccoon," I say. "I'm just easily startled at the moment." I grab one of our lanterns. "I'm going to go to the bathroom."

"Do you want me to come?" Eric's blue eyes glow in the dim light.

Part of me does want him to come. We can get Lauren, find the keys, and all leave together. I'm considering it when Eric rubs his neck, right by his diamond tattoos.

Where was Eric when Nick went missing? Or when we

found Dana? Even when they found Jennifer, Eric was off checking the caretaker's cottage. What do I really know about Eric except that he has stunning blue eyes, a wiry frame, and a birthmark on his ass? Nothing. I don't even know his last name.

"I'll be fine." I make an expression with my face, trying for a smile, but it feels odd. I can only imagine what it looks like.

Quickly, I make my way to the front door, tiptoeing through the hall so they won't hear me going the wrong way. I'm positive that's what Lauren's half circle motion meant, but she isn't there.

I open the heavy front door, trying not to make a sound. The rain immediately soaks into my clothes and my hair. I squint as rain falls from my eyelashes like tears.

Ice cold adrenaline shoots to my heart as someone grabs my wrist from the shadows.

Gabe

No one comes out from behind the tree.

No one rushes in from the bushes.

There isn't anyone lurking in the dark.

I don't know what I expected. Some grand confrontation with a psycho killer. With Wyatt James himself. He could still be the one responsible for all the deaths. Allie's the only one who claims he was arrested again. She heard it on the radio, but what radio? I don't remember anything in the clubhouse. Who else would do all this but a convicted killer? But how would Wyatt James get an audio tape of Jennifer and I making love? How would anyone get this tape?

I lower my arms, feeling like an idiot. Rain runs down my forehead and into my eyes. The recorder is still in my hand, and with all my force, I chuck it at the tree looming over the campsite. It breaks into hundreds of pieces with a satisfying crack.

All my anger leaves my body with that swift movement. I'm so tired.

Bone-achingly tired.

My skin sits heavy on my body. I go back in the tent and toy with the idea of having a nip more of whiskey, but the steps involved—unscrewing the bottle, pouring, lifting a glass to my mouth—is all too much work. Instead, I reach for the lantern. At least I won't have to find my way back in the dark.

I drag myself toward the trail that leads to the backside of the clubhouse, the trail furthest from the lake. If I never see another lake again in my entire life, I'll die a happy man. Not really, but that's the saying.

The rain falls in relentless waves. The air smells clean, mud and smoke mixed with the fresh scent of pine. It reminds me of the palm reading girl I met in the park for some reason. I think she would like it here. She probably would talk about its clean energy or its aura. Do trees have an aura?

Looking up toward the clouds, I search for any breaks, any stars, but what catches my eye instead is a small stream of smoke. Actually, that isn't the odd thing. There are two, when there should be only one. One stream of smoke is coming from the clubhouse. Another is coming from the woods that face the back of the lodge.

I head toward the second one. Toward the woods. Maybe it's Lauren. She may have gotten lost and started a fire to keep warm. The lantern illuminates a small spot in front of me as I walk. There are footprints in the mud, but it's hard to tell how old they are. They look like tiny mud puddles dotted along the path.

As the trail winds its way around the dark woods, the smell of wood smoke gets stronger. A small red house is nestled at the end of the trail like a baby bird in a nest. So warm. So out of place among these unsympathetic trees. The front door is already open a little, so I push it farther, with a metallic creak of rusty hinges.

"Hello. Lauren, are you here? Anyone?"

There's no answer, no sounds but the crackles and pops of a

fire. Moving into the sitting room, I turn the little plastic switch on the lamp.

There's a roaring fire in the fireplace, but from this close, it smells weird. Not like the typical spiced wood. Not the pleasant familiar scent that drew me here like a lemming to the cliff. I lean in closer to see what's burning.

Photographs. Dozens of photos fill the fireplace. Black and white prints, all of them. I reach in to pull one out, and the hair on my arm singes. The pain on my skin is a sharp pinprick. I pull my hand back out, feeling dumb.

Rule number one: don't touch fire with your bare hands, Gabe. I grab the tongs by the fireplace and pull out a charred photo.

There's a loud clatter from the other room, and I drop the brass tongs. They hit the floor with an equally loud clang. Adrenaline shoots all the way to my toes, propelling me forward.

Someone is here.

I run to the hall and push through the swinging door to the kitchen.

But it's empty. Did the noise come from outside?

"Hello?"

A small radio on the table blasts static out of the speakers. It echoes in my ears like fingernails on a chalkboard. I click it off, but nothing happens. I open the little door with the batteries and dump them out. A radio? Did Allie find this cabin? Is this where she heard about Wyatt James? Why didn't she tell us about it?

There's a phone on the wall. A small pinprick of promise forms in my chest. I pick up the receiver. The feeling spreads into something a little like hope.

Silence.

No dial tone.

Nothing.

Dead.

I slam the receiver back down on the cradle, again and again, the plastic breaking, my hands splitting, until the phone falls off the wall. Tossing the phone aside, I wipe my bloody knuckles on my jeans.

Of course, the phone is dead. We're all going to die.

Heading back to the sitting room in a daze, I crouch by the fire. All the photos are crumbling to dark ash. I pick up the piece that's fallen to the floor with the tongs and hold the lantern up to it. The room tilts to the side, like a reflection on the water, everything murky and distorted.

It's Jennifer's face, her neck tilted to the side, her eyes softly closed, her rosebud lips parted slightly. And behind her, with lips pressed to the flesh behind her ear, is me.

Allie

With cold fingers on my wrist, rain water streaming down my face, rage flares in the pit of my stomach. Fuck this. I yank my arm away easily, the thin fingers letting go immediately. I turn, fist in the air, ready to punch someone.

It's Lauren. Soaking wet, but otherwise unharmed.

She puts both hands up. "Allie, it's me."

"Where the fuck?"

Lauren puts her finger up to her lips. I take a deep breath and move over to the corner she's in, out of sight of the door. More quietly I say, "Where have you been? You've been gone so long I thought…"

"I went to get help."

A tingle hums through me. "Did you find any?"

She shakes her head.

Shit.

"You left me! Alone. Why didn't you tell me where you were going?"

"Technically, you left me." Lauren sighs. "I took the bike. There was only one. You couldn't have come, and the more I thought about it, the more I thought maybe Gabe was lying about the landslide, to keep us here." Lauren heaves a great sigh. "He wasn't lying. About that anyway. I took the bike down the hill, it's like the road just stops. There was so much dirt and rock. Trees. There're actual trees on the street."

Lauren's breaths are fast, her chest moving up and down rapidly. I put my hands on her arms.

"Lauren, look at me. Breathe."

Our eyes lock, and we take some deep breaths in unison. Should I tell her about Joe? No. It won't help right now. Right now, we need to act.

Once she seems calmer, I say, "Do you think we could get around it if we had a car?"

"Maybe, but where would we get one?"

"Second problem. That's the second problem. Leave that one to me. I need you to focus on the first problem. If we were in a car, do you think we could make it around or over?"

Lauren's eyes are weary. Like when we were in college and I would suggest going to a dive bar after the club. She lets out a long breath. "I don't know. Maybe."

I nod. Maybe will have to be good enough. "Okay, we need to go find the keys to the car." Lauren's head tilts to the side, her perfectly plucked brows furrow. "Sheila's car."

It's like a light turns on. "Oh my god. Where do you think the keys are?

I sigh. There's a loud noise, but it's far away. I can't tell what it is. I hold my breath as Lauren, and I cower in the corner of the porch.

The sound is gone.

"Sheila must've had clothes she was wearing when she died," I whisper. "They have to be somewhere. The keys are probably in her pocket."

Lauren looks unsure. The rain is pouring down, pounding

the lake, making it look like a living creature. But the thunder and lightning have subsided.

"I can go if you want. You can stay here."

Lauren grabs my arm. "*No.*"

"Okay, let's go together. Now."

"How are we going to find anything? I don't even have a flashlight."

I want to go inside to grab another lantern. But I don't trust Joe, or even Eric for that matter. Do I trust Lauren?

It's too late to question that now. "I have this." I hold up the dim light. "We can find our flashlights at the campsites. Come on, we have to go."

We walk as quickly as we can in the dark on the slick mud. We stop at the first site, my campsite, and look inside the tent, but the flashlight isn't there.

We try at the group campsite, but the lantern there is gone too.

"Someone must've already taken it."

I sweep the light around the site. Near the tree, some shards of what looks like plastic catch the light. "Let's check the next site."

We make our way over and go into the dark tent. I grab the lantern on the bedside table and turn it on. There's an open suitcase on the bed with clothes spread all over.

Lauren picks up a shirt with the tips of her two fingers, like she's in junior high and it's covered in cooties. The shirt has a screen print of a skeleton drinking a beer on it. "I think this is Gabe's tent."

She throws the shirt back in the pile of clothes.

I don't remember Gabe wearing that, but I hadn't really been paying too much attention to him. It's a pretty common Dead Guy Ale shirt. We get them for free at the bar sometimes.

I'm about to suggest we leave, when a swatch of pink leather in the pile of clothes catches my eye. I pull the strap, feeling a slight tug of resistance as it snags on clothes. I give it a swift yank, and a pink snakeskin Prada handbag comes flying at me.

Lauren gasps. "Why does Gabe have a purse?"

Unzipping the top of the bag, I pull out a black leather wallet.

It's one of those compact wallets, all the cards stacked together. I riffle through them. A gym membership, a Sprouts rewards card, a business card for a private investigator with a hand-written number under all the printed information.

A wave of nausea washes over me as I flip to the next one. It's just what I thought, but seeing her actual photo feels different than I expected. A woman with shiny dark hair smiles in the small government issued photo. The name printed on the Texas driver's license is Tanner, Sheila.

Gabe

My hands are numb. The scrap of photograph slips through my fingers, floats to the floor like a dead leaf falling from a tree.

I back up.

Sink into the plaid couch.

Rub my hands on the slightly scratchy fabric, trying to get feeling back into them.

I spot a bar cart across the room and launch myself at it, taking a swig right from the bottle of whiskey.

Why are these pictures here?

Bringing the whiskey with me, I go sit cross-legged on the hardwood floor in front of the fire. The scrap of the photo's sitting a few feet away. On the back, there's a small circular stamp. I pick it up and squint in the dim light, the words are only partially there, but I can just make out Austin, TX, in the bottom of the circle.

More shapes from the burning photos stand out now. Flickers of her stomach. Bare thighs. My hairy chest. These are all photos of me and Jennifer together.

When were these taken? Jennifer and I were only ever together a handful times. None of them were in Austin.

One of the last times, well, before our romp by the tree and before I went to Portland for the bachelor party, had been when I came to visit Portland for Christmas. I stayed in a hotel, not wanting to crowd Jennifer and Ben at the condo and refusing to stay with my parents. I can handle visiting with my folks between the hours of 9 and 6, but if I had to hear at seven in the morning about Ben's latest promotion or upcoming wedding, I'd shoot myself in the face. I'd tried to get Sheila to come with me, we'd been dating for a couple months by then, but she had to work.

Jennifer snuck to my hotel a couple of times while I was visiting under the pretense of going to the gym. It'd undoubtedly been a workout. And there was once at their condo while Ben was out Christmas shopping. That time was so hot, even remembering it now on this cold dirty floor gives me a semi. Ben and Jennifer invited me over for dinner and Christmas movies. Ben texted me when I was already on my way to their place that he was running late, but that Jennifer was home and I should just head over.

When I got there, Jennifer was making mulled wine on the stove, the zingy scent of citrus and spice filling the air. She answered the door in a short turtleneck sweater dress that clung to her body in all the ways I wanted to. We ended up fucking right there in the living room, up against one of their fancy floor-to-ceiling windows. The whole time I pictured Ben walking on the street below us. Packages in hand. Glancing up and seeing us together. Or walking through the door finding me with his fiancée, dropping his carefully chosen gifts, watching his face as his life shattered. But he didn't. By the time he got home, arms filled with presents, just as I pictured, Jennifer and I were on opposite ends of the couch. An appropriate distance for soon to be in-laws. Mulled wine in festive mugs. Watching *Trapped in Paradise* on cable.

Another swig of whiskey burns my throat as I tip the bottle back once more. Could the photos have been from that time? Someone could've taken them from one of the buildings across the street.

But who?

I let out a long sigh as I throw the photo into the fire.

What does it matter? Jennifer's dead.

Nothing I do or say will bring her back. And she was right all along—I never really loved her. None of it was ever about her. I wanted her because Ben had her. I wanted to beat him, finally and irreparably.

Draining more of the bottle, I stumble to my feet, the room blurring at the edges, The whiskey dulls the jagged shards of my brain. The house creaks, the way old houses do sometimes, but I freeze, listening for more noises.

The pounding rain outside. The crackle of the fire. The whiskey sloshing in the bottle hanging from my hand as I sway.

I hardly feel the first cut. The knife is sharp. Not painful. Definitely forceful, as it plunges into my back. I gasp for breath, but it's like something is stuck, the air caught. Won't enter my lungs. I collapse to the floor and look up into the face of my killer.

I try to speak, but no words come out.

Allie

I drop the wallet like it's burning my skin.

Lauren picks it up. "It's Sheila's. I knew we shouldn't trust Gabe."

My mind's spinning. Did Gabe kill Sheila? Did Gabe kill all of them? I don't trust him, but I didn't seriously think he actually killed anyone.

Lauren digs through the clothes on the bed. "Is there more of her stuff here?"

Clothes fly through the air and fall to the floor, while I stand transfixed, lost about the timing of everything. Did Gabe kill Dana, and what about Jennifer?

The thing I keep coming back to, that my brain can't make sense of, is if Gabe killed Sheila, why would he tell us about the car? None of us had seen it yet. He could've gone in the night and hid it or drove it into the lake.

Lauren is still digging through the clothes. A shirt sails toward my face. I move quickly out of the way and jerk myself out of my spiral of thoughts, shaking the purse as I do. It jangles slightly. The muscles in my abdomen soften as I reach into the bag and pull out a set of keys with a yellow rental tag attached to the keyring.

Lauren's eyes double in size. "The keys!"

We head out of the tent, back into the night. The ground is still too slick to run, but we walk quickly down the trail. It's taking forever. My muscles feel heavy, trembling with the effort of navigating the slippery terrain. "Was it this far before?"

Lauren lets out a long breath. "I don't remember. I only went this way when we were playing the games."

Shit, that was another life, before we found the first body in the lake and everything changed. The first body—covered in so many cuts.

Something's been bothering me about that too. We found Sheila covered in diamonds. But when we found Dana, she didn't have as many. I didn't get the best look at Jennifer—I couldn't, I turned away as fast as possible—but from my brief glance, I don't think she had diamonds on her at all.

I have an urge to go check on the first body. But there's no time.

Finally, we arrive at the car, and I push the bodies out of my mind. Whatever happened, whoever did this, it doesn't matter right now.

Right now, we need to leave.

I unlock the car, get in the driver's seat, and put the key in the ignition. The ignition turns easily, the car purring to life. The vibration of the engine stirs something in my chest. This is going to work.

Lauren climbs in the passenger seat and claps. "Yes. Let's go!"

I pull out of the site and onto the narrow trail, just wide enough for the car, the headlights are dim, but in the dark night they're too bright. I want to turn them off, so no one can see us, but I don't think I can navigate the trail without them.

Once I'm in the roundabout, I stop the car, hesitating. Should I go back for Eric? He hasn't done anything wrong, well, besides insisting on coming to the woods with a virtual stranger. I can't leave him. But what if Gabe is with him in the lodge?

"Allie, what are you waiting for?"

Turning onto the road, I inhale sharply and swallow down my guilt. "Nothing."

My guilt, however, is unrestrained. The image of Eric's smile when we were fooling around that first day camping, his eyes twinkling with wholesome mischief. If I leave him here and he dies, that twinkle will be seared into my mind like a sunspot that doesn't go away even when you close your eyes. I'll replay it for the rest of my life. I'll never forgive myself.

Instead of maneuvering onto the road, I keep turning the steering wheel until I've made a U-turn back into the parking lot.

Lauren gasps like I slapped her. "Allie, what are you doing? The road is that way, girl."

"We just have to get Eric real quick." Lauren's shaking her head at me. "I can't leave him here."

The car jars over a large bump and the trunk flies open, completely blocking the back windshield. I stop the car.

"What are you doing? Let's just go."

"Lauren, I can't see."

The visibility is already terrible enough without taking the back windshield out of the equation. I grab my flashlight and get out to close the trunk. The rain falls in a steady stream through the beam of my light. With each movement of my head, water droplets soar, making me feel like a wet dog. I can't wait to get out of here. Get in a warm shower, then a fluffy robe with a monster glass of red wine. I walk around the car, the vision so strong I can almost smell the Cabernet. Putting a hand on the lid of the trunk, I'm about to slam it when I freeze.

My flashlight drops into a puddle, my head buzzes, as the unseeing eyes of Nick's dead body stare up at me from the trunk.

Eric

The fire crackles, and the rain drums outside. If I was here alone, I'd curl up with my notebook and write until dawn. If it was just me and Allie, it'd be romantic. The flashes from the fire cast long shadows on the walls, making everything look distorted.

Allie's been in the bathroom a long time. Way too long.

"I'm just going to go check on her," I say to Joe.

He waves a hand at me. I wasn't asking his permission, and I don't need his dismissive wave of approval. Maybe I shouldn't believe everything he said.

The hallway is dark, the wood floors creaky. I knock on the bathroom door.

"Allie, are you okay?"

There's no answer.

"Allie?"

I open the door to an empty bathroom. What is Allie doing? Do I really have to go after her?

I check the store and the office. There's no sign of her.

Goddamn.

Stopping for a second, I take a deep breath, letting the heat in my chest cool.

Once I've come back to myself, I head back to the game room. Maybe we crossed paths, somehow. But the room is empty. The sliding door is open a crack, rain blowing in and dripping on the floor.

Joe's gone again, just a beer can by the chair where he was sitting.

That episode of *Unsolved Mysteries* comes back to mind. Everyone disappearing, one by one.

Another gust of wind comes from the door. I go over, try to focus in the darkness. There's a figure walking off into the woods. They're so far away and it's so dark I can't tell who it is. Maybe Joe? He's not my concern.

Only Allie matters now.

I close the sliding glass door.

As the lock clicks, a searing pain slices through my skull, and a flash of light. My legs won't hold me up. I fall to the ground, and another thud sounds in my brain.

Ginsberg was right; there's an almost delicate sensation right before everything goes black.

Allie

Nick is lying in the trunk, the back of his head misshapen, his hand clutching something. I pull it out of his cold hand. It's glossy on one side, the feel unmistakable to me even in the dark. It's a piece of a photograph.

Adrenaline fills my veins. I slam the trunk closed and jump in the car.

"What is it? You look like you've seen a ghost," Lauren says.

I turn on the dome light and examine the scrap of photo. It's too small to figure out what it is beyond shades of grey shapes. It almost looks like it could be two people kissing. Almost exactly like the one I took in the dim hallway of the bar on the night of the bachelorette party. I thought I saw Jennifer with a man. She took his hand and pulled him into the bathroom. I snapped a photo right before they both disappeared.

When I asked her about it later, she said Ben stopped by. I didn't know who it was, but I knew it wasn't Ben. Was it Nick? Was she sleeping with him too? Why would he have this photo?

"We need to go, Allie."

She's right. I click off the light and put the car into drive. Trying to focus on the path and avoid the rocks and divots.

A figure jumps in front of the car, putting two hands on the dash, and leans toward the windshield. My heart is pounding in my temples as I slam on the brakes.

I let out a sharp breath and roll down the window. Ben comes around to the driver's side. "We have to get out of here now. Quick, I think he's after me."

Lauren leans over me. "Get in. We're going for help."

Ben's face, covered in sideways shadows from the indirect light of the headlights, has an expression I haven't seen on him before. I can't quite make it out, but he looks almost angry.

He climbs in the backseat, moving the suitcase to the side, brushing away some of the broken glass. "Where did you find the keys?"

Lauren lowers her head and almost whispers, "In Gabe's tent. Sheila's purse was on his bed with all his stuff."

Gabe's tent. Gabe's stuff. I shake my head. Why did we think it was Gabe's stuff? Because of the beer shirt? I can't remember him wearing it, though. Was that really Gabe's stuff?

"Gabe's? Are you sure it wasn't Joe's?" Ben sounds genuinely shocked. I glance in the rearview mirror but can't see his face in the dark.

I start to drive the car closer to the clubhouse.

"Where are we going? Aren't we leaving?" Ben says.

"I just want to get Eric really quick."

I flinch as Ben puts a hand on my shoulder from behind. He has a Band-Aid on the middle finger of his right hand that scratches against the fabric of my sweater. "Allie, we can't. Joe attacked him. I saw the whole thing. He came up from behind him and hit him with a lamp. I hit him with the pool stick and ran so he wouldn't come after me too, but I'm pretty sure I just knocked him out. Everyone's dead Allie. Everyone. Sheila, Nick, Dana, Jennifer, Eric. They're all gone. We have to go."

Joe. Of course it was him.

"We have to go see if Eric's okay," I say. This is all my fault. I should've never let him come.

Ben moves his hand. "He didn't make it, Allie. There's no way he could've survived that."

No. Ben can't be right. Eric is dead?

"Oh my god. Joe killed everyone?" Lauren says, startling me. "Allie. Please. Let's just go."

I'm not the praying type, usually, but I send up a silent prayer for Eric, and for myself, then turn the car around and drive to the road.

As I drive down the dark asphalt, rain falls in great sheets. The sky is no longer black, but a softer indigo. Have we been up all night? The windshield wipers make an awful squeak each time they move to the left, heightening the silence in the car.

The sky turns quickly to deep sapphire blue with purple streaks illuminating the clouds. The headlights bounce back at us as they hit a massive wall of dirt. I stop the car. There's no road ahead of us, just dirt and rock and a couple of trees with gnarled roots lying at odd angles, and a cliff to one side.

I scan left and right, but I can't see any way around it. We're trapped.

Ben sits back with a sigh. "It's blocked. We can just turn around. The only one left is Joe, right? Everyone else is dead. He can't hurt all three of us."

The hairs on the back of my neck prickle, I turn to the back. "And Gabe, right?"

"I couldn't find him." Ben shakes his head, tears welling in his eyes. "I searched everywhere."

"What are we going to do?" Lauren cries. "Maybe we can just wait here, in the car, until help comes?"

I look out the windshield, my nerves absolutely fried.

Joe did it. But for some reason, it doesn't add up in my brain.

The rain stops, and orange light shines on the great mound of dirt in front of me. If I gun it, will the car run into the rubble like a wall or go up it like a steep hill? I'm not sure. I close my eyes, wishing I knew what to do.

Ben touches my shoulder again. "Come on, Allie, let's turn back. We can wait for help."

Opening my eyes, I look up in the clouds, an eagle circles high overhead, its wings spread wide.

I take a deep breath.

It's an ideal day to be bold.

I whisper to Lauren, "Go."

Then, wrenching open the car door, I run.

Ben gets out of the car, yelling after me. "What are you doing?"

To be honest, I'm not sure. From the side of the mound furthest from the cliff, I climb, gripping rocks and trees. Sticks scrape at my knees, warm blood trickles down my leg, and the rubble shifts rapidly under my feet. But I keep scrambling up. Until I get to the peak and let myself fall.

I slide all the way down, using my worn out Van's as brakes toward the bottom. As soon as my feet hit the road, I run. A large rock slides down the hill in my path, and I narrowly miss it. Muffled shouts from Lauren and Ben drift down the hill to me, but there's no going back now.

My lungs ache and my legs burn, but I keep running down the road for what feels like hours. The soles of my feet ache.

Finally, a car is coming. I stop in the middle of the road and wave my arms. A dark-haired woman in a pastel pink suit and four-inch heels hurries out of the car, clacking as she does.

"Oh, my lord. What happened?"

Murder? What murder? Episode 189 July 20, 2024

"Holy Shit. Hold the phone. I have questions."

"Ha! I bet you do, Jules. So, Melanie, the wedding planner, found Allie. She called the police and help finally arrived. They cleared away the debris and came across the absolutely devastating scene. Sheila, Dana, Jennifer, Nick and Gabe were all dead."

"Wait. What about Eric?"

"Eric was in critical condition. He was in a coma for several weeks. But ultimately, he pulled through. And his testimony was the most damning for Joe, well, his and Ben's."

"Oh shit. Joe really did it?"

"Yep. Joe killed them all in some weird copycat revenge frenzy. Justice for Wendy. That's the theory, anyway. Joe has always maintained his innocence."

"What does he say happened?"

"Joe claims he found Eric on the floor, his head bleeding. He picked up the lamp to move it away from him and was hit on the back of the head. But his fingerprints were the only ones found on the lamp. They were also on the knife found next to Gabe.

According to all the forensic evidence, that same knife was used to kill Jennifer, Sheila, and Dana."

"Okay. That's a lot of evidence against him, but explain the photos to me. The ones from the fire and in Nick's hand."

"So, Sheila worked for a law firm that employed private investigators, and she became close with one of them. He agreed to follow Gabe on his trip to Portland a couple weeks before the wedding. He took photos of Gabe and Jennifer together all over town."

"Why didn't Sheila just break up with him?"

"Great question. I don't honestly know. Her friends think she was also seeking justice. Her father used to be a serial cheater, so it was more than just Gabe's betrayal. It brought up all those feelings too. She wanted to tell Ben what was going on. They think she tried to do it before the wedding. Her phone records showed calls to Ben dating back from when she first got the report."

"Shit. So why was Nick holding one of the photographs?"

"We don't know. Ben says he never saw the photos until the trial."

"Joe's trial?"

"Yep. Joe was convicted to three consecutive life sentences."

"I still have so many questions."

"Do you want to ask me, or do you want to ask our very special guest?"

"Oh, man. I forgot we were having company, well I want to ask them."

"They'll be here right after we talk a little bit about mattresses. Jules, do you like your mattress?"

Allie
July 20, 2024

My mouth is dry, and my heart is beating fast. Why did I agree to do this? I tuck my hair behind my ears and put the headset on, adjusting the size. I was hoping being here would give me some closure, but so far, it just feels like opening old wounds.

Barb puts a hand on my knee. Her eyes are warm, and her black hair hangs in soft curls around her face. "Don't be nervous. You got this." She makes such direct eye contact that it makes me even more unsure of myself. Not myself, really, but this decision. I nod and try to smile.

"Do you want some water, or I think we have kombucha or wine?" Jules offers, her blue eyes bright. Have I ever been as awake as her? She turns to her assistant. "Freddy, can you get some wine for Allie?"

I shake my head. "No, no wine, thank you. Just some water would be great."

I haven't touched alcohol since a couple months after Lost Lake. When I climbed up the landslide, all I could think about was a glass of wine. I needed to get Eric help and then get a drink the size of my head. I was taken to the hospital as soon as help arrived. No wine for me, just an IV of liquids and relentless questions from the cops. They kept asking why I ran. I was relatively safe in the car, with my friends, why not just wait for help? I couldn't explain it, still can't, but there was a buzzing inside me. I had to get out of that car.

During the time after, when we came home from Lost Lake, it was so hard. Hard isn't even the right word. Joe was the one locked up, but it felt like I was the one in prison. I would wake up in the middle of the night and feel like I was back there at the campground. I saw diamonds everywhere. On the map on the bus, on the menus at work, once I even thought I saw some carved into the tree outside my window. I hated that fucking tree. I had to look super close to see if the diamonds were really there. They weren't. There were no diamonds anywhere. You'd think that would be a relief, and it was in a way, but at the same time, it wasn't.

I started reaching for the bottle earlier and earlier, moving from mimosas in the morning to whiskey gingers to just straight liquor, whatever was in the kitchen. Drinking at work all the time was the norm, not just before closing. I stopped returning people's calls, preferring to drink alone. Preferring, more like *needing*. I needed to be alone.

Until one night after work, I caught sight of my reflection in the dark window, that stupid tree blowing in the wind behind my face. I leaned in to get a closer look, the bottle of whiskey I was swigging off of sloshing in my hand. Heavy bags, a week or two worth of tangles in my hair, and no light behind my eyes. No sparkle. I looked dead. I looked like Dana.

I opened the window and poured the bottle of whiskey out.

Freddy hands me a sweating bottle of water.

"You ready?" Barbara says with a reassuring smile.

I take a deep breath. "Yes."

"We're back. And we have a guest here with us. Thank you for joining us, Allie."

"Thanks for inviting me, Barbara."

"You look fantastic!"

"Thanks."

"Catch us up on your life!"

"Well, I'm a teacher. Lauren actually encouraged me to go into it."

"Are you and Lauren still friends?" Jules asks.

"We are. She's the godmother of my son. After Lost Lake I was...well, I was lost. I quit drinking and had to quit the bar in order to be able to do that. I couldn't be around booze. I'm strong, but not that strong.

"Lauren got me a job as an assistant at her elementary school. After a while, I went back to school for my degree, and now, I teach high school art."

"That's awesome," Barbara says. "I loved my high school art teacher. And you have a son? With Eric?"

I laugh. "No. Not with Eric. But we still keep in touch. I just saw him at his book signing last month."

"Ahh, yes." Barbara reaches for a copy on the desk behind her and holds it up for the camera. "For any of you living under a rock, Eric is Eric Barner is the author of the hot, hot, hot fantasy series *King of Swords*."

"So, how did you meet your husband?" Jules asks

"If you can believe it, in a hiking club."

"Wait, what? Hiking?"

"Yeah." I laugh at myself and at the look of complete shock and disgust on Jules's face. "I know."

"I would think after what happened you would want to stay the fuck out of the woods," Jules says.

"You are absolutely correct," I say. "But that's what got to me. I was in a café, pouring some cream in my coffee and I saw this flyer on their community board for a hiking club. The flyer had this beautiful picture of a trail in the woods, sun shining through the trees, and I started to feel panic. Red-hot panic. I was sweating. Every day for a week this flier made me feel like I was losing my mind. And one day, I said fuck this and I grabbed the flier, the whole thing not just those little papers at the bottom. I felt bad about that later. But I joined this group and started hiking in the woods every other Saturday. It was amazing. Like I wasn't going to let this thing that happened control me."

Barbara nodded. "You got your power back."

I let the truth of that sink in.

"I got my power back." I smile. "After about six months in this group, a new guy showed up with dark eyes and a thousand-watt smile and the rest is history. My son is eight years old, and he loves dogs, reading, and if you can believe it, camping. The kid freaking loves camping."

"No! Hiking is one thing. You take him camping?"

I nod. "I do. We do. We're actually going camping right after we're done recording today. If you had told me twenty years ago this would be my life, I would've spit whiskey in your face. I don't know if it's what happened or if I'm just old now, but I love it. I'm very happy in my small life."

Barbara shakes her head and touches my hand across the table. She makes that intense eye contact again. "No life is small."

"Okay," Jules says. "I have a couple questions about Lost Lake, a few, well, a shit ton, really."

I laugh. "I'll do my best. Fire away."

"So, Joe was Wendy Robinson's brother?"

"I guess so. He was a few years younger than Dana, Ben, and Nick so they didn't recognize him. They didn't really know him much in high school."

"And to be very clear, Joe didn't have anything to do with the Gem Cutter killings from before, right?"

"According to Joe, no. But he thought Nick had something to do with Wendy's death. He also says he didn't have anything to do with...well, all the killings at Lost Lake either."

"What do you think?"

What do I think? Eric came out of his coma, and he was so sure it was Joe. And Ben said he saw Joe. I found his ID, with his real name. He'd been lying to us all. Besides, if it wasn't Joe, then who could it be?

"Joe did it. I'm pretty sure. But I still quite don't understand why, and I'll be honest, that bothers me to this day."

"Well, our next guest has some thoughts on Joe's motives. We'll take a quick break and be right back."

Next guest?

Barbara gives me a reassuring smile. "You're doing great."

The door to the studio opens, and my heart bullets to my throat, lodging there.

Ben walks through the door. I haven't seen him since the trial. We were never really close to begin with. All of us tried to get together once after a particularly rough day in court, Lauren, Ben, Eric, and I, but it was awkward and sad. We never tried again.

The only one I have a real relationship with is Lauren. She gives me updates on everyone. After Lost Lake, Ben went back to school and became a psychiatrist. He still lives in Portland and is recently married. Lauren is friends with Ben's wife. They do a book club, and they always invite me to join, but I worried it would be too weird. Jennifer was supposed to be his wife.

Freddy takes Ben's olive-green jacket. He pulls down his threadbare T-shirt, the print of a skeleton holding a beer almost worn into oblivion.

"Thanks for being here, Ben."

"Of course." He comes closer and holds his arms out for a hug. "Allie. It's been a long time."

I untangle myself from the headphones and walk into his arms. He smells spicy and warm, like sandalwood.

We both get settled with our headphones.

"So, Ben," Jules says. "Why do you think Joe did it?"

Ben rubs a hand over his stubble and shifts in his chair. Something is bothering me about him, and I can't figure out what it is. He looks just like the day we got to Lost Lake.

Ben drones on in technical jargon, psychobabble really, on reasons he thinks Joe could've done it.

"Wow. What led you to become a psychiatrist?" Jules asks, leaning forward.

"Well, my mom always suffered from what we called 'spells' when I was a kid, but I now know they were most likely panic attacks. She must've had acute anxiety disorder brought on by stress."

"Stress?"

Ben laughs. "My brother, god rest his soul, was a handful at the best of times."

The three of them keep rehashing details of the case, but I'm lost. I can't take my eyes off Ben. Watching him shift in that stupid T-shirt so worn and thin, his brown eyes shimmering with tears that never quite fall, my pulse races. Suddenly, the picture is coming into focus, and I can't unsee it.

I feel like I'm back there, the details flooding back so vividly.

That shirt he's wearing looks exactly like the one we found. But can it really be?

It is. Lauren and I found Sheila's purse in a suitcase with Ben's shirt with that idiotic skeleton drinking beer.

Ben grabbed my shoulder in the car with a Band-Aid on his finger, and I found a torn nail in Dana's clothing. Is that why he had the bandage? Did he tear his nail off when he was killing Dana?

Ben was the key witness in putting Joe away, when Joe had no real motive besides a complete mental breakdown and what they say was revenge for Wendy.

There's one more thing. I can't believe it took me this long to realize it.

"Allie, are you okay? You look pale. Do you need more water?"

I shake my head. "Ben, how did you know Nick was dead?"

He whips his head to me like I slapped him in the face. "What?"

"In the car. You, me, and Lauren were in the car, and you said the only one left besides us was Joe. How did you know Nick was dead? How did you know Gabe was dead? We didn't even know that."

"I just...I saw you shut the trunk with Nick inside."

I shake my head. "No, you didn't. You weren't anywhere around then. There's no way you could've known, unless you put him there."

Jules sucks in a breath, and Barbara's eyes go wide.

"What are you saying?" Jules asks. "Are you saying Ben killed Nick?"

Oh shit. What am I saying? Am I really accusing Ben on a livestream? I am. We found Sheila's purse in a suitcase with a shirt, the shirt that Ben's wearing right now. But he's never going to admit it. When the cops searched everything later, the purse was gone.

No sooner does the plan form in my head than it's out of my mouth. Just like when I jumped over that railing to grab the keys, just like climbing a fucking landslide—the ground shifting under my feet, and my hope that I'm quick enough to outrun it.

"Remember that fingernail I found snagged on Dana's underwear?"

Ben just stares at me, his face a wall of stone.

Barbara nods. "That's the only piece of evidence that doesn't add up. The DNA doesn't match Joe's."

"Right," I say. "But at the time, they had so much other evidence against him they didn't test the fingernail further. But I have a buddy on the force, and he tested it against all the rest of us. You, me, Lauren, and Eric."

Ben shakes his head. "How did you get my DNA to test?"

Shit. How would I? Lauren. "Lauren got some from your hairbrush the last time your wife hosted a book club."

Ben crosses his arms tightly around his abdomen, a gesture so close to Jennifer that it stings.

"It was a match." I hold up my phone and pray no one wants a closer look. "The fingernail is an exact match to your DNA. How do you explain that?"

Ben runs his hands through his hair and then starts to laugh. It is an honest to God belly laugh. Once he's done, he looks at me with fire in his eyes. "Allie, are you drunk?"

"I'm actually twenty years sober."

Barbara is making frantic eyes at Freddy, while Jules has completely curled into her chair.

"Did you kill Wendy all those years ago, too?"

"What the fuck are you talking about? I didn't kill anyone. This is absolutely ridiculous." Leaping from his chair, Ben yanks the microphone off his shirt.

"All those phone records. Sheila called you," I say, feeling the pieces of the puzzle start to fit together but not quite. "Oh my god, the scrap of photo. Why was Nick holding it if it was from Sheila? Did he see you two talking?"

"I'm leaving. I don't have to listen to this." Ben moves

toward the door just as it opens and Eric steps in. He's blocking the door. Was he watching the livestream? Is that why he's here?

"Why put the diamonds on the map?" I ask as Ben and Eric have some kind of staring contest by the door.

Ben doesn't respond. I can hear sirens in the distance. I look around, and Freddy is hiding under a desk, his cell phone lit up in his hands.

Ben points to Eric. "Maybe Eric did it."

"That's not how DNA works, Ben." I shake my head, keeping up the lie. In all honesty, I don't even know if the cops kept that evidence. "It's a match for you."

Ben crouches down as if to fix his shoe but comes up with a small knife. In one swift movement, he grabs my arm and pulls me close to him, the cords of my headphones yanking out, the knife's tip pointing directly at my throat.

"You are all going to let me get in my car and walk away."

Barbara and Jules nod silently, but Eric doesn't move from the door.

Ben marches me closer, touching the knife to my neck. Eric gives me a look, an apology with his eyes, and steps aside.

We walk out the door and down the stairs.

Outside, the sunshine is too bright.

"What now, Ben?"

The first cop car arrives, lights flashing, sun glinting off the windshield. Ben looks toward it, and while he's momentarily distracted, I use all the self-defense, all the Krav Maga, all the kick boxing I've taken over the past two decades since Lost Lake.

I stomp on his foot and elbow him in the ribs hard as I tuck myself into a ball and roll into the street. I pop up and run, my boots clacking on the road. Eric runs out of the building just as officers jump out of their vehicles with guns trained on Ben.

Eric runs straight over to me and pulls me behind one of the cop cars. My knee hitting the concrete with a smack.

"Are you okay?" Eric asks, his blue eyes bright in the light.

I was better before he decided I needed saving. But he meant well. He always does, as misguided as that often is. "I'm fine."

I crouch and peer over the hood of the car.

Ben has his hands in the air. The officers handcuff him and put him in the back of the squad car. A tear mixes with my mascara as it rolls down my face.

They're going to take him in. But who knows if they'll be able to hold him.

Killer Mysteries Season 13 Ep 9
June 11, 2026

"Kayaking, friendship bracelets, s'mores. It's hard to believe anything else could take place in this pristine setting but idyllic summer days and nights spent by the fire."

A man in a dark suit and khaki trench coat walks in front of a sparkling lake, the sun catching Mt. Hood in the background.

"But something else did happen here, over twenty years ago.

"Nine friends set off on a camping adventure, one that was supposed culminate in a wedding, but it was a wedding that would never take place.

"They were trying to recapture some of the magic of summer camp. The friendships formed among the trees can last a lifetime. Nature, proximity, lack of outside distractions all work together to form an unshakable bond. But in this instance, it ended up being a pressure cooker that led to their demise.

"I'm Toby Goliath, join me as we revisit the deadly case of The Lost Lake Murders. When we first aired an episode exploring this twisted and deadly tale, we had it all wrong. Today, we have an exclusive interview with the real killer."

Toby is now in a director chair. Across from him, Ben in an orange jumpsuit sits in an identical chair.

"Thank you for agreeing to talk with us, Ben."

"It's my pleasure, Toby." He holds up a hand, shakes his head. "Not pleasure. Duty. I owe it to the families."

"What drove you to murder?"

Ben sighs. "What drives anyone to do anything? Love. I was blinded by love."

"Love?" Toby shifts in his chair.

Ben shakes his head, tears forming in the corner of his eyes. "It all started with Wendy. I loved Wendy. I could never hurt her. She was so nervous about that stupid math test. I just brought her a couple of my mom's pills. To help her. She wasn't supposed to take all of them at the same time. In the end, it just made it easier for Wyatt James to murder her, and it was all Gabe's fault. If he'd never run away in the first place, mom would never have been taking those stupid pills. All of it was Gabe's fault."

"You killing your best man and your fiancée was Gabe's fault?"

Ben swallows hard. "No. It was mine. I am taking responsibility." Ben pauses, smoothing hair. "But I knew Gabe was sleeping with Jennifer. She was glued to her phone. Like I didn't know her passcode. I read every dirty text. Saw every grainy photo.

"I was just going to kill them. Just Jennifer and Gabe. They could be together for all eternity. I was going to make it look like an accident. But then Sheila called me. No one else could know they were sleeping together."

Toby nods. "It'd give you quite a motive. Why not just leave Jennifer? Confront Gabe? Why did they have to die?"

Ben laughs. "I couldn't very well break up with my brother. No. If I left Jennifer and"—Ben makes air quotes—"'confronted'

Gabe, as you say, then everyone would know. I'd be pitied. My parents. My mom, she couldn't handle it." He sighed. "Gabe had already put them through so much. He would just keep fucking up. He needed to be out of our lives, for good."

Ben takes a deep breath. "No. No one could know what happened. It was better they died. It was going to be a tragic accident. But then Sheila called me, and I had to come up with a new plan, quickly."

"Sheila called you..." Toby checks his papers. "Several times. But why did Nick have to die?"

"I didn't want to kill Nick." Ben pauses, and the camera pans to Toby and back. "He saw me with Sheila. She wanted to meet me before we went up there, but we were already at the brewery. I told her to drive ahead, and I'd meet her at the campsite. She was supposed to drive the car around the bend into the trees. Where no one would see it. Nick followed me when I went to meet her. I remembered the news report about Wyatt James escaping, and I thought if anyone found her, they'd just think he did it. A terrible coincidence, sure, but totally plausible. It could cover the whole thing. Nick saw me. Then he wouldn't help. He told me I was sick. I wasn't even thinking, I just swung my flashlight at his head."

Toby nods, his eyes at the same time warm and guarded. "Why put the diamonds on the map?"

Ben's eyes shoot daggers. "Are you listening? Like I said, Wyatt James could be the reason all of them died. And he always had some kind of map, right? That man took everything from me once. He could give me this. It just all seemed to be too perfect to pass up."

Toby nods. "And you thought you could get away with murder?"

Ben sighs. "I've learned a lot since then, but I did. It's actually the title of my book coming out this fall..."

Allie
June 12, 2026

Despite the breeze blowing through the art room, my palms are sweating as I slam my laptop closed. I don't know why I thought I could watch that and be unaffected.

I rise from my desk and wash the brushes soaking in the sink. The students are long gone for the day.

The podcast asked me to come back. For a follow-up show. A recap on what really happened.

Part of me was dying to. I didn't want Ben to get the last word.

But I've spent the last two years diligently protecting my child—my family—from all this. It was hard enough with the trial, the reporters, the press coverage.

I couldn't go on the show again.

Ben was arrested after the podcast interview. The process was long. Eventually, he made a full confession. Maybe because around eight hundred thousand people watched the livestream where he led me out of the cramped office at knifepoint.

I still wonder if my life and Lauren's would have been spared had we stayed in the car that fateful day at Lost Lake. In my gut, I know the answer. No fucking way. He would've killed us, just like the rest of them.

My story about the fingernail DNA testing had been a complete crock of shit at the time, but after they arrested Ben, they did test it, and it was a match. It's fortunate that it was a fingernail because the keratin protects the DNA.

Ben killed everyone. Even while the pieces were coming together, my brain still had such a hard time believing it. I thought he was such a nice guy.

Now that nice guy is serving five consecutive life sentences, and yet still finds the time to tell all to Toby Goliath. On the show, he made a formal apology to Nick's family.

I shake my head.

Not to anyone else's. Not even to Dana's. I thought they were really close.

Emotional detachment at its finest. Ben was only ever really looking out for himself.

It's sobering, knowing that if I had kept going the way I was I would've ended up the same. Not killing people, of course. But not letting anyone get close to me, either. Only looking out for myself.

Ben's book, *I Thought I Got Away With Murder*, comes out next month. Netflix already bought the rights.

Eric is also releasing a book about his time at Lost Lake. Hopefully, people will buy his novel over Ben's.

To be honest, I don't give a fuck what Eric writes. Or Ben. For me, it's over.

I pack up my sketchbook but leave the laptop. I won't need it where I'm going.

Swinging the door to the art studio open, I tilt my face to the sky, close my eyes, and let the sunshine warm my skin. A honk brings me back to the high school parking lot. I wave to the packed up Subaru with my husband waiting for me in the front and my son in the back.

He gives me a sidelong look. "Did you watch it?"

I nod.

"You said you weren't going to."

I let out a small breath. We both know I was going to. "But I did."

My husband's eyes are warm as he puts his hand in mine. "Are you okay?"

I look in the back, my son with his nose in one of his adventure books, dark hair falling across his forehead, and warmth spreads through me. There is a core that will always be me, but I'm not the same person I was in Lost Lake. I'm not even the same person I was ten years ago, let alone over twenty. And as awful as it is, I can't help but feel—grateful.

Not for what happened. But for who I am because of it. I know in my bones I would not be in this car with the two people I love most in the world, sober and happy, if it weren't for Lost Lake.

The radio is playing Brittany Spears's "Toxic," and I quickly change it to the college radio station. "Lives" by Modest Mouse fills the car. I pull my hand away from the tuner, placing it back in my husband's, and smile.

"I'm okay. Come on. Let's go to the woods."

The End

Acknowledgments

Thank you reader, for joining me on this new adventure. I have two loves, mystery and romance. For a while I thought I had to pick one, and stay in my lane, but as a true Libra I can't just pick one. Sooo expect some more mysteries and thrillers from me. If you are a romance fan you can check out my Fortune Falls series.

I wrote this book years ago and edited it forever! It's had so many versions but this one is by far my favorite. Thank you Samantha for loving it, asking about it and encouraging me to put it out there. Love you boo!

Thank you to everyone who has worked on this book and read it over the years. Thank you to Mary and Francie I will always remember laughing on that call with you about so many bodies. Because of your wise advice there's like three or four less.

A huge thank you to Robin Blackburn And Stephanie Paul. My ride or dies in this crazy writing landscape. Thank you for always being there for me and being willing to read when I have yet another book.

Thank you Alaina for reading this book several times over the years. Your encouragement means the world to me.

Thank you to Andrea Halland for the proofreading.

And thank you again, reader, for being here and reading my books. I hope you enjoyed it.

About the Author

I received a BFA in mixed media studio art. With a degree in the arts and no solid plan, I've had the opportunity to hold many different jobs; video store manager, barista, photographer's assistant, toy store clerk, and yoga instructor at a retreat in Puerto Rico are just a few. Hands on research for her books.

Currently, when I'm not writing, you can find me working at a title one elementary school library, crafting with my little girl, or hosting the podcast, *So I Wrote a Book...Now What,* where I interview fellow authors about their revision process.

Want to join my newsletter?

Also by NC James

My alter go is NC Barton and writes Rom Coms

The Now in Forever

The Art of the Meet Cute

The Road Not Taken

The Shipped Trip coming in May

Meet Me at the Loch

Thrillers:

Next one coming soon

Check it out on my website.